the
SWEETHEART FIX

MIRANDA LIASSON

Entangled Publishing, LLC
644 Shrewsbury Commons Ave., STE 181
Shrewsbury, PA 17361
Visit our website at www.entangledpublishing.com.

Amara is an imprint of Entangled Publishing, LLC.

Edited by Lydia Sharp
Cover art and design by Elizabeth Turner Stokes
Stock art by MilanMarkovic78/Shutterstock,
dien/Shutterstock, Kheat/Shutterstock
Interior design by Toni Kerr

Print ISBN 978-1-64937-142-3
ebook ISBN 978-1-64937-164-5

Manufactured in the United States of America

First Edition December 2022

AMARA

ALSO BY MIRANDA LIASSON

BLOSSOM GLEN

The Sweetheart Deal
The Sweetheart Fix

SEASHELL HARBOR

Coming Home to Seashell Harbor
Seaglass Summer

ANGEL FALLS

Then There was You
The Way You Love Me
All I Want for Christmas

THE KINGSTON FAMILY

Heart and Sole
A Man of Honor
The Baby Project

MIRROR LAKE

This Thing Called Love
This Love of Mine
This Loving Feeling
Can't Stop Loving You
Can't Fight This Feeling

*For Marissa and Mara, and all those
who help us with our mental health*

At Entangled, we want our readers to be well-informed. If you would like to know if this book contains any elements that might be of concern for you, please check the back of the book for details.

CHAPTER ONE

On a warm Thursday in early October, Juliet Montgomery ran her hand along the gray-washed surface of her brand-new IKEA desk, inhaled its fresh wood scent, and whispered…*"I finally made it."* She just knew that, after so many years of being AWOL, the karma of the universe was finally by her side.

Her one minute of revelry at being in a real office with her name on the door ended with a firm knock.

"May I come in?" her boss and mentor, Char Gohara, said, poking her head around and giving a little wave.

"Of course. Have a seat," Juliet said, thrilled to be able to actually *have* a seat for someone to sit on. Office furniture was thrilling! It would be to anyone who had made her own way through college and grad school. After ten years of working in her family's tiny bread shop, tutoring and doing odd jobs, she'd finally earned her graduate degree in marriage and family therapy.

A gentle autumn breeze wafted in through the open window, carrying with it the distinctive earthy scent that arose from the rows of crabapple trees that marched in two straight lines down Blossom Glen's Main Street, their leaves golden in the sunshine. A parking ticket on Juliet's desk flapped in that breeze, anchored by a pink lotus paperweight her sister Vivienne had gotten her for good luck, reminding her it was due today. She made a quick mental note to run over to city hall and just pay it at lunchtime before it killed her perfect-office vibes.

"It looks very nice," Char said, glancing around.

"Thank you."

As Char took a seat, Juliet sat back in her comfy ergo chair. Everything about her new office was wonderful. From her name and credentials on the door to the fresh pack of pens and sticky notes she'd stocked in her center drawer.

A real job. The job of her dreams. Now she could finally leave her past behind. She would help people, have the respect of the community, and everyone in town would forget the mistakes of her youth. And not-so-youth.

With her stylish short, dark hair, artfully tied scarf, and easy smile, Char projected professionalism and confidence. She was everything Juliet aspired to. And one of the therapists in Headspace, Blossom Glen's only Psychological Services practice, that she admired most.

A piece of paper rattled in Char's hands.

"Is that the form from the mental health center about my credentialing?" Juliet asked. "I just faxed that over to them." Yep, she was *on it*, and she wanted Char to know she would do everything, *anything*, to succeed.

"No. It's…something else."

Juliet picked up immediately on the concern in Char's voice. And her serious expression. Her heart gave a sickening little jolt.

"Is this about…last night?" Juliet blurted. Char had known her for years. She'd helped her family through their own mental health crisis when she was a teenager, pointing them to therapists and resources. She'd counseled Juliet about her college major and graduate programs as she sought to enter the mental health field. She'd even written letters and helped her find internship opportunities. And then she'd hired her.

Char had been a mentor in every way.

And now, the look in her eyes was wary and guarded. Her lips were pressed together hard, as if someone had just asked her to chug a bottle of vinegar. All of which triggered a big whopping *uh-oh* in Juliet's head.

Char looked her directly in the eye. "In part."

"I know I didn't handle that interaction well. I—"

Char held up a hand. "Juliet, please let me speak, okay?"

"Okay," she croaked. Already, she could feel the flare and itch of hives on her back, where they always started. Soon she'd be covered with them. That's how she knew this was bad. Really bad. She fought the urge to scratch her back on her chair like her sweet yellow tabby cat Ellie would do.

"Chris called me this morning with a complaint."

Chris was the female half of the couple Juliet had been counseling last night. Her very first couple in her new job. She knew the session hadn't gone well, but oh, to have a client go to her boss? How humiliating. A rush of heat flooded her face. "I—I got caught off guard. I...blanked." She forced herself to breathe. "It was a one-time thing," she added hastily.

Okay, she was sounding too eager to please. But she was finally living her dream, a dream she would protect at all costs. To return home to Blossom Glen to work as a therapist. To help people the way *she'd* been helped as a desperate teen in a small town in Indiana where sometimes the needed services didn't quite reach.

She sat up straight in her chair. "It won't happen again."

Char's look was not unsympathetic. "Chris put you on the spot. She brought up your...romantic history during the session. Specifically, the three engagements."

Juliet winced. "Two and a half," she whispered, which made Char frown.

"The number's not important." Her perceptive brown eyes flickered to Juliet's. "Or maybe that *is* the issue—clearly it still matters to you."

Juliet leaned forward in her chair, hands splayed out on her brand-new leather-bound desk pad that not coincidentally matched her new organizer. "Chris questioned if I was qualified to counsel them. Actually, her words were, 'Why should we listen to you? You've had three failed engagements.'"

Ouch.

Char shook her head. "You know how to deal with people who use projection to avoid talking about their own problems. You *are* a professional."

Juliet clutched her chest, which was suddenly burning worse than if she'd just eaten a bowl of her brother-in-law's chili-pepper-madness bucatini from his amazing Italian restaurant downtown. And she really shouldn't have devoured that 85 percent cacao chocolate bar for breakfast as a substitute for coffee, because it was making her shake all the way down to her toes.

"I *am* a professional." Her voice sounded watery and diluted, like she was trying really hard to convince herself.

That self-assurance she'd tried so hard to hone was circling the bowl fast.

"And…" Char added, "professionals don't say 'You're right.'"

Oh dear. She *had* said that, hadn't she?

"You were supposed to be helping this couple deal with their marital problems. Instead, you took their comments personally and injected your personal point of view."

"I'm so sorry," Juliet whispered. She'd screwed up. Badly.

Char stood up and paced the tiny office, past the real rubber tree plant from her grandmother, past the basket where she hid her stress knitting. Char was usually calm and not easily unnerved, but now she was clearly on edge. Like, maybe she was questioning hiring Juliet. Could she lose her job before she even got a chance to do it properly? She grasped onto her beloved desk, as if someone were going to burst in and cart it—and her—away.

And she hadn't even opened her pack of rainbow-colored sticky notes yet.

"None of us is perfect," Char said. "I'm divorced, but I have a lot of expertise in conflict resolution. Plus, I've worked on my own wounds. You have a master's degree in how to do that, too, and I know you've worked on yourself in therapy, but apparently you're missing something to go along with it."

Juliet had put in the hard work and got the stellar grades to prove it. She loved people. She got along with nearly everybody, the result of being the middle child of three sisters. "What am I missing?" she asked.

"Confidence."

Ugh. Of course, it wouldn't be something she could easily obtain to set things right.

"Are you letting me go?" Juliet asked, her voice coming out more like a croak, choked and foreign sounding. Her airway was closing. And the hives had now reached her ankles. She used the base of her desk to scratch them.

Char sighed. "I'm not letting you go."

She paused, and Juliet managed to breathe again.

"But I'm suggesting that you take a break from relationship counseling. Take some time to work on your own traumas and attitudes and get an armamentarium for when this might get brought up again."

Juliet fought the urge to bang her head against the desk. This was too much, and all before coffee. "I'll work on it," she said. "I'll be sure it doesn't happen again."

Char frowned and held out the paper she'd been holding. The plain white sheet was just that—completely blank.

Wait a minute...her name was at the top.

Char was holding up Juliet's schedule for the week—which was whiter than her grandma's French table linens. The few clients actually in time slots were referrals from school counselors for family therapy. Thank goodness she had those.

"Yes, it's a small town and everyone knows you," Char said. "Now it's your job to figure out how to be okay with that. I'll help you in any way I can, you know that." She walked to the door. "You can still take on your family clients. And Jordan's going to take your couples temporarily. But take today off to regroup, okay?"

"Wh-when—how long—I—" The tightness in her chest felt suffocating. Jordan Greer was a high-achieving, beautiful, and put-together colleague from grad school who had also wanted this job. And once she started taking Juliet's clients, Juliet might never get them back.

"Do what you need to do to get your head straight," Char said definitively. "Then we'll talk."

As soon as she was gone and the door shut, Juliet broke out in a cold sweat and lifted up her blouse to give her now-giant hives a scratch. The room was spinning. She felt flushed and woozy. She was a failure in her own hometown, a place where it actually counted what people knew.

She figured she had about a minute before she dissolved into a hot mess. Dumping the entire contents of her purse out on her desk, she found her bottle of antihistamines.

Tears were already stinging behind her lids. Her nose was running, something that always happened before she started to ugly cry. And her face was burning like she'd forgotten to wear sunblock all day at the beach. Except she knew that meant the hives were about to pop out there, too.

She had the day off now. But what would she do?

Not give in to the crying. Or the hives. Juliet had come too far to give in to despair.

A paper on her desk fluttered again in the breeze from the open window, catching her eye. Her overdue parking ticket. This, at least, she could fix. "I'd better go pay you while I can still afford to," she muttered, then snatched it up and headed out the door.

CHAPTER TWO

"You don't have to have kids to be a great teacher, right?" Juliet said to herself as she climbed the wide marble staircase inside the quaint, clock-towered town hall. "You don't have to have tooth decay to be a good dentist. You don't have to overcome a lisp to be a good speech therapist. You don't have to—" She paused halfway up to catch her breath as the truth she'd been avoiding hit her hard.

How could she be a good relationship therapist when her own romantic life was a disaster...and everyone knew it?

She could have gone to her very pregnant oldest sister's new pastry shop, Contessa Bakes. Tessa would feed her something delicious and soothe her worries, as she'd been doing ever since their dad died when Juliet was fourteen.

Or she could have visited her mom and grandmother at Bonjour Breads!, their family's longstanding boulangerie. Again, food and comfort there, too. But both those options had vibes of a thirty-year-old running to mommy, and she really didn't want to do that.

Even her younger sister Vivienne was nearby, working at the year-round Christmas shop down the street. Christmas was always comforting, right?

But she just couldn't face family now.

Her best friend, Noah, worked as a head de-signer in the town candle factory, but she couldn't go barging in there. And her good friend, Emily, was in grad school, studying to be a child psy-chologist, but she was preparing to defend her dissertation. And all her other friends were in the middle of their workdays.

As she should be.

Soon, everyone in town would know that she'd botched everything.

Apparently, no one wanted someone they'd watched grow up from a toddler to be their mar-riage and family therapist. Especially one they still called *Lulu* from when she couldn't pro-nounce *Juliet* when she was three.

If only it was just that. The gruesome reality was that no one wanted someone as their thera-pist who couldn't take her own advice.

Like, two point five broken-engagements-worth of not taking advice.

Except everyone in town rounded up to three. The third, while a near-miss, was not *technically* an engagement. But she might as well wear three scarlet *E*'s on her sweater, each a shining, neon beacon that kept all her clients away.

Three failures. Three men that weren't right. Looking back, she *knew* they weren't right... Why had it taken her so long to figure that out each time?

Juliet focused on the giant staircase sprawling before her, remembering how, as a little girl, when her dad brought her along to renew their vehicle licenses, she'd loved counting every step out loud.

She'd walked beside him so proudly, holding his hand and dragging her favorite doll along in her other hand. Twenty. Twenty-one, twenty-two…

Dad, I miss you. She never seemed to stop missing him.

What would he say to her now?

She imagined him holding her by the shoulders, looking her in the eye, and saying, *You got this, Jules. You can do anything.* And then he'd pull out a lemonhead from his pocket.

When life gives you lemons…

But she wasn't a kid anymore. And she didn't need a lemonhead. In fact, right now she could really use a drink.

Somehow, she'd ceased to believe those words about herself. She'd allowed her personal mistakes to impact her therapist-self. She really had lost her confidence.

Juliet reached the top step, number thirty-one, same as her age, and turned left into the municipal offices' wing. Sharon, the mayor's secretary, sat behind her desk in a central, open area, her bright scarlet hair and heart-shaped glasses visible amid a jungle of potted plants.

"Hey, Sharon," Juliet said to the older woman as she slid her parking ticket across the desk.

Sharon glanced at the ticket and then back up at Juliet. "Weren't you going to contest this?"

Juliet shrugged. She'd waited until the last day to pay because she'd been debating that. But right now, she lacked the strength to fight.

While Juliet waited for Sharon to process the ticket, she tossed up a prayer to her beloved dad.

Help me, Daddy. Send me a sign.

A sign of what? That this was just a bump in the road, that she was meant to be a therapist, and she'd find some way to earn her community's trust?

That staying in Blossom Glen had been the right thing to do?

That her future didn't completely suck?

But there was no sign. Only her ticket shining in the sunbeam across Sharon's desk. And her dad's voice—how she imagined it in her head, anyway—telling her in his no-nonsense way that she was going to have to dig out of this one herself.

But where would she go after this? What would she do? Visions of eviction from her apartment loomed. Of her brand-new furniture being carted away. And of Ellie, her rescue cat, glancing up pathetically from her soon-to-be-empty bowl.

Okay, she wasn't that desperate—yet.

All of that made her clutch her roiling stomach.

Just then, two men pushing dollies full of boxes exited out of a door beyond the mayor's office.

"What's going on?" Juliet asked.

"Oh, Councilman Friedman is moving to a bigger office thataway." She hiked her thumb behind her shoulder. "Not sure yet what we're going to do with an empty one." Juliet must have looked a little dazed because the older woman said with a fond smile, "Hey, babe. You okay? It *is* almost Friday, you know."

Juliet forced herself to smile at Sharon's

optimism. "Well, the smell of that coffee is making me feel better." The strong, unusually fragrant aroma filled up the office space, reminding her she hadn't even had her morning cup yet. Which would soon be giving her a headache. Not that she would notice on top of all her other woes.

Sharon looked her up and down with her sharp gaze. It wasn't an accident that she'd manned the head desk of all the city offices for the last twenty-five years. "The world treating you bad, baby? Just remember, all you need to do is unleash a little Lulu, and it will all be all right."

Juliet couldn't help laughing. She ran a hand over her face, checking for hive bumps, but found none. "Do I look that terrible that you had to remind me of that?"

She flapped her hand dismissively. "Oh, I know you hate that nickname. I just don't want you to forget your own power, is all. We all need to embrace our inner Lulus. And not try to tamp them down. There. Did Mama Sharon help make it better?"

She couldn't help laughing again. "Thanks, Sharon. I love you."

"As I do you. We redheads have to stick together. Now, about that coffee. Mayor insists on premium brew for forum mornings." She dropped her voice. "He thinks I got it from a fancy coffee subscription service, but truthfully, I bought it from George at the hardware store."

George Teeter was selling bags of coffee at the hardware store? Well, this was Blossom Glen. And George was a creative.

"It smells amazing," Juliet said weakly. And suddenly, she wanted the simple pleasure of coffee more than anything.

"And it tastes even better. Anyway, Mayor hopes it will put everyone in a good mood for the forum."

Mayor Jack Monroe, also known as Mayor By-the-Book, *would* try to control the chaos in his forums with indulgent coffee. He was more rigid than the massive center-pivot irrigators used by all the farms outside town. And he probably should have stuck to being an architect instead of running for mayor. Oh, he was hardworking enough, and full of charm, but he sometimes came across as impatient or brusque. Her therapist side had characterized him as someone who just didn't deal well with day-to-day emotions.

Which was literally what she did all day long.

And what would you call a man who wore a Stetson every day in central Indiana?

Clueless. Yep. The same kind of clueless that believed good coffee was just the right thing to soothe the souls of the townspeople at his forums. Juliet would certainly need more than that if she had to deal with Mr. Grumpus every day.

But Jack was her brother-in-law Leo's best friend, so...she had to be nice.

"Oh, darn, my computer's down." Sharon tapped the side of the monitor, as if that would shake some sense into it. "Tell you what"—she gestured toward the mayor's office—"why don't you go pour yourself a cup while I deal with this."

Juliet craned her neck to see through the door,

where several people were filing in. "Oh no, that's okay." She waved her hand dismissively. "It's for the meeting."

The last thing she wanted right now was to talk to people. Or, God forbid, the mayor.

"Oh, hardly anyone's in there yet. Go on, honey." She gave a wink.

"What exactly *is* the mayor's forum?" Juliet asked as she inched toward the delicious aroma. "Is it, like, where people air grievances?"

"Yep. Something new. It's twice a week." Sharon dropped her voice. "Mayor's very honest and kindhearted, but between you and me, he's a *terrible* arbitrator."

Honest? Kindhearted? Were they talking about the same person? Jack had imposed a beautification fee on all the shop owners on Main Street to maintain the tidy and quaint appearance of the street, including the upkeep of flowers hanging from the light posts. But the shop owners, like her mom and her sister and just about everyone else on the street, had balked at the cost. To be fair, Juliet thought the fee was probably a good idea, but Jack was too abrupt with his presentation—clearly, he'd never heard the catch-more-flies-with-honey lecture.

Juliet wandered into Jack's office, which was a largish room with a big oak desk in one corner in front of some bookcases stuffed with books. Not to mention the enormous...what in the name of Blossom Glen was that animal head with giant horns mounted on the wall? A ram, maybe?

Ugh. He hunted wildlife, too?

A few small rows of folding chairs were scattered behind two upholstered chairs in front of the desk where some townspeople sat, chatting. A rectangular table stood opposite the desk and held a full-scale model of Blossom Glen—all the streets and every business on Main Street represented in 3-D, corn fields dotting the outskirts of town. There were even little cars driving in the streets and tiny clay pots of flowers in front of the shops. Leo had told her that Jack hovered over that model, pacing and fretting and moving things around whenever he had decisions to make.

Jack Monroe was one weird dude.

Just as Juliet was pouring herself some of Sharon's hopefully-magical elixir from the party-sized coffee urn, the door shut beside her with an aggressive *boom*. Someone rushed by, leaving a scented trail of cedar and spice.

That certainly awakened her nostrils. In a fresh-pine-forest kind of way.

"Hey, everyone," the mayor said in his usual good-ol'-boy manner, greeting people left and right as he passed through the crowd to his desk. "It's hotter than a honeymoon hotel out there and it's already October."

She couldn't help rolling her eyes at his Texas talk, wondering if she could sneak out with her coffee and not be noticed, but something halted her in her tracks.

It was the sight of him in softly worn jeans as he blew quickly up the aisle. Or rather, his butt. It was a beautiful butt, indeed, filling out those Levi's in a *fine* way, showcasing his lean form and nicely muscled legs. For a few seconds, her inner sense of crisis stilled, and she found herself almost smiling at the best thing she'd seen all day. Well, make that in *quite a while*, since she'd sworn off men completely after her hideous, heart-wrenching breakup last summer.

The idea that Juliet was staring at his butt embarrassed her. She'd known him for years and had never taken a second glance. Maybe it was the fact that he seemed to have left his rock band T-shirts behind when he got elected.

Mr. Six-Feet-Two-Mayor was tall and saved from being lanky by just the right amount of muscle. He wore those jeans with boots and a blue plaid shirt, and yes, his Stetson, as if he'd been out on the ranch wrangling cattle all morning.

A strange mixture of irritation and fascination overcame her as he took off his hat and sat down, revealing slightly longish, wavy, dark hair. She hadn't even known he'd *had* hair due to his long-standing buzz cut, let alone a glorious full and thick mane. Without fuss, he ran his hand quickly through it, cleared his throat, and fidgeted with a clipboard on his desk.

Which also struck her as interesting. Because Jack Monroe *never* looked uncomfortable. He'd been full of swagger from the day he'd set foot in Blossom Glen from Abilene, Texas, at the beginning of seventh grade. And from what Leo implied, Jack didn't fail to put that natural-born charisma to good use with the ladies.

But what would she know about him, really, because he barely spoke to her at family gatherings? He struck her as the kind of man who avoided intelligent women.

She'd always thought of him as annoying. But now that she was seeing him up close for the first time since last winter, when they'd all been at Tessa's sweet little house in the Blossom district for Christmas dinner, she had to confess—he was hot. Even without the Stetson.

His astute gaze strayed over the room. He seemed to purposely not look in her direction. "Let's come to order, and then I'll hear your grievances." He smacked down his gavel—yes, a *gavel*—and read from a paper in his hands. "Sam Iverson and Jerry Caldwell, come on up."

Come on up? He was there to do business, not MC a game show. But the two elderly farmers he'd just called walked up and sat down in the cushy chairs in front of his desk.

"I'll start," Sam said, stabbing his finger in the air at his neighbor. "His tree is on *my* property line."

Jack flipped through some papers. "You two have been neighbors for over twenty years?"

"Yes, but the tree's been there for ten," Jerry said calmly. "It's a fine young tree."

"It might be beautiful," Sam shot back, "but it's on my property." He tapped his hand on Jack's desk. "And it's stopping me from putting up a fence in my garden. And it sheds on my driveway. And it might be smallish now, but it's going to grow a whole lot bigger. That tree needs moved, Mayor, plain and simple." He made a sweep across his throat with his index finger. "Or axed."

"Thanks for your opinion, Sam," the mayor said in a neutral tone, which Juliet had to admit seemed appropriate. "Now let's give Jerry the floor."

"It's a thriving tree, Mayor," the other man said. "And it took a long time to get it that way. It's only a few inches over the property line." Jerry used his hands to demonstrate a distance of about eight inches. "That little tree isn't hurting anyone."

"Every tree is beautiful," Sam said. "But it's at least twelve feet high. And it's throwing shade on my garden," Sam said. "My tomatoes won't grow."

"Yeah, well," Jerry said, tapping on his own chest, "you're throwing shade on me. Can't you just be a little neighborly and move your tomatoes somewhere else?"

"I haven't got anywhere else," Sam said.

"You can plant them in my garden. I'll make you a spot."

Sam rolled his eyes. "No."

Jerry's face turned a deep shade of red as he leaned over ominously. "I'll show you just where you can plant those tomatoes. Somewhere the sun don't shine."

"Why you—" Sam hovered menacingly over his more slight-of-build neighbor.

Jack went to stand between the two men. If this were Dodge City instead of little Blossom Glen, Jack would be the sexy sheriff about to drag both of them to the slammer.

Sexy sheriff? Oh, she must really be under duress to conjure that image.

"Can you trim the tree, Sam?" Jack asked with barely contained impatience. He sounded like a mom—*her* mom—as she had complained often in raising three girls, *Can't you all just get along?*

Judging by the way the mayor shuffled his papers, tapped his fingers together, and generally looked like he'd rather be anywhere but here, he appeared to be a handsome, arrogant, impatient man.

"Won't help," Sam said. "Besides, the trunk is half on my property line. It's got to go."

"I just don't see why you can't be more tolerant," Jerry said. "We're talking about eight inches. Longer than your—"

"Jerry, I understand about the tree," the mayor interrupted quickly. "But a property line's a property line."

Delores Teeter, who owned Christmas Every Day, which attracted people by the hordes as they traveled through their state on the turnpike, raised her hand. "I vote to keep the tree."

"I second that," her husband, George called out. He caught Juliet's eye and waved. She gave a tiny wave back. George was a sweetheart. He'd helped her fix her bike last year, even though bicycle supplies were not in the hardware store's inventory. And sometimes she watched George and Delores's little Yorkie, Stella, when they were out of town. Good people. Even Ellie would agree, since she'd developed a special affection for Stella.

Well, okay, if not affection, at least tolerance.

"No one's voting here, folks," Jack said to the

small audience.

"Isn't that why we're here?" Jamar Peterson, a retired councilman, asked. "We vote to save the tree."

"You heard the mayor," Sam said, looking nervous. "We're not voting. The tree's got to go. Or we'll be finishing this in court."

"Why don't we ask our resident psychotherapist how she would handle this?" George suddenly called out.

What?

Juliet, who'd just taken a big swig of coffee, froze and forced herself to swallow. George pointed right at her, a big smile on his face. Before she knew it, everyone had swiveled their heads to stare at her where she stood in the back of the room.

"What do you think, Lulu?" George asked.

Her cheeks flamed at the ridiculous nickname. Lulu, a.k.a. the infamous toddler who made national headlines for scaling all one hundred and fifty feet of the water tower just outside of town.

An amazing feat for anyone, not to mention a three-year-old.

And quite possibly the most spectacular thing she'd ever do in her life. Which was…a little bit sad. To have peaked before kindergarten.

The mayor used his gavel again. *Smack, smack, smack!* Which gave her the very strong urge to tell him about a little psychological term called "compensation." He could smack that thing all he wanted; it still wouldn't give him the ability to sort this out.

"Hey, everyone," he said, "let's please have some order so I can get to settling this thing."

Ugh, he really was an *awful* arbitrator.

"Let Lulu talk, Mayor," George insisted. "Maybe she's got some wisdom."

That was just the problem. She had *no* wisdom, including any for herself, and also, she was just there for the coffee. Her knowledge about property lines or legal disputes was about the size of Ellie's paw.

But she *did* know something about feuding neighbors, because for years, her family didn't speak to the Castorinis, who owned the Italian restaurant next door to their boulangerie.

And…she did happen to know something about this particular tree.

Plus, the mayor, smokin' hot though he was, appeared to be about as sharp as a mashed potato in dealing with these folks.

She set down her coffee near the urn and walked up toward his desk. "Hello, Jack," she said, all business. Startled, he looked up and over Sam and Jerry's heads, right into her eyes. He probably remembered the last time they'd confronted each other before her sister Tessa's rushed wedding, when he accused her of being a protective pit bull for her sister (which she actually took as a compliment), and she accused him of being…well, a bad mayor. Because who would agree to impulsively marry his best friend and her sister without any family present?

She tried not to notice that his eyes were as blue as his jeans. Or that the spicy, cedary scent was back, which somehow really fit that cowboy theme he was vibing. Her brain involuntarily went fireside in a cabin somewhere in the pine forests of Colorado—and for a moment, wanted to stay there.

But not. With. Him.

She was just…lonely. Confused. And sex-deprived. That was all.

Those baby blues held a little bit of confusion as well as a little bit of annoyance, and, if she wasn't mistaken…a little bit of heat.

No, no. Not that. It was just this train wreck of a day playing tricks on her. And it made her think even worse of him, because if he figured she could be easily swayed by his charm, he was dead wrong, *buddy*. That might work well on some women around here, who went for faux-cowboys, but not her. No, *ma'am*.

"Juliet." He stood and greeted her cautiously, his voice deep and gravelly, containing a tiny pinch of Abilene, the combination of which was scarily mellow and pleasant. Yeah, his voice was as sexy as his butt. And now he was looking at her the way someone might look at a ticking bomb.

Yes, she *was* that hysterical person who'd made town history by dumping her college sweetheart right here in the municipal building after tearing to shreds the marriage certificate they'd just paid a hundred bucks for. The resulting argument in front of city hall caused a car to graze the hydrant, causing water to shoot fifty feet in the air and create a massive flood that shut down Main Street for hours. Not to mention they'd had to pay the damages for the hydrant, which was a lot more than the cost of the marriage certificate.

She'd also fought with Jack over that Main Street business fee, and her sister's wedding, and was the one who...well, who didn't see eye to eye with him on anything *at all*.

Guilty as charged. He might be funny and chatty and attractive in front of Leo, but otherwise...he just...didn't get it.

Forcing herself to be all business, she reached the desk and pulled him aside.

"Yes, *Counselor*?" he asked, a well-defined brow raised. Which, in the politest version, she took to mean: *Why are you here in my mayor forum?*

She dropped her voice to a whisper and leaned in. A mistake, because he happened to smell better than the candle factory's amazing Christmas collection. "I feel I need to let you know, *Mayor*, that Jerry's kids gave him that tree ten years ago after their mom died of cancer. They planted it in her memory because Paula loved magnolia trees. So this is about a whole lot more than a property line."

"Thanks for letting me know," he said in a borderline condescending tone that made her force her eyeballs to keep from rolling toward the ceiling, "but as mayor, I can't allow emotions to cloud my decisions. I have to maintain order and be fair. As I said, a property line's a property line."

"And a memory is a memory. A person is a person." Juliet found she was waving her hands. Trying not to strangle him. "People count, *Mayor*.

In my opinion, decisions can't be made without emotions. But maybe being sensitive to people's feelings isn't in your wheelhouse."

He didn't say anything, even though she'd insulted him. But insult was better than strangle, right? Plus, he was making her so angry. Why didn't he *do* something? Jerry was distraught. It seemed so obvious what was needed. She could solve this problem in a heartbeat.

The mayor leveled that deep blue gaze on her. Yes, he had very beautiful eyes. But when he spoke, his voice was full of irritation. "I'm not sure how else I can make them both happy unless I go over there and move that tree myself." Darned if that sexy little drawl didn't send a little chill up her spine.

It was just that she'd always had a thing for cowboys. In movies. And romance novels. But *never*, past or future, in Blossom Glen.

Juliet was a grown-up now. She wasn't going to make any more mistakes when it came to men. And especially not with men in this town. She was going to focus, grab her coffee, pay her damn ticket, and get the sam hell out of Dodge.

But before she left, she was going to irritate him right back. "Now, we're finally getting somewhere," she said triumphantly, stabbing the air.

It took him a second before his eyes widened in surprise. "Landscaping is not. My. Job." He poked the air right back. "I'm trained as a greenspace architect, not a landscaper."

Oh. That was interesting. She'd known that he was an architect, but an environmentally conscientious one? How out of character. She leaned over the table a little farther. "How about you just send a city maintenance crew over to help?"

"Because their job—paid for by taxpayers, I might remind you—is to maintain our city, not get involved in private vendettas."

"Well, *your* job is to guide the town and keep the peace. *Mayor*," she breathed.

His thick, well-defined brows knit down deep. "Look, I don't need an overly emotional—"

"Stop right there," she said, splaying her hands. "If you say the words 'overly emotional' and 'woman' in the same sentence, I cannot be held responsible for what might happen to you next."

He sighed heavily. "Juliet," he said with measured patience. "I appreciate your trying to help. But I've got this."

She hooked her fingers in the air. "Don't say 'help' like it's in quotation marks."

"Come on, Mayor," someone in the second row called out, "I need to get back to work in fifteen minutes."

"Yeah, what's the hold up?" someone groused. "We've got four more sets of people waiting to have their disputes settled, too."

"May I please try my hand at making peace here?" she asked pretend-sweetly. "After all, it's what I do for a living."

Wasn't that what counseling was? Helping people make peace with themselves? But that often took years. This was much simpler stuff, the kind she felt sure she could handle.

"If you really think you have a magic wand," he said, gesturing to the two men, "have at it."

"I sure do, Mayor Jack." She smiled sweetly and swirled her hand around in a spell-making gesture. "It also happens to match my broomstick."

She didn't wait for his reaction. Instead, she pushed off from the desk and faced the men. "Jerry. Sam. The fact that you two have been neighbors for a long time means something. That you can take the time to listen to each other and find common ground." Creating shared meaning and focusing on the positives were straight out of her marriage counseling handbook.

"The only common thing I want to focus on," Sam said, crossing his arms, "is how nice it's going to be when that tree stops shedding on my driveway."

"We've been neighbors," Jerry said, "but the kind that never interact." He turned to Sam. "I liked you better when we never talked."

Okay, so maybe the positive affirmations and attempting to find common ground weren't impressing them.

"Nice, Counselor," Jack, who somehow ended up right behind her, whispered in her ear. Which sent another shiver up her spine. What *was* it about this guy? He was obnoxious. But apparently her body didn't think so.

"Stop calling me that," she whispered back over her shoulder. "I'm a therapist, not a lawyer."

In front of them, Minnie Bartoe from the garden center was waving at her. So was Alicia

Gonzales from the candle factory's famous storefront shop. That gave her a little confidence. This was her town, too. She loved it, and she loved her neighbors. She truly cared about them. And she wanted to help. *That's* why she'd become a therapist.

More importantly, she wanted to use her hard-earned degree. And if that meant she had to win everyone's trust from here to Chi Town, she was going to start. Right. Now.

She waved back, took a breath, and addressed the two men. "Gentlemen, I have great news. It's come to light that the tree under dispute here was planted in memory of Jerry's wife." She gestured to Jack. "Because it's a special tree, Mayor Monroe is willing to move the tree over a few feet. Minnie, maybe you can recommend some fertilizer and transplant techniques and tell us where to get a…" She hesitated. A what? A backhoe? A bobcat? An axe? She had no clue. "…the equipment we need to move it. The tree lives, the memory is saved, and it's off your property, Sam. And nobody has to pay for the transplant."

The room was shocked into silence. Jack looked like he was, too, which struck her as a little bit funny. But her job was done here. She was going to grab her coffee and run.

And she didn't give a 'coon's tail what Jack thought. This was his town, too. He could get a little involved, right?

"I didn't know the tree was special," Sam mumbled to Jerry, his tone conciliatory. "Why didn't you say something?"

Jerry shrugged. "It's a private thing."

Sam cast a glance at Jack. "If Mayor's willing to move the tree, I accept."

"Fair enough," Jerry said. "You'd really do that, Mayor?"

Jack's cheeks looked a little bit on the high-color side, which was hard to tell through that ruggedly tanned skin, as he placed one hand on Sam's shoulder and the other on Jerry's. "Yes, I'll do it. Because…" He cleared his throat. "Because it would be a shame to see you two good neighbors lose sight of your friendship."

He sounded like he was trying to swallow a horse pill, but hey, progress.

"So, gentlemen, let's shake on it," Juliet said.

As the two men reluctantly shook hands, Jack moved back to her side. "Thanks a lot for offering my services," he said in a low voice.

On this particular day, Juliet literally had nothing left to lose. "I actually solved the problem, Jack. Without bloodshed or lawsuits." She crossed her arms in defiance. "And maybe you don't see it, but this is an opportunity to boost your popularity. Which you sorely need. *You* should be thanking *me*."

CHAPTER THREE

Jack would certainly thank the pistol of a woman in front of him, all right...as soon as he escorted her sassy self straight out his door. Juliet Montgomery was trouble, from her wavy auburn tresses and full lips down to her soft curves hidden under her unapologetically red blouse, black pencil skirt, and heels. He knew her as the passionate and emotional Montgomery sister. Prone to impulsive decisions. Everything life had taught him to shy away from.

Never trust a woman with red hair, was what his momma would say.

But then, his momma hadn't really trusted anyone.

Sharon, who must have entered the room while he was arguing with Juliet, walked up to him. "Sorry to interrupt," she said. "But that developer's been calling about the land again. He wants to set a date to present his case in front of the zoning commission. His minion wanted to walk right in here, but I stopped him. People like that should be"—she glanced up at the horned beast above his desk—"strung up and put on a wall somewhere like that longhorn." Sharon tried to hide a barely disguised grin.

Jack sighed. He seemed to be surrounded by women who gave him sass from all sides. In normal times he might have laughed, but her words made Jack's heart sink. *The Land* with a capital L was his granny's land—the reason he became mayor in the first place.

"Oh, so *that's* what that thing is," Juliet said, gesturing toward the cow's head. "I thought it was a ram."

"A *ram*?" She thought his longhorn was a *ram*? "No," he said, making a curvy motion with his hands. "Rams have curly—"

She interrupted before he could explain. "It tells me so much about your personality that you hang dead animal heads on your wall."

"I'll have you know that there was no cruelty in the fate of my longhorn," Jack said. "My college buddies said Bevo Jr. keeled right over and died after UT Austin lost the 2002 championship."

Juliet stared at him with green eyes that were as brilliant as the Irish hills. "And it's named after a rock band?"

He must've looked exasperated, because Sharon said, "Juliet's not a football fan, Mayor."

Yes, but didn't everyone know who Bevo was? "Bevo," he said. "With a B. Not *Devo*. He's named after the mascot for UT Austin."

"What's the Jr. for?"

"Well, the real Bevo weighs sixteen hundred pounds." He pointed at the beast on the wall. "This guy only weighed fourteen hundred."

The two women exchanged glances that were an eyelash shy of complete disrespect. "What would you like me to tell the Omnibuild guy, Boss?" Sharon asked, proving that she might give him sass, but she always had his back.

"Tell him that the zoning commission meets in three weeks, and we'll see him then."

And then he winced. Because just like that, he'd set himself up for a ticking time bomb.

He'd run for mayor and endured all of the resultant aggravations for one reason only: for his dear, wonderful, frustrating-as-all-get-out grandma, whom he would die for. She'd saved his life by raising him, and now it was his turn to do something for her. All he had to do was keep the untouched field and forest land that had been in his family for two hundred years from a determined developer, which appeared to be well-nigh impossible, because his grandma's shady accountant had A) failed to pay her taxes for years, and B) stolen her money. And now the auction for her property was just weeks away.

He'd taken a two-year leave from his architecture job to become mayor and try to do something about it. But so far, being the mayor had only served to showcase how bad he was at handling all this personal stuff attendant to the job. All these complicated...emotions.

He looked at the roomful of people surrounding him. He was going to need their support. And somehow convince them not to be swayed by Omnibuild's porky promises of money for their community. Then he had to prevent Devin Chambers, the cocky head developer, from taking his grandmother's land. Simple, right?

The townspeople respected him, for the most part. But he needed more than that. He needed to be liked and listened to. Because he was going to need all the help he could get.

"I'll hear the next complaint," he said, getting back to business. A glance out of the corner of his eye showed him that Juliet was talking to Jerry in the aisle.

"Thanks, Juliet," Jerry was saying to her. "I—I hadn't wanted to mention that thing about the tree, but—it helped a lot, didn't it?"

"I'm glad you and Sam worked it out." She was smiling kindly and touching his arm. As the two men walked out, side by side, a surprising thing happened: the entire room clapped. Including Juliet. And was that a tear in her eye? All the citizens seated in front of him were smiling.

Smiling? He got respect, but *smiles*?

His heart sank. Apparently, things had been resolved to everyone's satisfaction. But he was completely screwed. He wished he could remember what Henry Jackson's favorite beer was. Because it was going to take buying his city maintenance supervisor a case or two to get him to let Jack take a backhoe off of city property.

Juliet turned to go. Suddenly the room erupted in applause again, and he realized that everyone was clapping for her. Congratulating her. And asking her how she was doing.

They *liked* her. Even though her marriage-therapy gig was in trouble—because her romantic life was an epic disaster, and everyone in town knew it.

In his opinion, she was an outspoken pain in the ass.

But what a wonderful ass she had.

Okay, scratch that for being unprofessional. But he couldn't help but notice. Not that he was interested. She was his best friend's sister-in-law, which was the equivalent, as far as he was concerned, of being his best friend's sister. Which meant she was off-limits. Not that he wanted her to be *on*-limits. And also, he had to treat her politely, even if he didn't like her. And even if, as they said in Texas, she was more stunning than a pink evening primrose.

She grabbed her coffee cup, topped it off to the brim, and walked over to him.

"Thanks for helping," he said. But the wheels of his mind were churning. This annoying, brassy woman was a gold mine in disguise. One he couldn't let slip away.

"You're welcome." She waved to a few more people gathering around his desk. "Well, see ya. Have fun!"

"Wait," he heard himself call. "Want to have a seat?" The desperation seeped out of his voice like water from a leaky garden hose.

She turned back, her brows shooting up. "Did you just ask me to *have a seat*?"

Oh, the attitude. "Um, yeah," he said, clearing his throat. "That is…in case I need more background on the next case. I mean…I wasn't born here, like you." *You suck at this, Monroe. You really suck.*

She frowned, hands on her pretty hips. "You moved here when you were twelve." She pretended to count on her fingers. "That's almost twenty years ago."

"But you're a native. And…you know people. You knew that was a memorial tree." He rubbed his neck nervously and lowered his voice. "I—maybe you can stay?"

"Why on earth would you want *me* to stay?"

He dropped his voice. Moved in a little closer. "People *like* you."

There. He'd told the truth. Everyone in town called her Lulu for some ancient reason involving the water tower on the edge of town, and they all had great affection for her. Maybe she could help smooth out more rough edges. *His* rough edges.

If Jack knew anything, he understood his faults. He just had trouble expressing them. Like he did his emotions.

Ex-girlfriends had accused him of not feeling enough, but that wasn't true. He just didn't put stock in a lot of flowery sentiment that only served to embellish the truth.

He was a sincere man, and he didn't use flattery and sweet-talk. He used words sparingly and only when he really meant them.

Before she could say *no fricking way*, he ran and got a chair and placed it next to him at his desk. Then he slid his clipboard over to her.

"You want me to take notes?" she asked incredulously, as if he'd just asked her to perform brain surgery.

"Just so I can keep track of everybody."

He looked up. The next two people were already approaching the desk. Louise Howard, who worked at the candle factory gift shop and was recently widowed, was holding a little, fluffy white dog, and Doug Johnson, an accountant in his forties, was rocking back and forth nervously, hands in pockets.

Juliet turned to go. He rose and caught her arm. "Wait. I—please." Her arm was soft, and she looked at him with a mixture of surprise and annoyance. And something else, too. Vulnerability.

She seemed…troubled. A little tired. Something.

Nah, must be his imagination. She certainly wasn't acting vulnerable. More like waspish to him.

Realizing he shouldn't have touched her, he dropped her arm like quickfire. Then he dropped his voice to make one more plea. "I—I really need this forum to work. I need…help." He felt himself turning red. He was not winning awards for elegant locution today, that was for sure.

As she narrowed her eyes at him, he should have felt threatened, but instead he noticed that she smelled great. Not like the overly flowery scents his mom used to wear before she went out on dates. But a citrusy scent with a little edge. Just like her.

He forced himself to stay on track. "Please." He choked a little. Because saying that had almost killed him.

She crossed her arms. "You're sweating," she said, pointing to his brow. "That *please* really cost you, didn't it?"

"I—I can pay you."

"Really?" She seemed to perk up at that. "How much?"

Oh geez, she was going to make him negotiate

right here. The fluffy white dog barked.

"Anything you want, okay? Within reason," he added.

"Can we get this started, Mayor?" Doug asked, stroking his beard.

Juliet searched his eyes, evaluating him. Maybe wondering if he was serious or out of his ever-loving mind. "Fine," she said. "I'll stay for now."

Maybe he *was* out of his mind to keep her here.

Or maybe she was just what he needed.

Either way, he released a sigh of relief.

"That dog is a nuisance," Doug said as Jack sat down behind his desk and Juliet took a seat, too. Doug pointed to the alleged criminal offender, who promptly ducked his furry head under Louise's arm. "I work from home, and it barks all day long until she"—he pointed at Louise—"gets home from work."

"Look, I told you," Louise said, "Daisy is a rescue. She was a puppy mill dog, and she's very skittish. She gets upset when I leave."

"But you're gone eight hours a day." Doug gestured with his arms.

"Mrs. Howard," Jack said, "have you thought of a dog-sitting arrangement for Daisy?" There, that was a decent solution that showed sensitivity, didn't it? Daisy, however, wasn't impressed, as she continued to lay low.

"It takes her a long time to trust people," Louise said, stroking the dog's head.

"Poor baby," someone from the audience said.

"My mom and I watched her that one time," Juliet said.

"Oh," Louise said. "When I fell and sliced my knee open on the sidewalk and I needed stitches. I forgot about that. Yes, you did."

"Daisy did great at the bakery. The customers loved her."

Next to Jack, Juliet tapped her pencil in deliberation. The Saints only knew what she was going to come up with next. He grabbed the clipboard and scribbled, *Please do not volunteer me to dog sit*. He loved dogs, but just to be crystal clear, he was not going to go about his business being trailed by a barky animal. A man had to draw the line somewhere.

She wrote something herself and handed the clipboard back. She'd drawn a giant frown emoji. Wearing a *Stetson*.

Half of him wanted to strangle her. And the other half wanted to…no, he did not want to touch that silky dark hair that fell a little past her shoulders. Or watch how she tapped the pencil against her full lips when she was thinking. *Why* had he invited her to stay again?

Because soon he'd be transplanting trees and dog sitting dogs. Or worse.

She was wearing the slightest smile. Wily as the Mona Lisa, that woman was.

"Daisy is a really sweet dog," Juliet said to Doug. "You're just not seeing her sweet side because she's terrified to be alone. She's a people-dog."

"Exactly," Doug, unmoved, stabbed the air to make a point. "Not sweet when she's barking up a storm all day."

Juliet stood, then walked around the desk and

said something to the dog that sounded like baby talk. The dog poked her head out for a second and blinked, sizing up Juliet. "I could take her to work for a week or so. Until you can work on a different plan."

"You'd bring her to work with you?" Louise asked in a hopeful tone.

"Would she be okay in my group sessions?" The dog allowed her to pet its head, inclining toward her for more. Even animals seemed to love her. "Clients love emotional support dogs." She spoke to the dog. "And when they hear your story, it might make them feel that they could be strong like you, right, Daisy?" Juliet glanced up at Louise. "And you can pick her up on your way home from work. Easy peasy."

Well, okay, a resolution. One that thankfully didn't involve him. That is, as long as that dog didn't attend his forum. Which he'd make sure of.

"That sound okay to you, Doug?" Jack asked.

"As long as I can get some peace and quiet," Doug said.

"Thank you," Louise said to Juliet. "You're a sweetheart."

"You're welcome," Juliet said. "But I think you two should shake."

She might as well have told them to kiss and make up. Because that was essentially what she was asking them to do.

"I am sorry about the barking." Louise offered her hand.

Doug hesitated, but then shook it. "It's all right. I think we found a solution."

"All fixed," Juliet said as the neighbors walked off, and she sat down next to Jack. He must've been wearing a serious expression because she asked, "Don't you like rescue animals?"

"Sure. I love animals." They'd gotten Henry, the dog he grew up with, who happened to be the Best Dog Ever, from a shelter.

"I have a rescue cat named Ellie," she over-shared. "Her full name is Elle Woods."

Of course it was. He didn't have time to respond, because once again, everyone clapped like they were watching a play. Which might say something about what people did for entertainment in this town. But it also showed that Juliet clearly had a talent. Of doing sweetheart fixes. One that potentially involved giving both of them extra work, but still. As they left, people were chatting with their neighbors, smiles on their faces. That was something Jack hadn't been able to accomplish on his own.

In the next ten minutes, Juliet told someone to please roll the trash cans up the driveway for their elderly neighbor with a bad hip who never seemed able to pick them up from near the road. And then she asked the same angry-but-able person to please take the cans down *before* garbage day, too. She gently asked two neighbors with dueling political signs to tolerate each other's differences until the election.

He had a feeling that if she'd really asked them to kiss and make up, people would comply. She was *that* good.

And then suddenly, it was over. A handful of

people left were standing around, chatting and sipping coffee like it was social hour.

"Hey, Mayor," someone said, holding up his cup, "How about bringing some donuts next time? To go with the coffee, that is."

"Or popcorn," someone offered.

Yeah. He'd have to see about attracting a movie theater back to town, because these people were *desperate*.

"Okay, everyone," he said. "Ten-minute break, then I'll sign the permits, okay?"

"Permits?" Juliet asked. He noticed that her brows crinkled together in the middle of her forehead when she was puzzled, which was sort of adorable.

But *he* didn't need a sweetheart fix, that was for sure. So, no noticing adorable things.

"For vehicle sales, alarm systems, dogs, food trucks, and fishing." He counted it all off methodically on his fingers. "That kind of thing."

"Oh," she said faux-innocently. "Things you could handle."

"Ha ha." He'd barely managed a scowl when Mr. Teeter came up and patted Juliet on the back.

"Maybe you should do this kind of thing along with your counseling, Lulu. You're a natural."

Jack didn't miss her cringe at the nickname.

"Thanks, George," she said with a polite smile.

"I don't care if you *did* have three broken engagements," Mrs. Henderson, the retired town librarian, said. "You did a fine job today, dear." She dropped her voice. "Was it really *three*? Mabel from the candy shop said four, but I didn't think you were *that* old."

Juliet stiffened.

"Now, Mrs. Chester," Jack said before Juliet could answer. He wrapped an arm around the older woman's shoulder. "It was only two-and-a-half, and in my book, three's a charm, and so two-point-five is just a hare's tooth away from true love. And same as the number of wins I heard you had at bingo last week."

"You heard about my big wins, have you?" Mrs. Chester waved her arm nonchalantly. "Oh, Lulu knows I'm just curious."

"Sure thing, Mrs. C.," Juliet said. "Have a nice day." She said it so amiably, like it hadn't hurt. But Jack could tell it had.

He had a compulsion to tell Juliet that he understood how she must feel. That it was uncomfortable trying to overcome your past, especially in a town as small as a donut hole, with a long memory for mistakes. But he barely knew her, and he shrugged it off as his propensity to always jump to help someone getting beat up on, figuratively or not.

As the silence stretched awkwardly between them, he said, "I didn't remind her that she's been divorced three actual times." He smiled. "Not two and a half."

She crossed her arms. Half of her mouth tried to lift in a smile but never quite made it. "I thought you didn't know the histories of people in town."

"Oh, maybe not like you do. But I know enough. Sorry about that."

"It's okay," Juliet said. "She didn't mean any harm. But...thanks."

"Maybe you shouldn't be so forgiving," he said. "Or at least, not so polite. Some of these folks should know you don't like them poking fun."

She blinked and gave him a curious look, as if she were discovering for the first time that he might be human. But then Delores Teeter came up to chat and drew her away, talking a mile a minute like she always did. As Jack looked up, he saw a sight that made his blood turn to ice.

CHAPTER FOUR

Devin Chambers, the head developer of Omnibuild, strutted down the hall like the big rooster in the barnyard with his custom suit and bajillion-dollar Rolex. Jack ran to intercept him before he could set two feet into his office.

"Well, look what the cat coughed up," Jack said as Devin peeled off his Aviators and narrowed his eyes.

"Hello, Jack. Sorry I missed your forum." He didn't sound sorry at all. "Hope you're having fun playing small-town mayor, but you can't avoid that little land issue forever."

"Bring it to the zoning commission meeting," Jack said sternly.

Devin laughed. "We're going to buy that tax-lien land at auction and develop it into a world-class golf course complete with high-end shops and restaurants. Oh, and a big old hotel. When I present my case, everyone is going to love it because it's going to make your town flush with cash for posterity. Now, who wouldn't want that in exchange for knocking down an old house and some scrubby woodlands?"

Jack gave what he hoped sounded like a nonchalant chuckle. "There's a lot more at stake than money, and you know it."

"Come on, Jack," he said. "Your grandmother can't possibly use a hundred and fifty acres. Do something for everyone's benefit. Get the burden off her shoulders and ensure that your town will still be thriving in a hundred years."

"See you at the zoning meeting," Jack said sternly. "That is, unless you want to stay and watch me sign fishing permits."

Turns out he didn't. As Devin left, Jack took a deep breath and repeated a vow he'd made to himself a long time ago. The day he allowed anyone to touch one speck of gravel from his grandmother's property, let alone turn it into a golf-course-plus-whatever, would never come.

Except his idea-well of how to get out of this mess was bone-sucking dry. If he didn't figure out something soon, his grandma was going to get booted out of the home she'd lived in for the past fifty years. The place where his grandfather was buried. And then Jack would never forgive himself.

He returned to his office, where another line had formed by his desk. Sharon had taken Juliet's seat, ready to help him with the permits, and he had no choice but to get to work.

Fifteen minutes later, just as he'd ushered the last person out, he turned to find Juliet right smack in front of him, dangling a piece of paper in his face. "What's this?" he asked, taking it and looking it over.

"A parking ticket I never should have gotten." She lifted an elegant brow. "Since you're signing stuff, how about you waive this fee for me real quick?"

He sighed heavily. But then also noticed her

scent again, something light and fresh and delicious. Well, Juliet might smell good, but that
fragrance disguised a bitter core. "I did say I'd pay
you, but that didn't include waiving your traffic
tickets."

"I double parked for five minutes to help my
grandmother move some boxes. *Five minutes*."
Juliet tapped the toe of her red heels on the old
wood floor.

"That's five minutes too long," he said with a
smile. "Take it to traffic court."

"You're so black-and-white," she said with dis-
dain.

"There is no gray with the law."

She snorted and pulled the piece of paper out
of his hand. "Fine. I'll pay my ticket."

"There you go." He pressed his lips together to
avoid smiling. "That's called being a good citizen."

She spun around, and as she walked away, he
realized something. That everyone said goodbye
to her. The older ladies chatted her up; the
younger men—and older ones, too—were flirting
with her. The community clearly embraced her.
Even if they didn't seem to trust her as a therapist.
And even if she hated being called Lulu, it was
clear that they meant it...fondly.

"Wait," suddenly came out of his mouth, and
he found himself going after her. "I have a propo-
sition."

She halted and looked over her shoulder.
"Excuse me?"

Her eyes, as pure a green as brand-new grass in
spring, showed irritation. And annoyance as he

led her back to his desk. But looking into them made him want to confess all his headaches, his troubles. Of course, he couldn't tell her the truth, that he was in over his head, and he didn't have a clue how to save his grandma's land. All he knew was that he needed people to like him and rally with him for that land.

"I need a town counselor," he said. "Someone to come in a few mornings a week and help me sift through the personal grievances, exactly like today. And then follow up with them. This is right up your alley. And I—uh—I know talent when I see it."

She gave a little laugh and waved her hand in the air. "What was *that*?"

He looked around, but all he saw was a bunch of town folk socializing in his office. "What was *what*?"

"The empty flattery you just gave me. Didn't anyone ever tell you that flattery won't get you anywhere?"

He crossed his arms. "I don't *want* to get anywhere with you." Immediately regretting that, he hastily added, "If that's what you're thinking." Did he actually just say that? Geez, that was bad, even for a person who was prone to putting his foot in his mouth. "Just to clarify, this is strictly business. I'm not hitting on you."

"You'd better not be, Mayor."

He'd stuck his gavel in his pocket, with the knob sticking up. She set her ticket down on his desk, reached over, pulled the gavel out, and tapped it against her palm, smiling an overly sweet smile.

"Or, to borrow a line from Jerry," she said, mischief sparkling in her eyes, "I'd have to stick this where the sun don't shine."

He ignored her cheekiness. "If you come back next week, I can pay you a stipend that might make it worth your while." He could feel her assessing whether he was serious. Again, he thought he saw something—worry, sadness, *something*— and his gaze lingered a little too long. "This could solve your PR problem," he added quickly, making sure to break the eye-lock spell and stay professional. "You did a bang-up job back there. You could develop your reputation as a mediator—in a way that could help your career."

"My PR problem," she said slowly and carefully.

He shrugged. "Well, it's no secret that you might possibly have a credibility problem." He knew he'd just delivered a blow. But he needed to pull out all the stops.

She blanched. "H-how did you hear about that?"

Her obvious discomfort made him feel even worse. "I'm just talking about the fact that the town is more interested in your love life than your ability to counsel people."

"You didn't hear anything else?"

"No. Of course not."

She heaved a sigh. "Char just told me she doesn't want me to take any marriage clients until I resolve my own issues." She couldn't hide a wince. "Which I *will* do, of course. But for now, my schedule is pretty empty."

"I'm sorry," he said. Because he'd just been a jerk. And he felt terrible. "Look, I fully admit I need some help, too." He waved his hand toward where the crowd used to be. "All these disputes. These arguments. I'm not the best at dealing with these kinds of things."

"Because they involve feelings?" she asked.

Okay, so she hadn't lost her bite.

"Because I'm a man of *action*. I'm good at... acting. Doing things." Talk was cheap. Getting things done was what counted.

She swallowed. "Doing things?"

Hmm. That was interesting. There was a tiny movement at her throat as she swallowed, as if she might be thinking some mighty unprofessional thoughts herself.

"Yes," he said, pulling back a little. "Like leading town council, managing the board of trustees, securing essential services for the city, and in general, keeping the safety and well-being of all the town's citizens in mind at all times."

He wanted to make clear that she understood that *doing things* did not mean doing things—private or otherwise—with *her*.

"Thanks for the job offer," she said with sincerity, "but do you really think I don't know about your grandma's land? It's not a secret that it's about to come up for auction. I'm not sure getting me to help you with your popularity is going to change the outcome of that."

Busted. She certainly had a knack of calling him out on his bullsh—

He heaved a sigh. "The zoning commission meets in just a few weeks. I need the town on my side. I want people to see me as a compassionate human being. Which I am, but...sometimes my words don't quite make people think that."

Just then, Shelby, the woman he dated-in-quotation-marks (meaning, they didn't date at all, they had casual sex) waved from across the room. She was wearing a body-hugging black dress and matching red lipstick, and she looked like a knockout.

His gaze flicked back to the woman in front of him, who had just called his bluff. Shelby, on the other hand, never gave him grief. Probably because they just didn't interact like that. No arguments, no unpleasantness.

But no real emotional connection either.

He could practically hear the opinion his granny would have on that issue. It would be a loud and clear one at that.

He sensed that Juliet would never make an arrangement like that. He could tell even from their limited interactions that she was by-the-book, a stickler for the truth.

He decided to do something he didn't do very often. Be completely open. "I'm just trying to do the best I can," he said.

His voice cracked a little, belying his stress.

She searched his eyes. "I don't like you, but I respect what you're trying to do." She paused before continuing, "If, say, I *did* accept your offer, how about giving me that empty office space down the hall?"

He should have known she was going to push his limits. "You're valuable, but not that valuable."

"I need a place to work." She wasn't giving up. Digging in her claws like a sand crab.

"This is a temporary, part-time position," Jack said. "I can't give you an entire office. Besides, lots of people work from home these days." Geez. Give the woman an inch, and she asks for all the space.

"The truth is," she said, "I'm doing some public info sessions on mental health topics and the church basement where I'm holding them is being renovated. I need a temporary space."

"I'm not sure an office in city hall is appropriate for that purpose. But if I think of any ideas, I'll let you know." He tried to forget that she'd just seen right through him. And he felt an unwelcome twinge in his heart because—why didn't she like him? For some reason, he wanted her to. Before she could turn away, he said, "So, what do you say? A forum to handle disputes, complaints, and other problems twice a week. This could benefit both of us, you know." *Please say yes*, he prayed.

She gave a huge sigh. Tapped her shoe. Crossed her arms. Looked everywhere around the room but at him. "Okay," she choked out, as if she were swallowing every single ounce of her pride to say it.

"Okay?" he asked, not sure he'd heard right. "Was that a yes without sass, lip, or putting up a fight?"

"I do have one condition." She reached onto his desk and picked up her ticket.

He tugged it from her fingers. "Fine, you win," he said. "The cost of doing business. I'll pick you up on Saturday at nine sharp. Wear boots."

She frowned. "Wait." She halted him with a hand at his elbow. "There's no mayor's forum on Saturdays."

"Correct. We're not going to the forum. We're going to transplant a tree."

CHAPTER FIVE

Juliet pulled her car up a gravel driveway past a pretty gray-frame Queen Anne Victorian to her detached garage apartment, praying that her all-seeing landlord, Mrs. O'Hannigan, would not be in the mood to chat.

But the likelihood of that was about as high as someone in town not knowing that she'd just been benched from having real clients.

When she woke up this morning, she'd had a shiny new job and an office with a beautiful new desk. Now her job was on hold and she'd been offered a…well, a very strange one, doing little more than she'd done her whole life, settling disputes between her sisters.

Weird.

Juliet hadn't yet hit the bottom stair up to her apartment when Jacqueline O'Hannigan came running out her back door to greet her.

"Hello, Juliet," the rather straitlaced, gray-haired woman said, a little breathless from hurrying. "I just wanted to remind you that your rent is due."

"Hi, Mrs. O." She forced a smile, because her mom and grandma had taught her to be kind and polite. "It's not even the middle of the month."

"Yes, but last month you *were* a day late, dear. Your sister Tessa always used to pay on time."

Ah yes, her older sister. The Perfect One. "I'll

make certain to leave the check in your mailbox," Juliet said.

"Also, I just wanted to take a minute to make certain you understood the apartment policies."

What on earth? If Mrs. O was telling her to get rid of her cat, she was leaving, that's all there was to it. Juliet had moved into Tessa's old apartment almost a year ago, after her last disastrous break-up, and Ellie had come with her. Mrs. O'Hannigan liked things neat and tidy and, ideally, pet free. She only tolerated Ellie because she'd allowed Tessa to have her cat, Cosette. But then, Mrs. O loved everything about Tessa.

"I just want to make it clear that there will be no gentleman callers after hours."

"Oh, okay." Since she'd sworn off men for all eternity, she didn't anticipate that being a problem. Also...*gentleman callers*? Was that Victorian-speak for boyfriends?

If she were more on her game today, she would have protested that demand. Because...geez. It reminded her of her gran talking about dorm mothers at colleges in the 1950s.

But today, she was too defeated to protest the rule.

She only hoped that this upcoming check would be one of the last ones she'd hand Mrs. O. She dreamed of moving on, into a real apartment, one that hopefully didn't include her somewhat confused younger sister Vivienne, who was still crashing on her couch after almost a year. Or a landlord who watched every move she made. And critiqued it using Tessa as the gold standard.

"My sister rents her garage apartment," Mrs. O said, "and her tenant has a man friend, and it's become a real problem."

First of all, *man friend* seemed to be an oxymoron. Maybe it should be *man lover*. That made her bite back a chuckle. "Why is that?" she couldn't help asking.

Mrs. O leaned forward and cupped her hand near her mouth. "The *noise*."

"Like, from the TV?" Surely, she couldn't be talking about...

She shook her head adamantly. "No, dear. An entirely different kind of noise." Now Mrs. O was nodding her head vigorously and wiggling her eyebrows.

"Oh! Well, no worries with us!" Because as far as Juliet knew, Viv wasn't getting any either.

"I just wanted to make sure we were clear about that. Because of your...history." There went the eyebrows again.

Juliet felt the hair rise on her arms. Not for the third time today. That would be the last blow to her dignity. "My history?"

"Your three past engagements. I just don't want any man trouble here."

"No worries," Juliet said. "No man troubles. I promise." Juliet told herself Mrs. O was elderly. She was alone and maybe even somewhat frightened of dealing with tenant problems involving big, burly male visitors...which, now that she'd just thought that, a certain man came unwillingly to mind. Wearing a Stetson and not much else.

Gah. She needed wine, her pj's, and a large

dose of *Grey's Anatomy*, stat. And she didn't even care if it was barely noon.

Mrs. O was also most definitely lonely, because Juliet had never known her not to be home. Her purple PT Cruiser was parked in the old garage under Juliet's apartment, shiny and unused. And she never missed an opportunity to seek Juliet out the split-second she pulled up the driveway.

When all that attempt at understanding didn't calm Juliet's blood pressure down, she thought of one last thing that would rein in her tongue: she needed a place to sleep tonight and had no money to go looking for another one.

"By the way," Mrs. O'Hannigan said as Juliet turned to go. "Your younger sister…is she all right?"

"Viv?" Just then, she saw her friend Noah's silver Camry hybrid making its way up the driveway, which instantly untied a few jangled nerves. "She just started working at the Christmas shop. Why?"

Mrs. O shrugged. "Oh, just wondering how she was doing, with her new job and all."

Christmas Every Day had not exactly been part of Viv's life plan, who'd come home after a stint in Paris, studying art, didn't work out as planned, and the whole family was a little worried about her. She'd helped out in the boulangerie last year, but she'd never enjoyed it like Tessa had, and now that her mom had finally hired help, Viv only worked occasionally. Plus, she had a gluten sensitivity that Juliet knew made her feel at odds among all the family bread lovers. The gluten problem wasn't so bad that Viv couldn't work there, so long as she didn't eat anything. Which was difficult, even though their mother always carried a few gluten-free items. But Viv was fine, as Juliet witnessed every night when they had dinner and hung out together. Why did Mrs. O'Hannigan always have to talk in code?

"Mrs. O, if there's something concerning you about my sister, I hope you'd tell me."

"Of course. It was just…well, she might have been crying the other day."

"Oh." Viv was crying? That was concerning.

"For about an hour. I heard her over my soap opera. I wasn't sure if I should knock on the door. But I thought I'd let you know."

"Thanks," Juliet said. "I appreciate that." Okay, so maybe there was an upside to twenty-four-seven surveillance after all.

Just then, Noah got out of the driver's side of his car. Tessa, who was almost eight months pregnant but looked more like twenty, took a little more time extracting herself from the passenger side.

Then Tessa came barreling over, a concerned look on her face. She waved to Mrs. O and gave Juliet a giant squeeze. "Hi, sweetie," she said. Then in a whisper, "Are you okay?"

As Juliet hugged her sister back, she couldn't help but smile a little. Tessa was going to be a great mom, because she'd been a second mom to her and Viv their whole lives.

"I'm fine." She tried to sound like she hadn't been a second away from bolting up the stairs, digging out her old bottle of cooking wine, and guzzling it all before lunch. While crying her eyes out. Silently, of course, so as not to attract Mrs. O's radar.

"Hi, Jackie O." Noah waved vigorously. "You look positively ravishing today," he said with a flourish. "You are totally rocking that flowered apron." Noah had come straight from work. He was impeccably dressed in a shirt and tie and brown pants with a faint plaid pattern. Dark-rimmed glasses and hair that was short on the sides and longer on top completed his cutting-edge, fashionable look.

Mrs. O blushed and even cracked a smile. Mrs. O *smiled*? Well, to be fair, her favorite person was here.

"Hey, Mrs. O'Hannigan." Tessa handed over a little brown bag. "Brought you some warm croissants."

"Oh, why thank you, dear. How thoughtful. You have a glow."

"Aren't you sweet." Tessa, an expert at cutting conversations short from working in the bakery all those years, grabbed Juliet by the elbow and marched her straight up the stairs. "You'll have to excuse us," she said over her shoulder. "I don't have much time before I've got to get back to work. See you later!"

A minute later, they were settled on Juliet's brand-new teal couch and fuchsia chair. Juliet had snagged her gross, opened bottle of wine from her fridge door and brought it with her to the couch, but Noah confiscated it and took it into her bedroom. Ellie hopped up on the couch next to Juliet, delicately pawing at her before padding onto her lap and settling in.

"Hey, Ellie," she said as she brushed dark cookie crumbs off her new couch, noticing the box of Oreos her sister Vivienne had left on the coffee table. She loved her sister and didn't have the heart to boot her out, but she was sort of an awful roomie.

"Nice furniture," Noah said, running his hand along the arm of the chair. He had an excellent eye for detail. "When did you buy this?"

"Does it matter? Because it's all going to get hauled away when I can't pay for it." Since Viv had been camping out on the sofa, Juliet had invested in a really nice couch that pulled out into a bed so that Viv could sleep on a real mattress. Except Viv still slept on the couch and never pulled it out. *Sigh.*

"Oh honey," Tessa said, giving her a big hug from where she sat next to her. "We heard about your job. How are you doing?"

Sort of okay. Maybe. Not really. And also, word traveled fast in Blossom Glen, but this was practically lightspeed. "I'm all right," she said. "How did you two…know?"

"Jack told me," Noah said in a low, don't-kill-me voice.

"Of course, he did," Juliet tried to tamp down her anger. She and Noah had been friends since kindergarten. But he also hung out with Jack and Leo. Therefore, he could not be fully trusted. Although, to be fair, he usually walked that line very judiciously.

"He's the one who told us you might need to be checked on," Noah said.

"Like I needed to be *checked on*?" Jack was... impossible. And clearly underestimated her. How could so much irritation come in such a handsome package?

"Look, don't kill the messenger. He said you were having a bad day. He wanted to know what else he could do. I suggested caramel crunch ice cream, but instead he sent me."

She was having a bad day. Perceptive of him, but still. She could summon her own friends, thank you very much. And as for her favorite ice cream...it was also her favorite comfort food, but she was unfortunately out.

"How would Jack be the one to know you're having a bad day?" Tessa asked.

"I walked into his mayor's forum, just to get some coffee, and somehow ended up helping him solve disputes. Now he wants me to be the town counselor." This was a very odd day. That's what she got for summoning help from her dad. Maybe some heavenly signals had been crossed and she'd gotten help from someone with a very dark sense of humor instead.

"First of all, Jack seemed genuinely worried about you," Noah said. "And second, everyone, not just Jack, is talking about the forum. They said you were amazing, and they're telling everyone to come back on Tuesday."

Really? "I just helped out. Also, he seemed a little desperate. I mean, who just goes and invents a sudden magical town counselor gig?"

Noah fell uncharacteristically silent. "You'll have to ask Jack that. But I think it's because he sensed you're good at something he needs help with."

Tessa took up Juliet's hand. "Did Char really tell you not to see any couples for a while?"

She nodded, grimacing. "A client questioned me about my own relationships and my credibility, and I stumbled—badly."

"You poor thing," Noah said. "It's not like you murdered someone."

"Noah's right," Tessa said. "Your private life isn't anybody's business."

"So I made some mistakes in my past, right? I mean, who hasn't? I was young."

She slid a glance at her sister, who was biting down on her lip.

"What?" Juliet held her breath. "Oh no. Not *the pact*."

"What pact?" Noah glanced from Juliet to Tessa and back. "Is this a sister thing?"

Juliet nodded, noting Noah looked way too excited. "Our mom made us swear that we'd always tell each other the truth. Because we're family, and that's what your sisters do for each other."

And Tessa was definitely giving her the Truth Look now.

"Is that for real?" Noah asked. "Because if it is, then I want sisters."

"You do have sisters," Tessa said. "Us."

Noah, who literally was a part of their family,

smiled warmly. "Aw, that's so sweet, Tessa."

Juliet rolled her eyes. "You know we love you, Noah," she said sincerely. Turning to Tessa, she said, "Just tell me already!"

"You already know what I'm going to say," she said quietly.

Juliet had her pride, so the least she could do was explain herself. "You're going to tell me that yes, I've made mistakes, but there was a reason I let those relationships get so far, and it's a cop out to blame it on being young."

"You actually weren't that young for the last engagement," Noah said. "Twenty-seven. Plus, last year you thought Jax was about to propose and—"

"You were young with Ryan," Tessa said, referring to Juliet's college sweetheart, "but I don't think youth was the main reason you ended that when you were nearly at the altar."

Ryan was now a fourth-generation farmer who lived outside of town with his wife and four kids. He'd been the first person to really care about Juliet after her dad died in high school, and they'd dated clear through college.

"And then there was Tyler," Noah said. "Parents are willing to commit crimes to get their kids into his kindergarten class."

"In my expectant mom group," Tessa said, "some of the women are starting a waiting list."

"He *is* nice," Noah said. "In a bad way. He's practically a saint, and everyone in town loves him."

"Why is that bad?" Juliet asked.

Noah rolled his eyes. "Brakes don't work on an

icy road, girlfriend."

"What does that even mean?" Juliet asked.

"No friction." Noah waved a hand dismissively. "*Bo-oring.*"

"The point isn't that you broke up with those guys," Tessa said. "It's that you waited until you almost married them to break up with them."

How embarrassing.

"Maybe Jack likes you," Noah said. "Which is why he told us about you."

What was this, sixth grade? "Jack does not 'like' me," Juliet said quickly, slamming the lid of this discussion before it got out of hand. "He tolerates me. He needs me for…whatever. That's it, Noah." She thought of something else. "And I am totally, definitely, absolutely not looking for a relationship, for the first time in my life."

Noah sighed, Juliet thought a little sadly. "Well, I'm never going to find anyone in this town, so we'll just have to get cats together."

"I already have a cat," Juliet said. "And Noah, you're a gem. Keep an open mind." He shrugged like maybe he didn't quite believe that as she continued, "I know my issues, and I'm working really hard on them. It's just disturbing that they're spilling over into my job. My *new* job that I want to do so badly."

Tessa gave her a side hug. "You're going to do your job really well. You're only just beginning."

"Yeah." Noah hugged her from the opposite side, so she felt like a piece of lunchmeat between her bread buddies. "Better to get all your issues on the table right now and then sweep them off so you can have a fresh start. You're going to be an amazing therapist, Juliet. You're just having a bumpy start."

Aw. That warmed some of the cold dread in her heart. "Thank you both for coming over," Juliet said, hugging them back. "I'm going to give this a lot of thought."

She had to. Because she had to understand herself so she wouldn't make the same mistake again. And so that she could show her town that she was capable at her job.

"Except, Juliet," Tessa said, "you tend to be harder on yourself than anyone else. Just remember that. This is all going to blow over."

"As long as I don't make another mistake," she said. Which she would never, ever do. Juliet tucked a pillow under her chin. "You guys can leave now and let me drink in peace." A whole afternoon of binge-watching was starting to sound better and better.

"Sorry," Noah said, "but I tossed that rancid wine down the toilet. It was brownish and smelled like consumption would cause instant death. You can thank me later."

"I'm only going to find more." She half-laid down on the couch and swept her hand underneath, pulling out her emergency bottle. "Forget about *me*," Juliet said, righting herself on the couch as she had a sudden thought. "Mrs. O' Hannigan asked me if Viv was all right. She said she may have heard her crying. Do you know anything about that?"

Tessa petted Ellie's tail as the cat settled in at

Tessa's side. "To be honest, I haven't seen her much since she started her new job. She's been working until nine at night, then she stays after to close."

"She keeps collecting those," Juliet said, pointing to a big stack of shiny, colorful pamphlets on the coffee table. "France, London, Belgium, the Netherlands. I think she's restless. But she didn't strike me as upset or desperate."

Tessa flipped through the stack. "Maybe she's thinking of going back to Europe."

"I don't need her to go that far, but getting her own place might be nice," Juliet said with a slight smile. She loved Viv, but their living habits were completely opposite.

"Well, maybe she *was* crying," Tessa said. "But everyone's allowed to have a bad day."

"I'll try to ask her about it," Juliet said. She looked at Tessa, who was rubbing her belly, and realized she hadn't even asked her how she was feeling. "How's my little niece or nephew doing in there today?"

"Kicking up a storm. The only problem is that Leo and I have been so busy, we haven't painted the nursery yet, and we can't agree on a baby name."

"I can help you with the painting," Juliet offered. "Especially if Leo cooks for us." She grinned. "Have you decided on the color yet?"

That was a loaded question. Because Tessa had collected three million paint strips in the past few months and kept changing her mind.

"I've been reading all about nursery colors,"

Noah said. "Green is refreshing. Yellow promotes imagination. Gray increases productivity. Blue soothes but could be depressing or cold. And pink empowers."

"That all sounds wonderful." Tessa frowned. "But how do you decide?"

"Color is something I feel in my gut." Noah spoke with passion. "I think it's like picking the person you're going to end up with the rest of your life. You just know when you've found the right one."

"I really disliked Leo at first," Tessa confessed. "It really wasn't a you-just-know type of situation."

Juliet really didn't have a clue how to comment. So she was a little relieved when her sister and Noah got up to go.

"Just remember, babe. Montgomerys don't give up." Noah looked pleased as he glanced from Tessa to Juliet. "I've been hanging around you all long enough to know that." He turned to Juliet. "You've worked too hard to let something like this get to you."

She *had* worked hard. But this hurt to her core. Maybe because she didn't quite understand her past actions herself. And she certainly couldn't explain them very well.

And also, she hated to admit this, but she was starting to feel a little like the time when she was a teenager grieving her father and things had gotten worse—her grief had turned into a major depression and she'd needed mental help. Therapy and medication had saved her—and had given her an interest in helping people herself.

The parallel to now was that at the time, she'd felt like everyone—especially her friends in high school—had labeled her as...weak. She addressed Tessa. "I think I know how you felt after Sam broke off your engagement and started dating someone else. Everyone knows all my mistakes. My screw-ups. And they seem to think it's okay to mention them to me."

"They'll soon forget them and move on to the next bit of gossip." Tessa patted Juliet's knee. "You'll see. The important thing is for you to resolve your past for yourself."

"She's right," Noah said.

That was exactly what Char had told her, too.

On the way out, Tessa extracted the second wine bottle from her hands.

And they were gone—with her wine, no less— before she could say another word.

• • •

Friday at dinnertime, Jack pulled up at his buddy Leo's driveway to find him and Noah in the garage surrounded by a clutter of crib parts. Noah was staring at the directions intently while Leo looked like he was trying to figure out how two long metal bars fit together.

"Hey," Jack said. "Don't most people put cribs together in the baby's room?"

"That's what normal people do," Noah said as he placed some rails of equal length all together in a pile.

Leo gave Jack a frustrated look. "Tessa and I have both been putting in a lot of overtime in our businesses. The baby's room's not even painted yet, and she's getting really nervous that this crib's not together."

"Can I see those?" Jack asked, holding out his hand for the parts. As Leo searched the directions, Jack rotated the parts and grabbed a screwdriver. In a minute, he'd connected the two pieces.

Leo swatted him with the directions. "How did you do that?"

"It's intuitive. The elbow joint connects to the arm joint, see?" He pointed to the connection.

"And the knee bone's connected to the thigh bone," Noah chanted, waving his arms to the tune.

Jack rolled his eyes. "The *real* reason is that everyone knows Texans have superior intelligence."

"You mean superior *egos*," Leo said with a chuckle. "Thanks." He let the paper flutter to the garage floor. "I need a beer." He herded them both to the backyard. "C'mon. Let's go."

A minute later, they were sitting on Leo's brick patio sipping beer and listening to the crickets, which were partying hard, their last hurrah before the mild weather disappeared.

"I need to borrow some tools," Jack said, rubbing his neck. He really didn't want to discuss why, but he had to show up tomorrow with the proper equipment or he'd be a laughingstock.

"What kinds of tools?" Leo asked.

"Tools to cut around tree roots. And maybe a tarp if you have one."

"All right," Noah said, setting down his beer. "Where are you hiding the body?"

"It's not a body. It's a tree." He might as well come out with it. "I need to move a tree tomorrow."

Leo laughed outright. "Please tell us what this has got to do with being mayor."

"Well, it might have something to do with the fact that I hired Juliet to help me arbitrate my forum a couple of times a week." There. He'd just get that right out in the open too.

"Tessa told me," Leo said carefully, in a way that made the hair on the back of Jack's neck prickle.

"Uh-oh," Noah said, taking another swig of beer.

Having Leo worry about whether or not he was going to hit on his sister-in-law was exactly what he *didn't* want.

He made sure to look Leo in the eye. "We made a business deal, that's all."

"Ha!" Leo poked the air. "That's what I said last year." His mouth turned up in a giant smile. "And now I'm going to be a father in a few weeks."

Okay, Jack was absolutely not going to allow that insanity to happen to him.

On a brighter note, his best friend was going to be a *father*. He still couldn't wrap his head around that. It was amazing, the transformation in Leo over the last year. He'd gone from fun and carefree to... well, a little more serious and also fiercely protective of Tessa. And that protectiveness apparently included Juliet, too.

Jack shook his head. "Yeah, well, I'm not a softie like you. Juliet's just going to help out temporarily. You know, using her psych skills."

"You know she *is* my wife's sister." Leo leveled his gaze on him.

Jack put his hands up. "I know, I know. I'll treat her nice and fairly." He would never do anything that would come between their friendship.

"Right," Leo said, sipping his drink. "Just not *too* nicely."

Jack looked at his friend. Normally he had a goofy grin on his face. But it was clear now that he wasn't kidding.

Jack decided to be as reassuring as possible. "You have no cause for worry."

A million questions churned around in his head. Specifically, what was Leo's take on those two-point-five engagements? On Juliet herself? And why did her boss tell her she couldn't see couples' clients? What was that about? He couldn't ask without getting Leo's radar up.

"Juliet's sensitive," Leo said in a serious tone. "And she might fall easily. And…I love you, but this is a warning."

Jack gave a firm nod. "Warning heard and heeded."

"May I say something?" Noah asked. "Juliet's been through a lot and for the most part, she's come through with flying colors. And she's determined not to make any more poor choices. So Leo, you don't have to treat her like she's fragile. And Jack—she's way too smart to fall for you, but if she did, she'd challenge you in every way. She's…wonderfully complicated."

Jack put his hands up in defense. "Yeah well, we all know I stay away from complicated women." Juliet might be hot, and she might be interesting, but she was also a huge pain in his side. That's why he went for women like Shelby, who didn't expect anything from him other than fun. A good time.

"Hey, guys," Tessa said, entering through the back gate. She walked over to Leo and kissed the top of his head. He smiled at her and took her hand. "Did you guys get the crib together by any chance?" she asked Leo.

"We—um—read the directions," Leo offered, shifting in his seat.

"What he means is, they were complicated," Noah said.

"Yeah, like, really confusing," Jack offered.

Tessa sighed. "Okay, so…that means no crib yet."

Leo squeezed her hand. "I'll look at it tomorrow. I won't let our baby go crib-less, I promise."

"Okay." She smiled at her husband, clearly wild about him. "I'll hold you to it." Then she said good night and headed into the house.

"I have a suggestion for you, Leo," Noah said. "You might need to hire an interpreter to help us figure out those directions."

"Or just have George Teeter do it," Jack said. "He's mechanically inclined."

"Hey, I have an MBA, okay?" Leo said. "I can put it together. When I'm more rested."

As the conversation shifted, away from cribs and warnings, into safer, nonthreatening territory, Jack realized that he loved his friends, and he adored his granny. But his growing up had shown him that love was really nasty. People said what they didn't mean and they hurt each other, and then they hurt their kids. And so, he didn't need Leo's warning. Because he was going to avoid love at all costs.

CHAPTER SIX

Juliet was waiting at the end of her driveway when Jack stopped by with his big black Toyota Tacoma at nine a.m. on the dot the next morning. She hadn't spent time imagining what kind of vehicle a good ol' Texas boy like him would have, but the truck suited him perfectly. She hauled herself up and in just as Mrs. O opened her door and peeked out.

Whew. A near miss.

Jack handed her a giant travel mug, a gesture that warmed her from the inside even though she hadn't taken a sip. "Coffee!" she said, immediately perking up. "Thank you."

He looked pleased. "Well, a deal's a deal."

Fair enough. Juliet eyed the immaculate inside of his truck. There wasn't a piece of lint to be found on the gray carpet. The floor mats were so clean they were shiny. Who had shiny floormats? The dashboard and wood trim gleamed. Looking down at the cup holders, she noticed he'd brought a coffee for himself, too.

"You gave me the nice mug. The kind that keeps your coffee warm all day."

He shrugged. "Hearts are big in Texas."

She chuckled and took a sip. "Mmmm. The only reason I hang around you is because you make amazing coffee."

"I do other things amazing, too," he said as he

stared ahead at the road.

Okay…no. He was just trying to get a rise out of her, right? And it worked, if the flare of warmth she felt in her cheeks was any indication. She rolled her eyes. "Like relocate trees?"

He gave her a quick once-over before he turned his gaze back to the road. Which seemed assessing and also…she'd dated enough men to know that he liked what he saw. Even though they disliked each other. So why did she get the feeling this felt more like a date than a landscaping adventure?

"It rained last night and more's expected by noon," he said. "Sure you don't want to put some old clothes on?"

She glanced over her outfit, a bright yellow sweater, a jean jacket, jeans, and her new flannel-lined boots. Sort of a casual, lumber-jacky vibe. "Well, I heard the *Blossom Glen Gazette* was going to be taking photos. And I'm the new Town Counselor. I wanted to make an impression."

"You might have to get down in the trench with that root ball. Might be muddy."

"I mean, nothing's fancy or anything." She lifted a boot. "These are root ball-appropriate."

Turns out Jerry lived on the county boundary, past a lot of farmlands, and it took about an hour to get there. On the way, she learned that Jack loved the outdoors. That he was dedicated to greenspace architecture, and he planned to get back to that as soon as his mayoral term was over. And that every time he mentioned his granny, his voice grew soft.

"You must love her very much," she said, expecting a joke or retort.

"I do," he said. "She's the best." And he left it at that.

Finally, they arrived at Jerry's house, which was a tidy ranch nestled in a quaint, quiet neighborhood surrounded by fields, now golden with dry corn stalks and low, rolling hills.

Near the garage, there was a sizable garden between Jerry's property and Sam's. Juliet recognized the deep reds, whites, and yellows of mums among some faded summer blooms. In the center was a tree with coppery-brown leaves that stood about fifteen feet tall, with a slender trunk.

"That doesn't look too terrible," Juliet said, feeling just a little guilty she'd gotten Jack into this mess.

"What were you expecting?" he asked. "A sequoia?"

After the best eye roll she could muster, she noticed that someone had already spray-painted an orange line where the utilities ran underground. As Jack pulled up, a giant piece of equipment with a big arm and a metal bucket came into view, parked on the grass.

"How did you get that—machine here?" Juliet asked.

"It's a front-end loader. Or just a loader for short." Jack threw the truck in park. "The City Maintenance Director let me borrow it, but he had to go to a wedding today. So I guess I'm driving."

He *guessed*? "Do you *know* how to drive that thing?"

He looked at her with a dead-serious expression. "Honey, I drive my front-end loader just fine." Then he got out, leaving her to wonder just what she'd gotten herself into with a man who constantly spoke in double entendres. She fanned herself, because Jack was…too much. Yes, that was it. A handsome devil with the focus on *devil*. And she'd best remember that.

She met him near the cargo bed, where he was gathering tools—a shovel, a large spade, and a heavy-duty set of pruners.

He handed her the spade and looked up at the sky. "It's going to rain, so we'll have to work quickly." He stood up straight, leaning his arm on the truck. "I want to ask you to leave our personal differences aside so we can work together to get this job done."

"I will." She took a coil of rope from him. And smiled.

He nodded and smiled back. And somehow, she got caught in that smile, snared in his October-blue-sky gaze for a few beats too long.

"All righty then," he finally said, giving a slight nod. "Let's go move a tree."

She liked it better when they fought, because then she didn't have to deal with the giant flock of butterflies currently fluttering around her stomach.

While Jack and a couple of guys from town got busy hand-digging a wide trench around the tree, she chatted with the neighbors. A reporter took some photos of the tree. Everyone was cordial, including Jerry and Sam, and the neighborhood kids were really excited to see the machine—the *loader*—hauling all the dirt.

She had to admit it was a thrill to watch Jack drive. Probably because of hot construction worker fantasies she couldn't help having... And of course he hammed it up and waved to all the kids before he dug the new hole. The kids were loving the big equipment, the loud noises it made as Jack controlled the giant arm, and the bucket with silver toothy jaws as it tore through the earth. But even though the rain hadn't started, the spring mud was awful. She wasn't even working yet and her boots were covered with it.

"Will you pass me the pruners?" he asked her later from inside the trench, and she quickly hauled them over and handed them down to him. A few minutes later, he said, "Pruning saw."

She reached over and placed it—at least, the only thing around that looked like a saw—in the palm of his upturned palm. "Yes, Doctor."

He shot her a puzzled glance.

"You want the scalpel or the forceps next?" she asked pointedly.

He dropped his voice. "Look, you're welcome to come down here and dig, just saying."

She stooped down and lowered her voice, too. "I just want to feel like I'm being asked nicely."

He stood up to his full height. Which, admittedly, was a sight to see in his flannel shirt and jeans, his wavy hair all rumpled, and those hands...those beautiful working hands. As he stood in the trench and she bent over, their eyes were level.

"Juliet," he said, slowly and carefully. "There is one more thing I need—I have a blanket in my cab that I'd like to wrap around the trunk. Would you mind getting it, *please*? If it's not any trouble, that is."

She took pleasure in his annoyance. "Well, since you asked like that, sure thing, Mayor."

When she retrieved the blanket, the photographer asked her to hold it up as she stood at the edge of the trench. She posed, and he asked her to stand a little closer to the edge. "I'm glad we have a mayor who isn't afraid to get things done," she said, getting in some PR in front of the small crowd.

"Hey, be careful," Jack called from the trench. "It's slippery—"

As she turned her head to look at him, the soggy ground gave way and she slipped. And slid down the rim of the trench like a mini sliding board. On her butt.

A few seconds later, she lay at the bottom, stunned, icy mud seeping through her clothes. Jack looked down at her with concern, all traces of sarcasm gone. "You okay?" he asked, extending a big, strong lumberjack hand. Which she took.

And *oh no*, that hand was just as sturdy and strong and warm as she'd imagined. But the contact sent a wave of heat through her, despite the fact that she was cold and shivering. And made her tingly and a little weak-kneed, so that she stumbled a little on the way up.

Then, as he helped her up, he slipped, too. Suddenly they were both back on the ground, mud and water sloshing around at the bottom of the trench.

She was caught in his arms, lying on top of him, looking into his blue eyes up close and wondering what had just happened.

For a moment, everything stood still—the trench, the mud, the big loader, the laughter and buzz of the crowd, the snapping of photos. It was just the two of them, bound together by his strong grip and the current of electricity snapping between them that blocked out everything else.

"Somehow, I didn't see you as someone who'd want to mud wrestle," he said with a grin.

Juliet tried to scramble off of him but slipped again.

"I can see the headline now," Jack whispered as he struggled to right her. "Mayor and Town Counselor Get Down and Dirty."

She didn't have time to roll her eyes. "Hey, Mayor," someone called, "you digging your political grave down there?"

"Thanks a lot, Al," Jack said as the crowd laughed. "And you're right," he called from the trench. "Digging holes isn't in my job description. I should stick to cutting ribbons and holding babies, right?"

And then, above the hole, the reporter leaned over the brim and took a thousand photos.

"Can you confiscate those?" Juliet asked in a panicked tone as she tried in vain not to touch his warm, lean body in the tight space. His arm held her loosely, but everything in her body felt hot and tight.

"Not legally," he said under his breath. "So, for

right now, better just say cheese."

All righty then. Juliet held up the now filthy blanket and spoke to the crowd. "Just wanted to be sure I delivered it in person."

As everyone laughed again, a shiver went straight through her.

"You all right?" Jack asked, strangely concerned.

"Great. Just fine. No worries," she said as casually as possible as she looked for a hand out. Because Jack being nice was…well, she didn't want to think about what it was.

People helped them out of the trench, but by then, mud was her middle name.

While Jack moved the tree with the front-end loader and plunked it down in its new home, Jerry's daughter offered her a clean blanket and a cup of tea.

An elderly gentleman who walked with a cane approached her from the crowd. "Hello, Ms. Montgomery. I had to come out today and see for myself who the new town counselor was."

Juliet, huddled in the blanket, warming her hands with the tea, smiled at the white-haired gentleman, who was tidily dressed in a suit and tie. "Well, I'm afraid you're not seeing me at my best," she said, sweeping her hand over her muddy self. "But it's nice to meet you. I'm afraid I don't know who you are." Which was odd because she knew just about everyone.

"My name's Alfred. I had to come and see the young woman who was getting neighbors to act more neighborly and help everyone to work together for the good of our town. It reminds me of the old days."

Juliet shrugged. "Well, my dad always taught us that being kind was number one."

Alfred leaned heavily on his cane. "Indeed, it is. Well, thank you for your work. You have quite a way with people."

Ha. Clearly he hadn't heard about her mandatory couples therapy break. "You seem to be interested in the community, Alfred. You should come to one of the mayor's forums. A lot of times projects come up that need volunteers. Maybe you'd like to get involved?" Juliet knew how important it was for elderly members of town to stay involved. She didn't really know of any projects off the top of her head, but judging by how quickly she and Jack had gotten involved, she was certain there would be plenty more.

"That sounds lovely, my dear." He gave a little bow. "Thank you kindly for the invite."

And then it was done.

Jerry and Sam thanked them, then introduced all their family members who had gathered. Everyone was grateful and best of all, talking to one another.

She helped Jack gather the rest of the tools. "I saw you chatting with Mr. Blossom," Jack said.

"Mr. Blossom? Wait. *The* Mr. Blossom, as in, from the founding family of our town?"

"You bet. He doesn't come out too much anymore, seeing as how he lost his wife a few years ago. But he looked like he was enjoying himself."

Mr. Blossom had complimented her for being

town counselor? She slapped herself on the fore-head and groaned. "I can't believe it. I just suggested that he do some volunteer work. I mean, he practically founded every volunteer group in town."

"Well, you never know when someone can use an invite." Jack's lips turned up in a smile before he tossed the tarp into his truck and dusted off his hands. "Okay, we're out of here." He looked up at ominous gray clouds moving rapidly across the sky. "Not a moment too soon."

Gosh, did he have to go and smile? Juliet was shaky, shivering from the cold, but also overcome with another reaction entirely. Her heart was pounding uncomfortably, and everyone's voices sounded like an echo chamber in her head, because all she heard was her own voice saying, *Jack. Jack is hot. Jack is attractive. Jack is…*

No, no, no.

He was *not for her.*

She wanted nothing more than to get out of her muddy, wet clothes and flee far, far away from the tall, hunky faux-cowboy next to her.

Just as he began to haul his tools back to his truck, she came to her senses and grabbed his elbow. "You have to say something," she whispered.

"Like what?" he said nonchalantly. "The job is done. Everybody's happy." He swept his arm over where the crowd was gathered. "Plus, rain's on the way. Time to leave."

"Just remark on the peaceful solution to the problem or something. You know, like, be the *mayor.*"

"*You're* the town counselor," he shot back. "Why don't you say something?"

She crossed her arms and glared at him. "Just do it, Jack."

"I...um..."

"What is it?" Wet mud had seeped through her undies and all down her right leg and into her boot. And something dripped down her back under her jacket, making her shiver yet again. She needed to move this along before she turned into a mudsicle.

"Maybe I'll just go around and shake their hands and call it a day."

The therapist part of her saw something—that swaggerin' Jack Monroe was...nervous. "No, Jack," she said, not unkindly. "Sometimes people need closure. You did a good thing. Now just...preside."

"Preside," he said, as if he were thinking about what that meant.

"Do you have glossophobia? It's all right if you do."

He gave her a puzzled look. "Glosso *what*?"

"Fear of public speaking. If you do, I can recommend someone to work with you on that."

"No, I just... I'm not good with words."

Hmm. An admission that had clearly cost him something. "Just a few would mean a lot to everyone. Focus on the neighbors." She offered him the spade like it was a staff. Or a crutch. Whatever he needed it to be.

He took it and stood before the small crowd, just as the clouds darkened and a few giant raindrops splatted down. One landed on the top of her head, cold and large, followed by another.

"Okay, folks," Jack said, looking around nervously and clearing his throat. "I—um—" Jerry and his kids were all linking arms. Sam and his wife were inspecting the new space in their garden, looking pleased.

"Let's all bow our heads for a minute and think about what this tree means. For some of you, it will help you remember the joy your mom took in nurturing beautiful, growing things. Like how she nurtured you all. For others, you'll dream of the plants you can make thrive in this beautiful garden, and that will make you happy. So, let's be glad we have this beautiful tree, and may it thrive just like the friendships between neighbors. "

At that, he glanced up at Juliet, who gave a giant, reassuring nod. He had it in him, after all, to be touching.

"Amen," he added.

"A-*men*," everyone replied.

Amen? He'd said *amen*? Juliet didn't have time to ponder his speech-slash-prayer because suddenly the sky let loose.

"Want to come inside, Mayor?" Jerry yelled over the pouring rain, which was beating down in icy sheets.

Jack looked at Juliet. Who looked down at her mud-covered self and gave a slight shake of her head. "Thanks, Jer," he said, "but we're out of here. See you all. Everybody, have a nice weekend!"

Jack grabbed her arm and ran with her to the truck. Her body seemed to still be in that trench, feeling the warmth of his body next to hers, the rumble of his laugh, and his big hand helping her out of the mud.

Yep, she was going to need all the prayers she could get.

• • •

Everyone was yelling "Thanks, Mayor! Thanks, Counselor!" as Jack herded Juliet to his truck. She was cold and shivering, her hair hanging down in limp strands. He worried about her getting sick, *catching a chill* as his granny would say, but at the same time, his mind was on overdrive, remembering how she'd felt in his arms.

Delicious. Wonderful. Warm.

"Get in," Jack said, holding his truck door open for her. It was raining buckets, an icy fall rain that warned of winter peeking its head around the corner.

"No," that stubborn woman said, crossing her arms.

After all they'd just been through, couldn't she just listen for once? But no. This Saturday morning was dragging on into afternoon, taking all his good weekend vibes with it. Not to mention how discombobulated he felt by the mud incident. Those brief seconds of her next to him, soft and sweet-smelling and curvy. How the whole thing was so horrible and yet somehow…fun.

"What is wrong with you, woman?" he couldn't help saying. "Are you waiting for the rain to rinse off all that mud? Get your fancy ass in my truck."

His voice cracked on the last sentence, sounding desperate.

The moment the words flew out of his mouth, he knew he was in trouble.

"Excuse me? My fancy *ass*?"

Jack pinched the bridge of his nose. Prayed for patience. But none was bestowed. Instead, the heavens opened up and dumped what appeared to be gallons of water. To Juliet's credit, she didn't even flinch.

"You're wetter than a gator in a pond. So get in." He paused. "*Please*."

She moved the dripping strands of hair out of her eyes. "It's perfectly clean." She pointed to the inside of his truck, then waved a hand down the length of herself. "And look at me."

Oh, he looked all right. Her dripping hair, her bright yellow sweater streaked with mud, her jeans and new boots barely visible under a heavy coating of it. As she drew her arms over her chest, she shuddered. Looking more pathetic than a wet cat.

And yet...her eyes were a stunning green—jade? Emerald? He didn't know the exact shade, but they were soulful and full of warmth. And when he looked at her, he got lost, sort of like being stunned into stillness, making him awkwardly tug his gaze away.

Warm eyes, warm heart, his grandmother would say. That warmth was evident in how Juliet had treated Jerry and Sam today. She'd united them and their families. Somehow left them better neighbors than they'd been before. Made them feel like they'd both won.

And she'd talked him up to everybody, too.

Part of him wanted to scoop her up and set her in the truck. And part of him wanted to drive off alone, because frankly, this sopping wet woman felt like a threat to him in ways he didn't want to examine too carefully.

And no. He did *not* want to kiss her. Not after all that headache. Which was her doing, really. On his one day to work on his dream greenspace projects free from distractions. Instead…here he was. Drenched, hungry, cold. And his truck was about to become a mud pen.

"I don't care if my truck gets dirty," he lied.

"Yes, you do." She circled her finger in front of his face. "I can see it in your eyes."

He sighed. "Okay, I love clean things. And I do feel possessive of my truck. But trucks are made for work. For getting dirty. So, let's try this again, Juliet." Saying her name out loud caused it to reverberate in his throat in a weird way. Familiar, yet not at all. "*Please* get in my truck."

Something in her eyes appeared to soften. "Okay," she said, and got in.

Women. He'd never understand them. Especially not this one.

Once inside, he started the engine and cranked up the heat. Next to him, she hugged herself and seemed to be trying not to shiver—and failed. He was drenched, too, his hair dripping into his eyes, his flannel shirt muddied and soaked.

"I have one thing to say," she said.

"What's that?" he asked warily.

She tossed him a giant smile, and for a flash it was as if the clattering rain had stopped and the sun had broken out. "You did a nice job back there, Mayor. I even saw a few tears." She tapped her finger against her lips. "Hmm. Or were those raindrops? Anyway, it doesn't matter. I think our effort was a big success. Except"—she bit down on her cheeks, like she was trying not to laugh—"I didn't realize we were going to pray today."

And just like that, his anger and frustration evaporated, and he found himself cracking a smile. "I didn't either." But he'd done it. Made an emotional speech. Got through it.

"You did…all right," she said, plain and simple. No flowery words. It made him feel like she was telling the truth. And being sincere. "More than all right. I'd say you were a big hit."

"If anyone was a big hit, it was you." It was true. Everyone in town loved her.

"No, Jack," she said softly. "We did it as a team."

He gave a brief nod and tried not to think about how they'd actually managed to work together for good. Except for the problem of a growing attraction he couldn't seem to control.

Attraction or not, right now they both needed to get somewhere warm and dry. But town was an hour away. Fortunately, he knew of somewhere much closer they could go.

CHAPTER SEVEN

"You missed the turn-off," Juliet said a while later, looking out the window as fields of corn rolled by. Growing up in Indiana had taught her that it was dent corn, so named because of its hard, indented kernels that were used to feed livestock. The stalks were left to dry in the fields through October, turning them a familiar amber color that made her heart ache a little with its beauty.

"Thank you, Ms. Smarty-pants, but I did not."

She let her gaze rest on his profile as he drove. His brow was strong, his nose perfectly straight, his jaw square and obstinate to match his personality. "I'm going to ignore that misogynistic name you just called me because I have to ask, are you taking me somewhere where you can kill me and hide the evidence?"

"Now, how'd you know that?" The corner of his mouth turned up in a smile. But he still didn't say anything else.

"So?" she asked, not relenting. "Are you going to tell me where we're going? Because I'm getting nervous."

"I'm taking you somewhere close and warm."

"I knew it! You *are* trying to get rid of me, aren't you?"

"Actually, I'm trying to save you from catching pneumonia."

"Jack, I'm fine," she protested, just as a tickle

began in her nose. "We'll be back in no—no time—ah—" *Do not sneeze*, she told herself as she rubbed her nose with her finger to get rid of the urge. She inhaled a deep breath. Pressed her lips together. But all was futile as her whole body convulsed in a giant, eye-watering, noisy *ahchoo*!

"I need to ask you a favor," he said as he produced a tissue box from his middle storage compartment.

She blinked at him through watery eyes and blew her nose. "Okay, sure."

"I'm going to ask you not to protest, not to say anything. Trust me—just this one time. Okay?"

As he glanced at her, all the warm, fizzy feelings from inside the muddy trench came rushing back. He wasn't a half-bad person, as evidenced by the way he'd managed to help everyone back there, even if he did think he was a reverend instead of a mayor.

And he was being nice. So she found herself saying, "Okay."

"Great."

That was it. No explanation. He just stared ahead and kept driving. A couple of miles later, he turned onto a back road, then rode it until it turned into a winding, gravel drive that meandered through an apple orchard, then passed over a stream, now swollen from the rain. The drive began its ascent up a hill, where a picture-perfect white-frame farmhouse sat at the top, smoke drifting out of its chimney.

"What is this place?" she asked. "It's beautiful. Even in the pouring rain."

"This is where I grew up," he said. "It's my grandma's house."

He was taking her to his *grandmother's* house? Looking like this?

"Jack, please," she begged. "Turn the truck around. Look at me." That stubborn jaw was just as set as ever. She tugged on his wet sleeve to get him to listen. Except that was a mistake. Because under his shirt, his muscles were strong and corded. And his arm radiated heat despite her whole body being an ice cube.

And then, against her will, she sneezed again.

"That's precisely why I'm doing this," he said. "You're going to catch your death and we're still a half hour from town. Here, you can change into some dry clothes and warm up."

"Such a worrier," she said, although secretly, she was touched. "Anyway, you can't do this to her. Look at us."

He winked. "You don't know my grandma." He flicked his gaze up and down at her, which had the effect of giving her goose bumps. "You do look wetter'n a rat floating down the river, but Granny won't mind that."

She rolled her eyes. Mainly to deflect from the fact that his gaze rested on her in a way that made her feel calmer and more unsettled at the same time.

"Shouldn't we at least give her a heads-up?" Juliet asked.

"If I'd have called ahead, she would've fussed. Just trust me on this one, okay?"

The annoying man continued up, up the gravel drive.

"Wait a minute," she said as she stared out the window at acres of tall trees, currently showing off bright hues of yellows, reds, and oranges. The rain had brought the leaves down in a colorful carpet at their bases. "This is...*the land*."

And just like that, his expression changed to stoic and serious. "Yep," he confirmed with a heavy sigh.

"Oh, Jack," slipped out of her mouth. Because she couldn't say that this was the most stunning piece of property she'd ever seen, and to have it be ruined for chichi shops, condos, and a giant hotel and golf course was...an abomination.

A tiny muscle in Jack's jaw was working, and he was nervously tapping the wheel with his fingers. She decided to wait and let him talk about it on his own terms. Would Jack do that? She wasn't sure. But she could tell he didn't want to discuss it now.

A minute later they stood at a little door facing the gravel drive. The house was freshly painted, the yard edged and tidy. A small country graveyard sat on a small hill in the near distance.

Juliet knew, like the rest of the town, that the property was about to be sold off to the highest bidder. But she didn't really understand why, and she didn't know his grandmother well.

The rain was steady now, not torrential at least, but every drop felt as stinging as sleet. At her third "Ahchoo!" Jack cast her an uncomfortable glance, shifting his weight from foot to foot, and rapped louder on the door.

He seemed worried. He wanted to help her. It

was like every little kind thing he did chipped away at an invisible wall around her heart that she didn't want to come down.

Finally, the ruffled curtains over the paned windows parted, and the door opened. A tiny woman with short white hair appeared, wearing a blue flannel shirt and rolled-up jeans. Her blue eyes, very much like her grandson's, lit up immediately on seeing him.

"Granny!" Jack said with obvious affection as he reached over and gave her a big kiss on the cheek. "I'm gonna give you a giant bear hug right now…" He put his arms out, displaying his wet, muddy self, threatening to engulf her in a muddy embrace.

She laughed and pushed him away. "Why, you're a mess, Jack Herbert Monroe. Wetter than Noah and the animals themselves."

Herbert?

Jack's grandmother narrowed her shrewd gaze onto Juliet. "And who's this skinny, wet thing?" Despite the mud, she immediately took up Juliet's hands and squeezed them tight. "You're soaked through and ice-cold."

"Granny, this is Juliet," Jack said quickly. "She's a mental health therapist and she's been helping me out in my mayor's forum." He turned to her. "Juliet, meet my grandma, Adele Anderson."

"It's a pleasure to meet you, Adele." Despite Jack's granny's scrutinizing look, all Juliet could still think of was…*Herbert*?

There was a story there, for sure. But what made her want to hear it? She shouldn't want to know anything else about this man who'd dragged her to his grandmother's house in the woods because she was wet and freezing. And who was so openly affectionate.

Jack Monroe had a soft spot. Who knew?

"Is the mayor's forum how you two got so muddy?" his grandmother asked.

"Sort of," Jack hedged. "I'll tell you all about it. Okay if I let Juliet shower downstairs?"

"Go right ahead," she said, shooing them off. "I'll fix us some nice, warm lunch."

"That sounds like just what we need," Jack said with a nod.

"Thank you," Juliet said, but his grandmother was already gone.

Jack led her into a very tidy attached garage with a wall of tools all lined up on pegboard, and then down a set of stairs to the basement. She followed him with a mixture of trepidation, dread, and the urge to strangle him for bringing her here in this condition. But she was too icy cold to protest.

"Leave your muddy clothes right here," he said, pointing to the floor outside the door, "then you can just run straight into the shower." He pulled off his shoes and tossed them into a pile at his feet. And then, in one quick movement, he peeled off his shirt. Which was a huge mistake, as her gaze gravitated straight to his chest.

His naked, sculpted chest and his rippled abs. Which she could not *not* notice. And he definitely noticed her trying to not notice as her eyes suddenly darted anywhere else but *there*. Which was…confusing. Most of her was an iceberg, but her face could grill a cheeseburger. Well done.

He rushed to say, "I'm leaving. We're not going to shower together. *Of course.*" Could this possibly be more awkward? As he glanced quickly into what looked like a bedroom with an attached bathroom straight ahead, he said, "I need to round you up some towels, though. I'll just set them inside the door, okay?"

"Yes. Sure. Thanks," she mumbled. Her face must have betrayed what she was thinking, that Jack Monroe was quite the specimen. When she finally brought herself to make eye contact, he was assessing her quietly. Probably regretting this whole idea.

Once he disappeared up the stairs, Juliet stripped down and ran into the bathroom, closing the door and starting the shower. It was a small but clean room with fresh white tile, a black-and-white mosaic tile floor, and a shower with a curtain. The modern touches were cute and unexpected in a house this old. She stood under the spray, watching the muddy trail gurgle down the drain, letting the steaming hot water soak into her frozen bones.

A few rounds of shampoo and soap later, she heard a rap on the door.

"It's me," came Jack's voice.

Nerves made her grope for the shower lever and rotate it off. She clutched the curtain to her body, sticking her head out into the steamy room.

And there he stood, Stetson-less, halfway hidden behind the door, a pile of fluffy white towels in his big, tanned hands. A tiny blob of mud sat at his temple, which somehow managed to look endearing, not ridiculous.

For a second, he stood there, her own private fantasy of a man aiming to please. Also, his tanned skin against the white towels added to his already-proven hotness. But Juliet reminded herself that, while Jack was a beautiful man, the rest of him was not to be trusted. Even if he was nice, he was the kind of man who didn't do relationships, not that she was looking for one. And she was not going to fall for an outer shell of a man this time, no matter how gorgeous he was.

Mr. Mayor's emotional muscles might not be terribly developed, but his pecs and abs were *excellent*.

"I—um—didn't want to scare you." He stepped forward into the room, enough to push the bundle toward her.

She stared at him. Watching his very nice lips move while not really comprehending. Her mouth went dry and her pulse began to pound. Must have been the wave of testosterone that hit her broadside before she knew what happened.

"Thanks." Her voice was trembly, and she was too aware of the way he was looking at her. His expression held a mixture of curiosity and heat that had goose bumps rising on her newly thawed skin. She reached out and grabbed a towel from his pile.

"Warm in here." He cleared his throat. *Yes, it certainly was*. "I—I'll let you finish. Hope you're hungry. Granny's cooking up a storm." He averted his gaze and set the rest of the pile on the countertop.

Still standing in the shower, she quickly wrapped the thick, fluffy towel around her. "This is a very nice bathroom—updated," she said. Speaking to him probably prevented him from leaving. Why had she chosen that moment to discuss bathroom remodeling?

"I redid it a couple of years ago." He glanced around. "It needed it. Like, desperately."

"You did this yourself?" He handed her another towel, which she wrapped around her head. "Thanks. Except I have a teensy-weensy problem."

He averted his gaze. Which was sort of sweet. And that signaled to her that he might be a little flustered, too. "What's that?"

"No clothes."

"No clothes?" His voice came out a little strangled. He glanced up at her briefly and then hiked his thumb toward the door. "Oh, I almost forgot. I'll go grab you some sweats."

"Thank you."

"Welcome." He gave her a quick nod. And then he vanished.

Except after he left, the room felt even steamier.

Juliet unwound the towel from her head and dried off her wet hair extra hard to get her mind off of…him.

Physical attraction was only one of the things that had gotten her in trouble with men in the past, especially with her last boyfriend, the one who she'd believed was going to propose last year. But she saw that mistake for what it was. And it was one she could identify and correct, starting right now.

She was not going to fall for Jack. No matter how perfect Mayor Cowboy's abs were. Or all that hunkiness—and kindness—he happened to be hiding beneath the brim of that Stetson.

• • •

Jack was pacing the confines of his old bedroom when the door finally opened. Instantly, the scent of soap and shampoo wafted out on a cloud of steam, and when the mist cleared, there stood a freshly scrubbed Juliet, her hair hanging straight and wet, wearing his burnt orange and white Longhorns sweatshirt and gray sweats, looking like…

Well, like his eighteen-year-old self's secret fantasy.

Except he was thirty-two. And he was the *mayor,* for goodness' sake, and she was his employee. And this was his grandmother's home. Why had he brought her here again?

He'd been struck with the need to do something. His misdirected sense of responsibility was acting up again.

She crossed her hands nervously over her chest. "Thanks for the sweats."

"You're welcome," he said, once again unable to stop drinking her in. "I…wanted to warn you about a few things before we have lunch."

"Okaaaay."

He nervously followed her gaze as it flicked around the tiny room. He tried to see it as she did—gray walls, with a gray-and-white checked comforter. He'd taken most of his personal things out over the years. Except for a few.

And wouldn't you know, she homed right in on the photos on his bookshelves. He intercepted her, trying to casually lean against them as if he wasn't trying to shield her from seeing them. Which also left him standing right smack in front of her. Close enough to see a bead of water dripping from her hair. The delicate arch of her brows. The smattering of tiny freckles across her nose, now that all her makeup had washed off. She was shrewdly scanning his room, digging for clues of who he was. And he wasn't quite sure if he wanted her to find out.

"This was your old room?"

He adjusted his position to seem more casual. "Yes. From the time I came here when I was twelve."

"How nice for your grandma."

"Yes, well, she raised me. I was the lucky one." He cleared his throat. "So, about that warning."

"I'm happy to listen, but think you could spare me a pair of socks? I'm still freezing." She shuddered and shimmied her arms to demonstrate. He could think of a few ways to get her warm, that was for sure. All of which were inappropriate, so he tried to put them out of his mind.

Jack walked to his old dresser and rummaged through a drawer, handing her a pair of white sports socks.

But as he closed the drawer and turned back around, there she was, examining his photos with the intensity of a microsurgeon. She pointed to the one photo he did not want to talk about. "Is this your mom?"

This was why he *never* brought women home.

"Yes, that's my mother."

"Well, I see where you get your good looks from," she said as she straightened up. "She's beautiful."

Funny, because his mother always used to tell him he looked just like his father. His *deadbeat, good-for-nothing father*, as she liked to call him.

"Yes, she was beautiful." And frivolous and flighty and mercurial. Completely unreliable.

"Oh." Juliet brought a hand to her mouth. "She's...passed on? I'm sorry."

"No," he said in a low voice. *Just out of my life.* "Lives near Austin, in fact." He should have stopped there, but for some bad, unknown reason he kept on going. "She...remarried. Has another family now. She...had me young."

"You have siblings?"

He nodded carefully. "Two half brothers." Whom he'd never met. But it wasn't for lack of trying.

"Oh, that's great," she said as she perused his shelves. "I'm the middle of three, which was absolute chaos growing up, but I wouldn't trade my sisters for the world."

As she joked about how her dad had always said that having three daughters was an expensive blessing, he stared at the beautiful, terrible photo that he couldn't seem to take off his shelf. He saw himself at twelve again, at the train station, holding tight to his mom and begging her not to go.

"Go with your grandma, Jackson," she'd said firmly, scooting him away from her skirt, but he'd clung to her anyway. She stooped down to look him in the eye, smoothing down the lapels on his coat, dusting off a bit of fuzz. "I can't give you what a boy should have."

Did she have tears in her eyes? He didn't remember. It seemed to him now that she'd left breathing a sigh of relief to free herself from the ball-and-chain she'd carried around her ankle since she was eighteen.

"You come with me, Mama." He'd tapped her repeatedly on the arm. Being a pest, no doubt, but he was desperate. "We'll go to Granny's together, okay? You can get a job in Blossom Glen and I—"

She bent down and stroked his cheek. "There are no jobs in Blossom Glen, baby, unless I work in the candle factory, and I'd rather shoot myself than do that. I can't come with you, Jackson. I love you so much, but I haven't done a good job. Not the way a proper momma should do. But Granny will. You understand me? You go with Granny and become everything you were meant to become. A decent, solid, kindhearted man. You do that for me, okay?" Her voice had cracked as she cast a nervous glance at his grandmother, who stood behind him, ready to whisk him home.

"Come along now, Jack," his grandmother had said, placing a firm hand on his shoulder.

He looked up at her. "I can't leave my momma," he said, crying now. "I won't leave her."

"Jack, I'm sorry." His granny gripped his shoulders firmly, trying to reason with him. But he was beyond reason.

"No, Granny, no!" he wailed. "She can't leave me. You tell her that—that I belong with her."

"Best way to help your momma is to come with me." His grandmother tried to be firm but her own voice was cracking. "I know you don't understand now. But this is what we've got to do."

He remembered his mother on the train, wearing a big, stiff smile as she stared out the window. He'd stood there watching the train pull out, and his granny let him stay until it had chugged away, until it was just a speck in the distance.

Suddenly Jack was back in his old room, Juliet looking at him expectantly. "I'm not close with my half brothers." He had no idea what she'd just said, just hoped that was an appropriate reply.

Juliet seemed to search his face for clues. "Well, I can see your mother must have loved you very much."

"How do you know that?" She *couldn't* know. Because he himself didn't know it.

Juliet picked up the photo and examined it carefully. "See how her hands are fisted. Look at how devastated she is, even though she's smiling."

He wasn't sure if that look was sadness or discomfort at the fuss she knew he was sure to make. "You're right that she loved me enough to let my grandmother raise me."

And that had to be enough. Because all the other questions he'd been asking for most of his life simply couldn't be answered.

"You're good at reading emotions, Juliet." As for him—it often seemed that something scrambled between his brain and his mouth. He knew what he felt, of course, but he often failed badly at expressing it.

She shrugged. "Sometimes I get too into it. I didn't mean to pry." When she looked up at him, he almost had to glance away, because he saw pain in her eyes—for him. "I didn't know—I'm sorry, Jack." Before he could say something that surely would have been awkward, she sat down on the bed and put the socks on. "In my family, no one can stop talking about family and getting in each other's business. Sometimes I forget it's not like that for everyone."

He sat down next to her. Being careful to not get too close. Then reached for an old snow globe on the stand next to his bed and shifted its solid weight from hand to hand as he spoke. "My mother—she had a bad marriage—to my dad. And she started drinking. She left me with my grandmother because she knew I'd be better off and...and she was right."

That was the mantra he'd been repeating to himself for twenty years.

Juliet finished tugging on the socks. "Did your mom—is she—okay?"

"She got back on her feet." Jack turned the snow globe over in his hands. The scene inside was downtown Blossom Glen, a wintery wonderland. And, ironically, in the very center was the city hall building where he worked every day with its clock tower and parklike lawn, where a snowman stood surrounded by a sea of flurries. His mom had given it to him that last Christmas they were all together. He'd been too young to see the irony of receiving a snow globe of Blossom Glen as a gift within a year of being left there.

He didn't want to dwell on his mother, so he chose a more positive topic. "My granny is amazing. And shrewd. And she can smell a rat from a mile away."

"What do you mean?" Juliet listened attentively, color back in her face, bundled up in his sweats. He'd better get them upstairs, because it was way too easy to sit here companionably with her and spill all his secrets.

"I've led her to believe that the land thing is under control when…when it's not at all. So I'd appreciate it if you didn't mention anything about it. Or if it comes up, just say I've got it handled. Because…I will. Get it handled." She looked like she was forming another question, so he hurried on. "And make sure you taste her chocolate cake. She doesn't take kindly to anyone who won't have a piece."

"Why would anyone not have a piece of chocolate cake?"

"Well, I've had girlfriends she might have met at restaurants who were always dieting. That kind of thing. Granny doesn't take kindly to anyone who denies themselves the simple pleasures of life."

Juliet laughed. "I never met a piece of chocolate cake I didn't like."

He almost smiled at that. But he had one more

thing to say. "I'd also appreciate it if she didn't think we hated each other. I—I just don't want to have to explain stuff. We'll just tell her we're work colleagues and leave it at that."

"I can probably pretend not to hate you if chocolate cake is involved." She paused. "Plus, I don't really hate you. Too much. If you let me keep these sweats. They're awfully comfy."

They both laughed, but the laughter dissolved to a moment, quick as a heartbeat, where something electric passed between them that made Jack's pulse leap and his blood run hot and fast.

And made him think that Juliet definitely wasn't looking at him like she hated him. He forced himself to break the spell, to get up and walk fast toward the staircase, where he waited for her at the bottom.

As she passed him, she held up her thumb and forefinger pinched together. "Maybe just a teeny tiny bit." He must've seemed puzzled, so she added, "Of hatred. But don't worry." She gave a wink and lowered her voice. "I can hide it."

He chuckled and gestured for her to climb the stairs first. And he followed, watching her feet pad upstairs in his old white socks, her fine ass swaying in his gray sweatpants.

CHAPTER EIGHT

Okay, fine, Juliet told herself as she climbed the stairs, which were covered in a bright gold-and-red plaid carpet, the likes of which she'd never before seen.

Jack is not what I thought he was.

He was kind to his grandma and handy with a front loader. And he'd suffered hurts that were much deeper than she'd ever guessed.

And the attraction she was feeling between them was just…best not acknowledged at all. All she had to do was get through this lunch and then things would go back to being all business. Easy peasy.

She entered a big room with a beamed ceiling and a giant window. The room was lit up with autumn color displayed right outside the window, with a killer view of rolling hills and a winding stream. She had a feeling Jack had a hand in this room, too, which was clean and modern-looking. So maybe he just hadn't gotten to changing out that plaid carpeting yet. Beyond a big oak table was a cozy fireplace, a comfy couch slung with colorful crocheted afghans, and a big black dog with loppy ears, belly-up, with his tongue lolling.

As soon as they entered the room, the dog shook himself, rattling his tags, then rolled off the couch and galumphed over.

"You are a big guy," she said, bending to pet

him. "He *is* a guy, yes?"

"This is Henry," Jack said. The dog bounded over to Jack, jumping up until he was standing on his hind legs, nearly reaching Jack's shoulder. "Well, hello there, Hen." Jack rubbed the dog's silky back. "You have to be a showoff, don't you? I'll take you for a run later, I promise. You're a good boy, aren't you? The best, yes you are."

Hearing Jack lavishing love freely on a giant dog in an octave higher than usual was...just about as surprising as the rest of this day.

"You know why he's big, don't you?" Jack asked.

Juliet raised a brow. "Because everything from Texas is big?"

He belly-laughed at that. Which was also unexpected. "I was going to say that his father was a Great Dane. But I like that one better."

Juliet couldn't help smiling. And feeling a little giddy that she'd made him laugh.

"Okay, you two." Jack's grandmother shooed them to the table. "Come sit down before everything gets cold."

Juliet was warm and dry, thanks to Jack. And very, very hungry. So, she would stay and eat this fine lunch with his grandmother, and try not to think about this other, completely different side of Jack.

Then they would go back to being Grumpy Jack and business-only Juliet, and she would stop having lumberjack fantasies. And stop thinking of him as a human.

A nice human. Who hadn't gotten out of his

youth without being scarred, just as she hadn't. With a granny he loved and would die for, and a charming old house and a big old dog that he spoke in baby-talk to.

The big oak table under the beamed ceiling had been set for lunch. Actually, that was an understatement. More like for a Thanksgiving feast, and it smelled like it, too. Wonder what his granny would have done if he'd given her more time to prepare?

Jack's grandmother gestured for them to sit, then she took a seat, too, at the end of the table nearest to the kitchen. She folded her hands near her plate. "Let's bow our heads and give thanks," she said solemnly. "Jackson, you can lead us in prayer."

"Yes, Granny," he said, bowing his head as instructed. Juliet reveled yet again. How could this stubborn mule of a man be so obedient to a five-foot-tall, white-haired force of nature?

And his full name was Jackson. Which seemed…fitting, in a renegade-cowboy kind of way.

Jack's grandmother took up Juliet's hand. Which was sweet. But then she nodded to her grandson. "Hold her hand, Jack," she commanded. "We're not heathens here."

He had long fingers and a strong, firm grip, and for some reason it made Juliet's palm start sweating as if she were a teenager holding a boy's hand for the first time.

Then Jack bowed his head and said in his low, rumbly voice, "Thank you, Lord, for the bountiful meal, the good company, and the chance to be with family and friends. And *co-workers,*" he added with a wink and a squeeze.

Juliet wasn't sure which gesture got to her more, but she felt a little light-headed. Had to be the result of all that strong coffee and not enough breakfast, yes, indeed.

Juliet felt her hand squeeze—this time from his granny's side. "And thank you, Lord," she said, "for the opportunity to spend time with my dear grandson Jack and his very sweet, beautiful, and interesting friend, Juliet, whom I know he truly cares for. Amen."

Yikes. Juliet opened her mouth to correct that, but Jack beat her to it. "Grandma, just to be clear, Juliet and I work together. We barely know each other."

Jack's grandmother uncovered a steaming platter of—was that barbecue? Oh my, it smelled good, spicy and sweet. Her stomach grumbled in response. Apparently, tree-moving worked up quite an appetite. As his grandmother offered the platter to her grandson, she said, "Anyone who blushes when you hold her hand means something more than friendship."

Juliet smiled at Jack. "That's only because he was squeezing it too tightly, Ms. Anderson."

"I was just testing your strength in case we arm wrestle after lunch," Jack said as he dug into the food.

Adele served them barbecue, scalloped potatoes, green beans, and fresh, hot biscuits. Juliet had no idea how she came up with all that food so quickly, but she was too hungry—and it was too delicious—to care.

"I know your family's from France," Adele said after a while. "Your grandmother's told me all about it. I'm from Abilene. One year I came here to visit my aunt, and I met Gabriel at the Blossom festival. I stayed for love, and after he died, this land kept me here. I suppose I fell just as much in love with it as I did with him." She pointed in the direction of the front door. "He carried me across that very threshold on our wedding day, and here I am fifty years later. I never guessed that I'd become its keeper."

"It's truly beautiful." Juliet glanced at Jack. "I saw some of it on the way in."

"I'm sure Jackson would love to give you a full tour after lunch," Adele said with a wink. "If it stops pouring rain, that is."

"Juliet might be tired, Granny," Jack said. "We've been digging out a tree since early this morning."

"I'd love to see it all," Juliet said. Because it was beautiful. *Not* because Jack would be her tour guide, of course.

"You two dug out a tree?" Adele asked. "So that's why you were so muddy."

Jack entertained her with the story, omitting Juliet's role in strong-arming him to move the tree in the first place. And the mud wrestling.

"You forgot to tell her about the prayer," Juliet said with a wink. So, Juliet relayed that part herself. To which Adele positively beamed.

In the course of the meal, Juliet learned that

Jack had overcome a stutter, put himself through college and an architecture masters, and basically did all the maintenance and upkeep in sight. All of which didn't make her hate him more.

It was clear that Adele loved the company, the stories, and her grandson most of all. "How about I make us some coffee and we have a little fireside chat before you get on your way. Unless you're in a hurry?"

Jack looked at Juliet. "Do you need to get back?"

"I'd love to stay," Juliet said and meant it.

Adele took her hand and led her to the couch in front of a big stone fireplace.

Jack, who'd put on a rain jacket, paused with his hand on the door. "Now, Granny, don't be telling any of my secrets while I split some more wood, you hear?"

"I'd never do that," she said in mock horror.

"I'll hold you to it," he said with a semi-stern nod as he headed out the back door.

Adele chuckled. "He told me a few days ago about how you volunteered him to help out with the neighbors. I can't say he was too happy about it."

Oh, so he *had* told her. Interesting. "Neighbors were fighting, which was a shame," she said. "Sometimes they need to know someone's on both their sides. I think that's an important part of what a mayor does."

"Jack is good at doing things."

"Yes." One glance around at the updates, the tidy woodpile, and the immaculate yard told Juliet that was correct. Not to mention he'd moved a tree today.

"...and not so good at *saying* things." Adele wrapped a shawl around her shoulders. "I blame his father. The man never lifted a finger to help anyone in his life. But he could sweet-talk a chicken across a five-lane highway."

That was revealing. "Jack must have had a difficult time growing up," Juliet said. She recalled the photo of the beautiful, sad woman. She didn't recall seeing any photos of Jack's father.

"He did, and he has a few rough edges because of it." She paused a long time. "Maybe you'll be the one to break through to the real Jack."

Oh no, no, no. This conversation had taken a wrong turn. Juliet held her hands up in defense. "Honestly, we're just friends." To be *really* honest, they weren't even that. She barely knew Jack. Though, could she really say that now, after learning so much about him today?

"He's never brought a woman home before," Adele said.

Juliet couldn't help but laugh. "I'm sure a muddy, shivering one really impressed. He brought me here because he thought that I was on the verge of catching pneumonia." So lifesaving really didn't count as bringing a woman home, did it?

She nodded. "That's Jackson. He worries more than I do." After a pause, she added, "He's always been determined to go it alone."

Yes, that would also fit with what she knew about him. Hot guy, serial dater, not one to settle down. A lot of family turmoil. All that set her therapist's mind a-working.

Run, Juliet, her inner voice said. *Run, run, run.*

At least his grandmother clearly thought the sun rose and set in her grandson.

"I know all about you, you know," she said, "even though I live outside of town. You sort of remind me of myself when I was young."

With some people, those words might have been threatening. But somehow, Juliet didn't feel *too* threatened. Although talking about her past always made her uncomfortable.

"I have to tell you that I was a bit wild in my time, I must say. My husband always told me no one could tame me. And he meant it as a compliment." She gave a little nod to punctuate that statement.

"What did you do that was so wild?" She couldn't wait to hear.

"Oh, I worked the rodeo circuit. Chewed tobacco. Dated a rodeo star and broke a few hearts. Just like you did."

Juliet shook her head. "Maybe I broke one. And I made some mistakes. In our small town, I'm not sure people are going to let me forget them."

"Honey, sometimes you've just got to say *what the fudge*." She laughed. "How else can we learn anything in this life if we don't *live*? Embrace your past and everyone else will, too." Then she leaned close. "And honey, something must've been wrong with those men. Or you wouldn't have passed them up. Good thing you realized it before you married them."

Juliet barely got a nod in as Adele kept going. "Of course, I settled down with Gabe. We worked the land and raised our animals and our kids. And I went to school and got a social work degree. Jack and I would sit around the kitchen table and do homework together, how about that? But Gabe died when Jack was just fifteen. First his mother left and then Gabe. He had to grow up too fast."

Juliet had never heard the story about Jack's mother from anyone in town. "I'm so sorry," she said.

"My daughter left Blossom Glen when she was just eighteen. Headed straight to Abilene and fell in love a rodeo star, Jack's dad. But that was a bad match." She sighed heavily. "She was alone and struggling with alcohol, and she had the good sense to realize she needed help. That's when I took Jack. She got help and started fresh, but I believe shame's kept her away." Adele paused a long time, and Juliet could see traces of her own pain. "Life's no fairy-tale," she said. "But true love does make the hard times a whole lot less heavy. And someone who truly loves you makes you believe you can do anything."

Juliet cracked a smile. "I love hanging out with you, Adele. I get warm clothes, a fire, great food, conversation, and flattery, too."

"It's not flattery. I can tell you're a good person, Juliet. Use your experiences for good. Experience is what helps other people. Don't hide it, flaunt it. Embrace it."

On impulse, Juliet gave her a hug. "You've

made me feel very welcome. Thank you. I really needed to hear some kind words."

"Well, anytime. Jack would probably say some, too, if he had someone to bring out the best in him."

Juliet was trying to think of a polite way to tell her she didn't need Jack's kind words, thank you very much, when Adele suddenly gripped her hand.

The older woman leaned toward Juliet and dropped her voice. "I've got to tell you something before Jack comes back."

Oh no. Juliet did not want to be the carrier of secrets, and that grip told her that secrets were a-coming. Also she did *not* want to get pulled into Jack's personal life. But everything about Adele's demeanor conveyed a sense of urgency, and she was talking before Juliet could stop her.

"I know Jack's trying his best to have the town vote to not turn this land into a golf course and Lord knows what else, but I already know everyone's going to vote for it."

"Maybe not," Juliet hedged. Although she knew Jack was worried that the deal was too lucrative for the town to pass up. And honestly, the enormous economic boost from a golf course and its attendant attractions would be hard for the citizens of Blossom Glen to pass up.

"If my land gets turned into a golf course, the town will have tourists. Revenue. Airbnb business. Maybe the old hotel downtown will finally get a facelift. See, I know there's not enough good reasons to prevent that developer from doing what he wants to do. The fact that my Gabe is buried right over that hill, and I go visit him every morning, won't mean a hill of beans to anyone."

"Oh, Adele," Juliet said, still squeezing her hand.

"I know how hard Jack is working on my behalf. But I want you to know I'm tough. I can accept what is to be. I try to be positive in front of him, but I've reconciled myself to moving. And I don't want him to feel badly about that. That would break my heart."

Juliet struggled for words and swallowed past a sudden lump in her throat. Because it appeared Adele was just as concerned about Jack as he was about her. "He's not giving up on this, Adele."

"Juliet, you've got to make sure he understands when the time comes that it's okay." She patted Juliet's hand, her voice cracking. "That I'm going to be all right. He treats me like I'm fragile, and I'm not. I've seen a lot of trouble in my time."

"Adele, you may be tiny, but Jack does *not* think you're fragile. You're probably the only person on the planet that he obeys on command."

And speak of the devil…he came through the door just then, carrying a handful of firewood. Adele swiped at her eyes and stood up quickly. "I'm going to get us some coffee. To eat with our cake." Then she disappeared into the kitchen.

"You okay?" Jack asked Juliet as he filled a brass wood holder with wood and she came to stand nearby and watch him.

A voice called from the kitchen. "All I did was tell her about the remodeling projects you've done around here, right, Juliet?"

"Right, Adele," she called, biting back a smile.

"What were you two *really* talking about?" Jack asked.

"The story behind the longhorn over your desk." She counted on her fingers. "Your old girlfriends, how you peed your pants when you were post-op from your tonsillectomy when you were ten. That kind of thing."

He blanched. "You told her about the longhorn?" he called over his shoulder as his grandmother returned with a tray containing pieces of chocolate cake.

"No, child," Adele said with a grave tone. "That unfortunate story is for you to burden her with, not me." She set down the tray on a low table in front of the fireplace. "I'll be right back with the coffee." And she jetted away before Juliet could offer to help.

Juliet laughed at Jack's semi-panicked expression. But she didn't have time to wonder about the longhorn. "We mostly talked about your grandmother," she said. "And...she was—giving me professional advice."

"Well, I hope it helped."

"She's very wise, Jack."

"Yes, she is." He threw a log on the fire and dropped his voice. "You sure you're okay with staying for dessert?" He bent over the fire, poking at it with a poker, giving her a view of that fine butt again before he stood and dusted off his hands.

And just like that, dessert suddenly took on a whole new meaning. But she shook off that thought and said, "Sure. Mainly because I'm enjoying watching you do everything your granny says."

"You would." He grinned as he walked over to her, stopping in front of her. Which had the odd effect of making her dizzy. Because Jack Monroe's face without cynicism, snark, or seriousness was…a beautiful face. He smelled like fresh air and rain and suddenly, words failed her. She got lost in his nice blue eyes, and every thought she had flew right out of her head except what did that brilliant blue remind her of? The sky. The ocean. A big blue marble. All three.

His expression turned serious.

The fire was warm, and now she was, too, and his nice, full lips were so close. And his dark, wavy hair was shiny in the firelight. And when he bent his head, his full lips quirked up in the slightest smile.

Juliet felt her eyes close, her chin lift, and her body incline of its own accord toward his, every muscle tensing in anticipation.

Until an image formed in her brain. Of that big, blank schedule Char had held up in Juliet's office.

Her future passed before her. A future filled with more blank schedules and no patients because of her bad decisions. Ice-cold terror made her freeze. What was she doing?

She lurched backward, bumping into the couch. Jack caught her by the arm.

He was calm and steady, and his grip was firm, and he was looking right at her with a question in his eyes.

"Not the best idea," she whispered, holding her hands up in defense. "I—I never meant—"

"Of course," he said quickly, letting his arm drop. "I—never meant…yeah."

She felt her way safely around to the other side of the couch. "Let's-let's just forget that happened, okay? I mean, *nothing* happened. And it's just—I mean, it was an *accident*."

She did *not* fall for good-looking guys full of swagger just because they adored their grandmas.

"Right. Totally. Completely." Even calm-and-cool Jack seemed flustered, too.

Just then, Adele returned, carrying another tray with a little silver coffeepot surrounded by cups and saucers in an old-fashioned floral pattern. Juliet jumped immediately to help, taking the tray and walking it to the coffee table.

Her face was surely as red as the fire, which was blazing up and crackling up a storm.

"Now, isn't that a beautiful fire," Adele said, as they all took seats.

Juliet sat and bit into the cake and managed to keep up with the conversation, doing everything she could to show Adele how much she loved it, when she could barely taste it. Which was a shame, because ordinarily, she'd be stuffing it into her mouth as fast as she could and making moaning noises at how amazing it was.

How had it happened that she'd come within *an inch* of kissing Jack? Had she learned no lessons from her past?

It would never happen again. She was never going to figure out why she'd made the mistakes she did if she kept falling for hot guys who weren't her type. And Jack was definitely *not her type*.

He wasn't awful. But he had a lot of baggage, and frankly, so did she. But if she was going to get her dream job back, she had to stop doing the things that had gotten her into trouble in the first place.

• • •

"This is truly a beautiful property," Juliet said, looking out the window of Jack's truck as he drove them home. They passed thick groves of trees, the creek that passed through the property winding its way among them like a picture-perfect postcard. "Is that—is that the little cemetery your grandmother was talking about?" She pointed to a little hill, just a short distance from his grandmother's house.

Jack nodded calmly, but his head was whirling. What had possessed him to bring this woman home to his grandma? Oh yeah, she'd looked wet and helpless.

She was far from helpless, though. And worse, she was absolutely charming. His granny had seized on that, and with that gleam in her eye, she was probably already planning his wedding. And she'd been *waaay* too welcoming, taking Juliet under her wing and chatting with her and confiding in her like…well, like she was family.

So why the sam hell had he almost kissed her? Had he started that, or had she? He remembered joking around. And then suddenly, they weren't joking around. And he'd gotten…lost. In her eyes. And then he was reaching over and…she wasn't.

In fact, she'd practically hurled herself over the couch to get away from him. He had to admit his male pride was just a little bruised because...well, he hadn't had a brush-off like that since before he had a driver's license.

Juliet was still looking out the window...and still remarking about the property as they made their way back to the road. "I can see how you care a lot about your grandmother and this beautiful land."

She was so...chatty. His gut was telling him she was talking a mile a minute to avoid the awkwardness between them. He'd blurred the line between their work relationship and any other kind of relationship, and he had to get his markers out and draw that line back right quick. In thick, black, permanent ink.

He'd made a huge mistake. How had this day started with moving a tree and ended up with having Juliet bulldoze into his life?

"Have you thought of making the cemetery a landmark?" she asked. "Like, what do they call that?" She thought a moment, then suddenly held up a finger. "Oh, I know. Put it on the National Register of Historic Places."

"That takes a few years," Jack said. And he had what...a few weeks? Things had moved so fast— discovering the unpaid taxes, the foreclosure, the auction... It had been a whirlwind he was still trying to wrap his head around.

"There must be some way..." Juliet started.

To keep his granny in the home she'd known and loved for fifty years, he finished in his head.

"Believe me, I've been wracking my brain." He tapped his fingers nervously on the wheel. "I can't afford to buy her property outright. And I haven't got enough collateral to get a loan that big. And I don't know of anyone in town rich enough or crazy enough to outbid Omnibuild, but I'm looking."

"Look, Jack," she said, turning to face him. "Regardless of what…happened back there, I want you to know you can count on me to help."

"I know it. Thanks," he said. Somehow, he knew deep down that she meant it. Then, silence fell and became awkward. He turned on the radio to fill it and prayed for the hour to pass quickly. When Juliet dozed off for a while, he could only say he was grateful.

Finally, they were back in Blossom Glen. He pulled up her driveway and threw the truck into park. He knew he had to say what was on his mind. "Look, Juliet—" He spoke slowly and carefully. "I have to say 'thank you' for coming today. I think we made a good tree-hauling team, and thanks to you, everyone felt like they won." He meant every word. But he had to make it clear that this was where their relationship ended.

"I think so, too. I'm glad it worked out." She started to gather her purse and her bag of clothes, but he stopped her with his voice.

"I just wanted to make something clear. We have a business partnership. I-I didn't want you to think that the fact that I brought you to visit my grandmother changes our relationship."

She looked up, her brows knit down in a worried expression. "Jack, I totally get it. You don't have to explain any further."

Okay, so they were on the same page. But he wanted to make sure there were no hurt feelings. Actually, he was used to giving versions of this speech, where he let women down easy. "Look, I think you're a nice person. I just want to make it clear where I stand. You're Leo's sister-in-law, and I would hate to hurt you." He was being truthful—because he didn't do relationships.

Juliet straightened out, suddenly flushed. "Wait—you're assuming that *I'm* the one who's going to get hurt? And that *you* would do the hurting?"

"No, I—" He was trying to say that it was him, not her. He was trying to protect her from himself. Because he was a bad bet for a romantic partner.

But she didn't let him finish. "Is it because you think *I'm* the vulnerable one? Because I tend to fall too hard and fast?" She waved her fingers like she was casting a spell. "And then mesmerize men into falling in love and then manipulate them to propose to me? Well, don't worry, Jack. Because I don't want to date you. I don't even dream about kissing you. In fact, I'd rather kiss that obnoxious dead beast on your wall than you."

Then she got out and slammed the door.

As she walked away, he heard her curse under her breath. And mumble something about noise, and a landlady, and a kiss that never happened.

CHAPTER NINE

The absolute *nerve* of that guy.

Jack was patronizing. He was arrogant.

And the worst thing of all...he thought what everyone else thought about her. That she was an emotional rollercoaster with men. And he'd said he didn't want to hurt her, like he was the one who let women down because they couldn't help falling for him.

Well, she didn't want to have anything to do with him, either.

She collapsed onto her new couch.

She liked Jack. She'd felt they were becoming friends. They'd confided in each other. They'd had such a nice day. Well, until the almost-kiss anyway.

But then he'd gone and ruined everything.

As if *she* were the one who was getting too interested. So interested that he had to warn her away. Yet she was the one who'd pulled away.

This was really messed up.

And she totally agreed with him—she wasn't going to risk making the same mistakes as she had in the past.

But if she totally agreed, then why was she so...angry? The guy was a jerk who probably thought he was God's gift to womankind—he probably gave versions of that same I-would-hate-to-hurt-you speech all the time. So it was *much* better this way. And it was what she wanted.

Wasn't it?

All Juliet managed to do in the first five minutes she was home was scare poor Ellie under the bed with her stomping around. She made tea to calm down but couldn't drink it. Finally, needing some fresh air, she put on some clean sneakers and ran the three-fourths of a mile to her sister's charming little house in the Blossom District, close to downtown. She peeked through the wooden gate and found Tessa in her garden, sitting with her feet up in the afternoon sun, reading a book. The clouds had dissipated from earlier and the sun was out and shining brightly.

"Hey there," Juliet said as she released the squeaky latch on the back gate to the little yard, which consisted mostly of a brick patio surrounded by a garden where ivy and little ceramic garden gnomes ran rampant. Cosette, Tessa's cat, sprawled out on the warm bricks, occasionally flicking her tail in interest as she watched chipmunks scamper up the old trees.

Just then, Leo walked out of the garden shed with a shovel. "Hey there, sis," he said to Juliet. "Since when did you become a Longhorn?" He must've noticed that her face turned practically the same bright color of Jack's sweatshirt, because he said, "Oh, sorry—maybe I shouldn't have asked that."

And maybe if she hadn't been so upset, she wouldn't have forgotten to change. "It's not what you think," she said, then looked at Tessa. "I know you probably just got home from the bakery, but do you have a minute?"

Leo leaned on his shovel. "I think I'll make us some iced tea. And...dig up the garden another time."

"You're the best," Tessa said, shooting him a genuine smile.

It was wonderful to see her sister so happy. And so in love. Juliet was thrilled for her, but she couldn't help wondering if she would ever find love herself. Maybe she *would* be on an emotional rollercoaster with men her entire life.

"Thanks, Leo," Juliet called as he opened the slider door to the house. To Tessa, she asked, "You sure it's okay? I don't want to interrupt."

Her sister reached over to squeeze Juliet's hand. "Honey, I always have time for you."

"I know, but I'm really trying to be more mature now. To avoid making things into crises. To not come running to you with all my troubles."

Tessa held up a book. "If you get my mind off of this, I'll listen to anything." The title read *How to Have a Great Labor*. On the cover, a woman sat in a hospital bed, covered from the waist down with a blue surgical drape, smiling gleefully. "Did you know that if you go into labor by yourself, you should sort of sit up in case you have to catch your own baby?"

"Stop reading that book right now." Juliet grabbed a chair from the table set and dragged it over to where Tessa sat.

"Tell me about it." Tessa laughed and tossed the book onto the wrought-iron table. "So, what's on your mind?"

"Taking the town counselor job was a bad idea.

I'm trying so hard not to make mistakes. To be wise and sensible. To not let my emotions guide me straight into trouble."

Tessa sat up a little and frowned. "Exactly what kind of mistakes are we talking about here?"

Cossette walked daintily over and wound herself around Juliet's legs. On impulse, Juliet reached down and scooped her up into her lap and cuddled her. "I've only done the job one day, but I feel like I'm handling it fine. It's the faux-cowboy part that's upsetting me."

Tessa nodded toward the longhorn on Juliet's sweatshirt. "Jack."

"We moved a tree for Jerry Caldwell out near the county line, but we got stuck in the pouring rain, so Jack drove us to his grandmother's." She tugged on the longhorn to explain. "I had...I had a wonderful time. Jack was open and funny, and his grandmother was adorable, and she made us this wonderful lunch...but then...we almost kissed."

Tessa sat straight up. "You almost *what*?"

"I pulled away," she rushed to say. "I didn't kiss him. And then you know what he did? He gave me a lecture on how *he* didn't want to be the one to hurt *me*. How arrogant! Like he's thinking I'm the kind of woman who's just waiting to fall hard for the next guy who walks into my life."

Leo walked out with glasses of iced tea. "I'm not supposed to be listening. But I have something to say." He handed out the glasses of tea and grabbed a seat. "Jack's a great guy, but he's got his own issues. And maybe he pushed you away for those reasons rather than because he really wanted to push you away, you know what I mean? Maybe it's not about you at all."

Juliet felt a little lost. "Are you saying he wasn't pushing me away because of my issues, but because of his?"

"Exactly." Leo sat down at the table and rubbed his chin thoughtfully. "I guess what I'm saying is that I've never known Jack to have a real relationship."

Tessa sipped her tea. "My best advice is that I think you need to find your inner Lulu."

Juliet turned to her sister. She'd hoped at least her own sister wouldn't bring that up. "I hate my inner Lulu, Tessa."

Tessa laughed. "That chubby little toddler was *boss*."

Juliet threw up her hands. "She was ridiculous. She climbed a water tower. She was a spoiled little brat."

"Well, I'm only two years older, but I remember her being sweet and loving and giving everyone the benefit of the doubt, just like you do now." She paused. "And…little Lulu took chances."

"I wouldn't even be able to climb the water tower anymore. I'm afraid of heights, remember? Probably from the PTSD of scaling it the first time." She leaned forward, her elbows on her knees, rubbing her temples. But it wasn't taking away her massive, Jack-induced headache. "Where were our parents, anyway? Letting a three-year-old escape like that. Geez."

"Ask Mom. I'm just talking about following your heart and taking some risks instead of closing yourself off."

"I've taken chances in the past and look how those have turned out. I'm the three-engagement wonder. No one trusts me to be their therapist. Priority one is getting my job back on track. Besides, you can't possibly be telling me to take a chance with Jack."

"I'm all for taking chances," Leo said carefully. "But not necessarily with Jack. I mean, the man's my best friend and I love him like a brother, but he's a risk."

"Leo," Tessa said gently, "you were a risk, too."

He shrugged. "Well, you saw the best in me. But I know Jack too well. I just don't want Juliet to get hurt."

What was implied, but not said, was *again*.

Tessa shared a look with Leo. "You just know his romantic history," she said. "But Jack's a quality guy. And sometimes you gotta take a chance." Tessa turned to Juliet. "I mean, look at me. I met Leo again after all those years apart. Next thing you know I'm married, through pastry school, and starting my own business." She patted her belly. "Oh, and this business. All in the blink of an eye."

"You two are too cute." Juliet was really happy for her sister and for Leo. They'd overcome a lot and made it work. But Blossom Glen was small, and the chances of her finding a once-in-a-lifetime love were even smaller. Not that she was even thinking about that now. Because…she needed her job, food, and rent. She nudged the cat off her lap and stood. "Thanks for the talk. Bring Cosette over for a Caturday date with Ellie sometime, okay?"

As Juliet hugged her sister and brother-in-law and then walked back to the gate, she thought of a few things. One was, she couldn't afford to take the chances that Tessa had so cavalierly talked about. She wasn't going to ruin her life further by getting involved with someone who should come with a red-flag warning.

So she'd fallen in love impulsively a few times. Was that a crime? It had just gone way too far both times before she bailed.

She was going to set herself up for success. Do a great job as Town Counselor. And break her old patterns of picking men who were all wrong for her. Starting with staying far away from Jack emotionally. She would never make those same mistakes again.

• • •

On Monday, there was a water main break on the far end of Main Street, and the water had to be shut off to all the businesses. So Jack's day started with a flurry of phone calls and tugs in a million directions. He fought back a yawn and the unsettled feelings that had knocked around in his head all weekend about Juliet. And caused him to lose sleep.

They would soon pass. It was for the better. That near-miss kiss had been an accident.

That's what Jack had been telling himself over

and over. But he was honest enough to call himself a liar.

He was walking back to city hall after assessing the damage when he noticed the line for Christmas Every Day spilling out onto the street. Either they were having the biggest sale in history, or there was a problem.

Turns out the line also snaked through the store. And at its very origin, in front of the big antique cash register surrounded by colorful glass Christmas balls dangling from the ceiling, was a young woman in a silly elf costume whom he recognized as Juliet's younger sister, Vivienne.

A woman at the front of the line was talking very loudly over a sizable box which sat atop the counter. "I ordered a Santa hat, a Santa top with a belt, and Santa pants online. Not Santa *panties*."

Santa panties?

Vivienne righted her green-and-white striped hat, which had slipped down over her dark curls. "Yes, ma'am," she said politely, "but the date of purchase was three months ago. I'm sorry, but that's past the time our return policy—"

"I live in Chicago," said the woman, who was wearing a red-and-green sweater with pompoms dotted all over, despite it being an unseasonably warm October day. "I waited until I had to come back this way on the turnpike."

"I understand," Viv said calmly, "but this could have been mailed back within the return time limit."

"I've been a faithful customer for the past ten years," the woman said. "And I didn't order twenty-five pairs of Santa panties. I want to speak with the manager."

Jack walked up to the counter. "Hey there, Viv," he said. "Hey, ma'am. My name's Jack Monroe, and I'm the mayor of Blossom Glen. Thanks for patronizing our shop. Hope you don't mind if I borrow our little elf for a minute."

"Oh, hello, Mayor." The woman appeared a bit flustered, her pompoms swaying as she clapped a hand to her chest. "As long as you can set things straight," she said in a condescending tone.

Jack pulled Viv aside down an aisle. At eye level on the shelf, a Santa was popping out of an outhouse, waving a roll of toilet paper with a list of kids' names on it. It was just one example of the quirky Christmas stuff that was literally packed from wall to wall. And it was what made people flock here from six neighboring states. "What's going on?" he asked.

"Delores is on a buying trip," Viv whispered. "It's been one holdup after another because that ancient register is old and…useless. Someone returned like, fifty ornaments, and I had to punch in all the SKUs by hand. Now this lady won't budge. But if I let her return twenty-five pairs of Santa panties three months late, Delores will send me ho-ho-home with no job." Her mouth turned up in the slightest smile.

For a flash, he could see her resemblance to Juliet, which got him thinking about the great day they'd had. And how he'd ruined it, said something stupid that she mistook for an insult. But he pushed all that out of his mind.

Viv looked stressed but okay. And at least she was cracking jokes instead of crying.

"Delores is the kindest woman alive," Viv said, "but she doesn't allow *anything* risqué in the store. The panties are an online-only item. If I let the customer return them late, I'll have to eat the cost because we can't put them in our inventory and resell them here."

Jack frowned. "How much is it for a pair?"

"Around six bucks."

"Okay, how about this. You return her money. And I'll take care of the panties."

Viv rolled her eyes. "I don't even want to know what that means."

"It means I'm going to sell them."

"Where? On Ebay?"

He smiled as they walked back to the register. "Nope. Right here."

Jack cleared his throat and checked out the long line of customers. And the people happily browsing the tightly packed aisles. "Hey, everyone," he said in his mayor's voice. He waited until everyone had stopped talking and was paying attention. "We've got a seventy-days-before-Christmas special today. Come and get yourself a pair of holiday panties for just eight bucks cash right now. A limited-time offer, today only." He spotted Hector Gonzales, the owner of the Foggy Bottom, Blossom Glen's local watering hole, who could take a joke. "Hector, you know you want some for Gladys."

Several husbands, who looked like they'd rather be at the dentist than shopping in a year-round

Christmas store, wandered up.

Jack held up some samples, which were either red or green and had words printed on the butt. "We have *Naughty, Nice,* or *Ho ho ho.*"

Someone raised a hand. "I'll take a *Ho ho ho.*"

"Better hurry up, folks," Jack continued, "'cause this item is going to sell out right quick."

"What'cha got there, Jack?" Jim Levinson, who'd just retired from the bank, asked. "I'm looking for something for Sandra's birthday."

Jack rummaged through the box. He felt a little like he was selling popcorn at a baseball game, but hey, it was working.

"I'll take a pair," Jim said. Some women wandered over. A crowd of local retired guys from the coffee shop did, too.

"Cash only, folks." Jack held up some different-colored samples. "Relationship therapy for eight bucks." Someone chuckled. Followed by someone else making a *tsk*ing sound of disapproval. He glanced up to find a pretty therapist with a very large frown, which made him do a double take.

Juliet.

As usual, he reacted to her presence with a little zappy shock that ran all through him. Make that pretty, clearly still angry, and definitely not pleased at what he'd just said.

"Not that *regular* relationship therapy isn't important, too," he said nice and loud as an attempt to extract his foot from his mouth. "A good marriage needs both kinds, right?"

She started to turn away, so he held out the box and shook it a little. "One pair left and I'll give it to you for a steal. Need some *Ho ho ho* in your life?"

That earned him a giant frown. "You're ridiculous." Juliet shook her head and turned to check on Viv.

Okay, he was making everything between them even worse. "Juliet," he called. He wanted to talk to her. To explain. But she didn't hear him, because Tyler Wells, the most beloved teacher in town, had called her name at the same time.

Rumor was, he'd never gotten over being dumped by Juliet, and he was now single, having recently broken up with his longtime girlfriend.

"Jules?" Despite his arms being full of construction paper and vials of glitter, he embraced Juliet with a massive hug. "So great to see you!" he exclaimed, using his kindergarten-teacher voice. "I've been meaning to call you to congratulate you about your new jobs. Both of them. You look *amazing*." Another enthusiastic embrace.

Tyler certainly didn't have any trouble telling Juliet how *he* felt.

"Hey, Jack," Tyler said, finally seeing him. Jack nodded, suddenly realizing he was standing there with a pair of panties in hand. Ones that said *Bad Santa Baby*, which he quickly dropped back into the box.

Tyler was loaded with his hallmark energy. Parents did devilish things to each other to get their kids into his class. One year some mom had broken into the office and erased a child's name off the waiting list so her kid could move up. Who knew Blossom Glen Elementary's kindergarten could be so cutthroat?

"I'm so happy for you, Jules," Tyler said. "You're going to be the most *awesome* therapist *ever*."

"Thanks, Ty," Juliet said. "You look great, too. What brings you in here?"

"Autumn trees art supplies in a pinch." He held up the red and green construction paper. "I supplement these with other colors." As he put them into his hand-held basket, he said, "So how are you doing? You heard I broke up with Holly, right? Ever since then I've had more time to do art projects with the nursing home folks, and once a week I visit the kids' ward at the hospital. You should come with me some time. We could catch up."

Jack's phone buzzed with incoming text messages. Actually, it had been doing that for the past fifteen minutes, all from various city employees dealing with the water main break. Viv's register line was under control now and he was down to his last pair of panties, but water mains, police chiefs, and public utilities officials were not doing well at all. And he was filled with a nagging feeling that he'd screwed up with Juliet. Badly. Again.

On a whim, he tossed a ten into the box as well as the rest of the cash he'd collected and pocketed the last pair of panties. Mission accomplished.

But he felt…bad. Terrible, in fact. He hadn't meant to hurt her.

"You need help carrying that stuff back to school?" Juliet asked Tyler. "I'm headed that way."

"Oh, I'd *love* it," Tyler said.

"Bye, Jack," Juliet said with a wave. "See you at work. Good luck with the panties!" She gave him a faux-sweet smile. "However you might define that."

He forced a smile as she walked off with Mr. Wonderful.

CHAPTER TEN

Jack rushed back to the courthouse to find Hunter Kirby, the public utilities director, and Aaron Masters, the chief of police, in the open area outside his office, which was Sharon's territory, and therefore subject to her supersonic sense of hearing.

"I want to thank you both for your quick action," Jack said. "Nice job re-routing the traffic and getting the crews on the main break, fast. All in all, the water shut-off only lasted the morning."

Hunter and Aaron looked at each other, then at him. They'd all been friends a long time, and Jack knew when something was up.

"What?" he asked. "What is it?" Was his shirt buttoned crookedly? Did he forget to shave? He might be a little off his game, but he still knew how to dress himself. He glanced down to make sure.

"You're being...nice," Hunter said.

"I'm always nice," he said. Okay, he knew he could be a little abrupt sometimes. But he was trying to take a lesson from Juliet.

"Well, you're nice outside of the mayor's office. But sometimes you're...a little bit of a hard-ass," Aaron, who was tall with a build that would scare anyone on the street, said with a grin.

"Well, I...I want you guys to know that I...appreciate you." There. He'd said it. And he was still alive to tell about it. Juliet would be proud.

Ah, *Juliet*. Why could he not get that woman out of his head?

Hunter snorted. He and Aaron exchanged glances.

"You like, gave us a compliment," Aaron said.

"Both of us." Hunter held up two fingers. "Two compliments," he said, chuckling.

Sharon chuckled, too. But when he looked up, she was busily typing away at her computer.

"So, what's up?" Aaron asked. "Why the kinder, gentler version?"

"Maybe I'm like a good bottle of wine." He beelined for his own office, waving goodbye to his friends. "I mellow with time."

"And don't go spreading the word about that," he called over his shoulder to Sharon. "I'm the mayor. I'm nobody's friend. Got that?" He didn't want people thinking he was *too* nice, did he?

"Yes, Mayor." Sharon tidied a stack of papers on her desk. "Except you sound grumpy like my dad."

That made him stop. "Your dad isn't grumpy," he said.

"He was when we were teenagers. He used to say, 'I'm your father, not your friend' all the time."

Maybe Jack should take umbrage at being compared to a middle-aged father, but he had bigger fish to catch. He was looking forward to a calmer morning where he could get some work done in peace and quiet. And wrack his brain about potential solutions for the land problem.

And stop thinking about a certain town counselor who had him all discombobulated.

As soon as he entered his office, he ran into a soft, perfumy wall of…Juliet, who was standing right by the door, like she'd been eavesdropping and failed to move away fast enough.

He grabbed her at the elbows to steady them both. Which put them up close and personal. One glimpse in her soulful green eyes and he was hit with a wave of longing so powerful he had to suck in a breath. And there were those tiny little freckles again, mostly covered up but still visible if you looked hard enough. They were…cute.

"Glad things went well with the water crisis," she said in a chipper tone. "Hi, guys." She stepped out and waved to Aaron and Hunter, who were standing around Sharon's desk, talking.

"Jack's really chilled out since you've been Town Counselor, Lulu," Aaron said. "What's your secret?"

"It hasn't even been a week," Juliet said with a smile. "Maybe it's the new coffee."

"Glad somebody's a good influence on you." Hunter walked into Jack's office. "We're taking some of that coffee to go, by the way."

"Yeah, well, better watch how much you take," Jack said. "Taxpayers are paying for that."

"First he compliments us"—Aaron shook his head, biting back a smile—"then he tears us down."

"See ya," Hunter said, his mug now full. "We'll keep you posted on the main break."

As Jack's friends cleared out, he grabbed a mug from the shelf, poured the coffee into it, then offered it to Juliet.

"No thanks," she said. Her too-sweet smile that didn't reach her eyes. "I've already had some."

She was clearly still upset with him. And it was going to take more than a cup of coffee to fix things, for sure. It was going to take what he hated the most. *Words.* Lots of them. Ones he wasn't sure he had.

"Look, Juliet," he said. "I-I think I was a little harsh the other night and I wanted to explain—" She walked toward his desk. As he followed her with his gaze, what he saw made him blink twice. And took all the words from his mouth.

His office...his sanctuary, his place of privacy, had been transformed into...chaos. His beloved scale model of the town, which stood next to the wall, was gone. Gone! And in its place was what appeared to be a cheap folding table, the kind you'd use for a party—long, stretching along the wall, taking up *space.*

His space.

The table was covered with piles of paper, a laptop, and a desk lamp. And were those tiny cacti of some sort? As he stood there, mouth agape, she sat down, put on a pair of black-rimmed glasses, and started poring over papers, deep in thought.

He walked up to her little setup and placed his hands on the table. "Juliet," he said.

She looked up. Her glasses were...totally hot. "I agree we should be business colleagues," she said. "So I moved my work in here, since there's no other space available. I didn't think you'd mind." She tapped some papers on the desk. "You were tied up with the water main, so I took care of some things for you this morning." She handed him one of the papers. "Here's a summary of everything. Let me know if you have questions."

He suddenly noticed there was music playing. The kind for relaxing and meditating, but it was having the opposite effect on him now. A white-and-gray rug with a geometric design sat in front of his desk and a woven basket and…was that a tree near his window? And a giant pillow propped up against the wall.

A pillow?

And then something barked.

Daisy, Louise Howard's fluffy white dog, was cuddled into a dog bed in the corner that matched the rest of the decor.

A dog. In his *office*.

"Where—where's my…town?" he managed. He felt a bead of sweat trickle down his forehead.

"Oh." She looked up from her work and waved her hand around. "Well, something had to go, and that was it."

Jack surveyed the room in a panic. The architectural model was six feet long and four feet wide. Impossible to hide. "Go, as in, where?"

"Sharon helped me move it down the hall, to that nice empty office."

Okay, she was *definitely* punishing him. Was this the same woman in the Longhorn sweatshirt he'd thought was irresistible?

His heart sank. Because *irresistible* was a very strong word. But he'd definitely thought it.

"You don't really need a toy-sized model of

our town, do you?" Juliet tapped a pen on her makeshift desk. "Sharon says it's been in here for fifty years."

"Mayor Graves bequeathed that to me when I was elected. It's a tradition." She didn't seem to be getting it, so he said, "It helps me consider traffic patterns. Unused land. Parade routes, the 4th of July 5K race, building refurbishing funds...so yes, it's useful." And it helped him when he was trying to figure out what to do about his granny's land. Although, admittedly, it hadn't provided any clear answers. Yet.

"Well, we didn't pitch it," she said defensively. "We just moved it down the hall."

"Look, we said this was a temporary arrangement," he said. Judging by all the stuff she'd brought in, it looked like she was planning on staying a year. Or three.

"Yes, but the cases are piling up." She patted the pile of folders beside her computer. "And there's a *lot* of follow-up involved."

"Can't you work from home like everybody else these days?"

"Well no, because you have a people problem that I'm helping you solve, so I need to be right here. Where there's *people*."

"But do I have to be one of the people?"

"This setup is part of the solution. I've created us a very functional working space. For our *business* relationship."

"I liked my un-functional one," he groused. He shot her his grumpiest look, but she was smiling like she'd just won the Powerball.

She checked her watch. "I'd love to chat more, but I've got to get to work." Then she turned her attention to her laptop.

He sat down at his desk and turned on his own computer. Sharon had already sent him a dozen messages since they'd talked two minutes ago. He had an entire line of sticky notes on his desk and calls to make. And an upcoming meeting with the downtown business taskforce at ten. "Okay, look," he said, "how about we just focus on our work and talk about this later?"

"Okey dokey," she said, taking a sip from a tea mug that said *Namaste*.

He'd barely gotten through his first email when he smelled something. Something citrusy and pungent. He looked up to find that Juliet had lit a candle. Make that three.

"Candles are great for concentration," she said, blowing out the match. "Plus they support our local business."

"I find them distracting." He found *her* distracting. But today, not in a good way. And he also wanted his office back.

"You seem a little stressed." She turned from her computer. "Maybe some calming sounds would help," she said. "Would you like campfire, wind, or ocean?"

"None of the above," he said as he read the first sentence of an email ten times.

"I also have Aretha Franklin."

"Aretha Franklin is part of this…meditative work environment?"

"No, but everyone loves her."

"I draw the line at music. I like silence."

"Music is very—"

"If you say therapeutic, I'm going to—"

"You're going to what?" she asked innocently, batting her eyelashes to be funny.

Tarn your hide seemed like the kind of thing that if said out loud, might get him arrested. But it unfortunately made him think of her hide, which was quite an amazing one at that. "I'm going to… not like it."

She followed a cord on her desk to a little switch and turned something on. Suddenly, a desktop water feature, composed of water cascading over black stones, gurgled to life. LED lighting illuminated the cascading water, which was quite burble-y and loud.

"If you don't like music, water sounds are very soothing. And remember, this is a safe zone. I want you to think positive, encouraging thoughts."

"How about strangling thoughts?"

Okay, judging how her face was turning red and she was squinting down her eyes at him, he was making her angry. *Good.* Because why should she walk away from this scot-free?

"Aromatherapy, candles, a giant banquet table. Succulents. That's a whole lot of work to go through to invade my space. My *peace.*"

"Was your peace all that good, Jack?" she asked. He saw a flash of something in her eyes. Triumph. Like, despite the fact that this whole scenario seemed orchestrated to annoy him, what she'd just said had stabbed directly at the truth.

Strangely, when he thought of his life

pre-Juliet, it seemed light-years away. She'd filled up everything—his thoughts, his actions, his dreams. Ever since she'd showed up in his forum last week, he'd been on a merry-go-round, unable to get his feet on the ground.

And on top of all that, he just really hated the fact that she was upset with him.

Juliet stood abruptly. "You hired me to do a job. And I need a place to do it. If you don't want me here, the solution is simple." She leaned over his desk, bringing a vanilla scent with her. Which was incredible but anything but calming, if his bodily reaction to it said anything. He had no choice but to look into her fiery green eyes.

"And what might that be?"

"Find me another space." She crossed her arms and tapped her lip with her index finger. "For example, the model town and I could switch places. It comes back, and I get the office down the hall."

Of course. Her plan all along, no doubt. Also, why did he get the feeling that she was holding his beloved model town hostage?

And he'd bet a million bucks that Sharon was her accomplice.

Juliet innocently picked Daisy up, crooning to her like a baby. Then she grabbed her purse from atop her desk, slung it over her shoulder, and said, "Oh, and about the other day. Just to be clear, I feel the exact same way about you. You are as far from my ideal man as…as Antarctica. My ideal man would want to be friends. He wouldn't push me away after we had a nice day because he's an emotional snail. And he'd say what he really means, not make something up about not wanting to hurt me. I don't want a man with issues. I am issued out. So, you were right. Business it is."

She spoke to the dog. "C'mon, Daisy, let's go home. I'll get you away from this mean man right now."

Jack let out an exasperated sigh. "You are the most annoying woman I have ever met."

But she probably didn't hear him, because she was already gone.

CHAPTER ELEVEN

Jack walked out of city hall and straight down the street toward Castorini's Italian Restaurant, which was already hopping with the lunchtime crowd. It was a sunny fall day, and tourists were strolling along the sidewalks, sitting under the yellow canopy of leaves, eating ice cream. He walked past the crowded candle factory gift shop and Christmas Every Day. The smell of warm, fresh bread hit him even before he approached Bonjour Breads!, where he gave a wave to Juliet's mother, Mrs. Montgomery, through the window.

When he reached the restaurant, he walked around to the back door and into the kitchen, where the mouthwatering scent of garlic and simmering tomatoes hit him hard. Leo, wearing a white apron over his gray T-shirt and jeans, was stirring a giant sauce pot on the big, industrial-sized stove.

Tessa sat nearby, gently tapping a sieve over a large container of tiramisu, causing powdered cocoa dust to fall gently over a layer of whipped cream.

Tessa looked up. "Hey, Jack," she said with a smile.

"That looks amazing," he said, but his heart wasn't into it like usual. His new town counselor, in addition to sapping his mental energy, apparently had also attacked his appetite. What would be next?

No, not that. Certain other appetites seemed as raring to go as ever, especially in her presence.

Leo walked over to Tessa, putting a loving hand on his wife's back. "Rub lower please," she said, giving a stretch. "Carrying this little person around all day is hell on the back."

"You look great," Jack said. "You feeling okay?"

"Thank you." She smiled. "I have tons of energy and food tastes like an orgasm."

"Hey!" Leo said.

She kissed him playfully on the cheek. "I didn't say *better* than an orgasm."

He kissed her back. "Well, okay then."

They were so perfect together it was…sickening. Something tugged at his heart. Not jealousy, exactly, but the feeling that he'd never find what they'd found.

Wait…was he even looking for that? They were clearly exceptions to his rule that true love was all a fantasy, anyway. He wished them the best, but he knew better than to dream.

Jack surveyed the packed dining room through an opening in the kitchen where Leo's dad was busy placing beautifully presented plates. "Business is booming."

"Since Tessa took over the desserts," Leo said, "we've got people coming in just for those. Plus we've sold more cappuccinos and lattes than we have in months."

Tessa shook her head in disagreement. "I think it's that people take one look at the menu—and the hot chef in the kitchen—and end up staying a while and eating a meal."

"Hey, I heard that," Mr. Castorini called, giving Jack a wave. Jack grinned and waved back.

Tessa looked at her husband with moonstruck eyes. And he looked the exact same way right back.

"Am I...rigid?" Jack blurted.

"Rigid? You?" She assessed him carefully. "Well, you do take off your shoes whenever you come over to the house and line them up perfectly at the door."

"And I've never seen a paper out of place on your desk," Leo added. "And every time we go out and you take a shot, you turn the shot glass upside down and stack it. And when we go camping, you always do that weird thing with your sleeping bag where you have to fold it a certain way to put it away while everyone else just shoves theirs in the bag."

He shook his head to indicate *enough*. "Okay, I'm sorry I asked. Next time I'm going to ask people who don't know me so well."

Tessa finished sprinkling the cocoa on top of the sumptuous dessert. She reached for a nearby knife, cut a generous piece, and handed it over to Jack. "Sit down," she said. "You look like you could use some sugar."

Between the dessert and Tessa's kind smile, he couldn't resist the offer. Jack sat down at the worktable, and Leo walked up and glanced over his shoulder. "Well, if it's break time, maybe I'll have a piece, too. I'll get us some coffee." Leo looked at his wife. "Decaf?"

"Thanks, but I'll let you two talk. I've got to get back to the shop."

Leo kissed his wife goodbye and patted her growing baby bump in such a clearly affectionate way that Jack pretended to be checking out his phone. Especially when Leo said, "Oooh, hey, that was a strong kick. I think we've got a potential soccer player in there," and got a goofy, smitten grin on his face.

"Whatever our baby is," Tessa said, "I'd feel so much better if they had a place to sleep when we come home from the hospital. Oh, some names would be nice, too."

"I can come and help you paint that nursery," Jack offered. He looked at Leo. "If you cook, we will come." Leo had done this before; cooked up a storm and had Noah, Tessa's sisters, and Jack over to help paint their garage last spring, and it had been worth every bite.

"We might take you up on that," Leo said. Then he kissed Tessa again and saw her out the door.

Love had certainly hit his best friend hard. And Jack was truly happy for him—for both of them. But for the first time, he felt a little…lonely. Leo had always been his partner in bachelorhood. To see him reverse tide so definitively was scary.

"What's up, Jackie?" Leo said, slapping him on the back. He set down two mugs of fragrant, steaming coffee and sat down next to him.

"I'm really worried about my grandmother's land," Jack said. Which was always true. Also, the

land was a whole lot easier to talk about than trying to figure out how to articulate the rest of his
frustration. Especially when that involved Leo's
sister-in-law.

And what exactly was he supposed to say
about Juliet anyway? That he'd come a half inch
away from kissing her? That she had him all tied
up in knots? And was driving him up an ever-loving wall?

No. No, no, no.

It was the stress of this land thing, that had to
be it. No woman had *ever* tied him up in knots of
any kind. Square knot, fisherman's knot, or love
knot. None of the above.

"I thought you said the developer's plan was
coming up for a vote with the zoning commission," Leo said.

Jack nodded. "Yep. And I got an email this
morning confirming the date for the auction." He
stared down at the beautiful dessert, his appetite
all but gone. "I can't stop it, unless I somehow win
the lottery and buy the property back."

Leo took a sip of coffee, deep in thought. "I'm
sorry, Jack."

"Omnibuild's going to do a giant pitch to everyone. They'll say that a golf course and condos
and shops are going to be great for our economy."

"Will they be?"

Jack shrugged. "They're going to bulldoze all
that beautiful land. The forest. And I've been
chatting with my architect friends. For a golf
course, they'll have to re-route the creek. And of
course, my grandma's house will have to go, too.

"Devin Chambers is determined. And wealthy as Midas. And he pays no heed to environmental damage. But none of what he's doing is illegal. I think everyone's going to see the cash flow this is going to generate for the town and give it two thumbs-up."

"Is anyone else bidding on the land?" Leo asked.

Jack shook his head. "Chambers has made it clear he'll outbid anyone."

Leo tapped his fingers on the table. "What about that land on the south side of town that you mentioned? Where the junkyard was?"

Ah yes, the junkyard. Jack's last-ditch idea. "I made sure to apply for federal cleanup funding. A golf course is more suited to that site with less trouble. Except the land wouldn't be ready for another year or two. If I can convince Omnibuild that it's worth it to switch gears and use that land instead of my granny's, I might have a shot. But frankly, it's a longshot. Devin doesn't strike me as patient, compassionate, or environmentally friendly."

Jack's stomach turned sickly. The coffee smelled strong and bold, and Leo always made a great cup, but today it didn't appeal. The giant piece of tiramisu, his favorite dessert, might as well have been a pile of lard.

"It's okay if you can't eat," Leo said like the true friend he was. "Take it to go."

Jack scrubbed his face with his hands. "When I think of telling my grandmother that I can't fix this—I just can't sleep. Or eat. I've got to find a solution."

Leo gave him a concerned look. "Well, I'll do anything I can to help you. You know that."

"I do know that." Jack forced a smile, because he knew Leo would do anything for him if he could. "Thanks."

Jack continued to stare at his dessert. He scraped the cocoa from the top of the whipped cream.

"Jack," Leo finally said. "What else is bothering you?"

Leo, of all his friends, understood his difficulty in articulating his troubles. But that still didn't make it any easier to come out with it. "What makes you think there's something else?"

"Because I don't think the land problem made you fly down Main Street like your pants were on fire." He looked up at his oldest friend. "Is it Shelby?"

Jack snorted. "No. That ran its course a while ago."

His friend nudged him in the elbow and got a goofy grin on his face. "Tell Uncle Leo. Come on."

"You have to promise not to judge me."

"Fine."

"Your sister-in-law is…a challenge." That was the politest thing he could think of saying.

Leo lifted a brow. "Juliet?"

"Yes, Juliet." Jack put his fork down and made eye contact with his friend. Because he wanted to be honest. "It's been less than a week since I got her to help me with my forum, but she's gotten me involved in solving people's problems. And complimenting them for their good work. And my grandma likes her way too much."

"From what she told us, she likes your granny a lot, too."

He jerked up his head. "She told you that?" What he really meant was, *what else did she tell you?*

"Yes." Leo assessed him carefully, like he could see straight through all his grousing about Juliet. "Other than that, she mostly said that you were annoying."

Jack snorted. Of course she had. "She's sharing my office and asked me if I wanted campfire or ocean waves as a soothing listening background. And she has *succulents*. Not to mention she's dog-sitting Louise Howard's fluff ball."

"Wait a minute. Juliet's working with you *in your office*?"

"She asked me for an office of her own, but it's a part-time job and I figured she could take the paperwork home. Not only did she move herself in, but she also moved my town model out. That was the last straw. And you know what? I think she tortured me on purpose just so I'd give her office space down the hall."

"Everyone loves her," Leo said in a warning voice. "Be careful if you fire her."

"I'm not going to fire her, and the position is temporary anyway. She *is* loveable. And she loves everyone. She bends over backward to help any-body get along. Trouble is, her solutions usually involve me."

Leo appeared to be on the verge of laughing. "Is that a bad thing?"

"Well, yes. No. I don't know. I had this idea that

if I could connect more with everyone, they'd see my way about my grandma's land, but honestly, it's a long shot. Once Devin makes his case, I think everyone in town is going to go along with it."

"Juliet's been good for your image. Everyone's talking about you driving that front loader." He hid a sudden chuckle with a cough.

"What is it?"

"Have you seen the *Gazette* today?" Leo got up, grabbed a newspaper from his desk, and tossed it in front of Jack.

He took one look and groaned. The trench photos accosted him in all their muddy glory, he and Juliet close up and looking like…well, looking like they were having way too much fun. "She slipped and fell. It was muddy. I—"

Leo stared at him.

"She's so…emotional." He waved his hand in the air. "She laughs, she cries. She feels bad about the land." He sounded ridiculous, he knew.

"Right," Leo said. "It would be terrible to have to interact with a human being with feelings."

"She told me I have issues."

"You do, Jack." Leo smiled, then softened his voice. "And I tried to warn Juliet about them. But…I don't know." He studied the photos. "I can't believe I'm saying this but, I just see—I see potential in you, Jack. Just like Tessa gave me a chance. This might be *your* chance to leave your baggage behind and actually connect with someone. The question is, are you going to let your past get in the way of something good?"

Leo's words startled him. When Jack had said

he didn't want to hurt Juliet, she'd taken that personally. He got that. But all he was trying to do was to warn her off—to tell Juliet that he wasn't the kind of man she needed. He'd been trying to protect her from *himself.*

He was used to doing that—maintaining emotional distance with women. He wouldn't recognize himself otherwise.

"I'm not going to get involved with her," he told Leo. His best friend knew him better than anyone. And he'd never want anything to come between them.

"Okay, good," Leo said, calling his bluff. After Jack didn't say anything, Leo added, "You're acting smitten."

"My heart is safe. The last thing I need is a woman with big *emotions.*" He said emotions like they were something scary. To him, they were. "And saying this out loud has given me an idea how I can solve this dilemma right now."

He picked up his phone. "Sharon? Hey, it's me. Will you please give Juliet the key to room seventeen? Tell her she can move all her stuff down there ASAP. Okay, thanks. Bye."

He punched the end button. "There. Problem solved."

Leo shook his head sadly.

"What?" he asked, looking at his friend. "I mean, most relationships suck," Jack said as he hung up the phone. "I—I don't even know if I can be in one."

Leo sighed. "I used to think love was complicated. But it's really not. It is or it isn't, that's all."

What did that mean? "You sound like Yoda."

"It means that love can transform your life if you're open to it. And you *can* be in a relationship, Jack. You have a lot to offer. More than you think."

What had happened to his fun, single friend?

"But, Jack…" Leo continued. "If you're *not* open to it and you break Juliet's heart…" He made a slit-the-neck gesture that was straight out of *The Godfather*. Then raised his brows to make sure he got it.

Jack did. He was just surprised Leo didn't end with *Capisce?*

"Warning heard," he said.

"And also, Jack," Leo said. "You do know that giving Juliet an office isn't going to solve the problem, right?"

Jack heaved a heavy sigh. Giving Juliet a space of her own might get her and the fluff ball out of his office, but not out of his mind. He just had to make sure to do everything possible so that she didn't somehow find her way into his heart.

CHAPTER TWELVE

The following Wednesday evening, Juliet borrowed some folding chairs from a city hall storage closet and arranged them in a circle in her new office space. All the while, Daisy sat in her dog bed in the corner, watching her with wide eyes.

She'd asked Louise if Daisy could come to her group therapy session tonight. Daisy had done just fine this week, happy to be with people, and Juliet thought she might be an inspiration to her group.

"Don't judge me," Juliet said to the dog. "This will have to do until the church basement is done being remodeled."

The office wasn't as big as Jack's but was decent in size. Placing her rubber tree beside an old green metal desk helped. As did adding a few bright embroidered pillows she'd brought from home to the ancient puke-orange couch, but nothing in the world was going to help the half-a-century-old green shag carpet. She was just debating going back to Jack's office to snag the light-up water feature and some candles to get the musty odor out when she heard a noise coming from the hall.

Country music. She poked her head out to confirm the source. *Yep.* Jack's office.

A certain someone was singing—loudly—about mamas not letting their children grow up to be cowboys.

She glanced at her watch. Almost seven. Her group would be arriving any second. Surely, Workaholic Jack should be home by now, doing whatever Indiana cowboys—or small-town mayors—did in their spare time?

As Juliet went to shut the door, she found Tessa standing there, smiling and holding a giant tray heaped with freshly baked goodies. Vivienne walked in right behind her. "Fresh batch this afternoon," Tessa said, placing the tray on the empty desk and removing the lid. "Have one."

Juliet took in the mini eclairs and mini opera cakes, all coated with chocolate ganache. "Oooh," she said, snagging an eclair and taking a bite. "Amazing, thank you." She closed her eyes and gave a little moan. "This will put everyone in a good mood." She hugged her sisters. "Thanks for bringing my favorites."

"I've been experimenting with offering more gluten-free options," Tessa said, handing Viv a little box. "Taste test those and tell me what you think."

Vivienne opened the box and peeked inside, her pretty blue eyes widening. "Gluten-free mini eclairs? This almost makes up for the twelve hours I spent in an elf suit today."

Poor Viv. Juliet knew that she'd have to broach the subject of her job soon. But she'd probably omit the Santa panties debacle.

As Juliet closed the door, Vivienne hiked a thumb toward the hall. "When did Waylon and Willie move in?"

"Shhhh," Juliet said, dropping her voice. "I don't want him to know I'm here."

"*Him,* meaning Jack?" Viv asked. "No one can hear *anything* over that racket," she pointed out.

Tessa narrowed her eyes suspiciously. "What's going on? Why don't you want Jack to know you're here...with a group of people?"

"No reason," Juliet said, fussing with the chairs.

"Juliet." Tessa used her warning voice, honed from years of being Second Mother to her and Viv.

"Okay, fine." Juliet stopped messing with the setup. "I sort of made Jack so miserable with me in his office that he gave me this one. But he didn't exactly give me permission to hold my group here."

Tessa stopped pulling the wrap off her pastry tray. "*Didn't exactly* give you permission? Maybe you should go clear it with him right now."

Juliet sighed. "I had to negotiate with him for the space." She didn't say that she'd sort of held his model town ransom. "And he wasn't really happy about giving it to me. And he questioned if a psych info session would be appropriate in city hall. But on the other hand, he never really said no."

Tessa folded her arms and gave a frown. She was going to be a great mom.

"It's just until the church remodel is done. Besides, I've already told everyone the session is here." What was the worst he could do, boot everyone out?

Okay, that would be bad. But she had to keep

doing things in her profession, and giving information to the community was important. And city hall was a community building, right?

She couldn't help thinking her dad would be proud that she'd found some way to keep working in her field. It was a great way to show everyone that she was more than capable. And that would help her get her marriage counseling clients back.

Vivienne was surveying the stark office, the green rug, the orange couch. "Maybe you're going to have to ask your group tonight for forgiveness, too. It looks like the seventies are back with a vengeance."

"The desk is okay," Tessa said, walking behind it and lifting the dusty gray shade on the window to reveal a stunning salmon sunset, a backdrop to the streetlights on Main just flickering on. Juliet joined her at the window, opening it to let in the crisp fall air. The trees lining Main Street were a brilliant gold in the fading light.

"A Main Street view," Juliet said. "You can't beat that."

"You always find the positive," Viv said.

"It's a good omen," Tessa said, hugging her. "Viv and I would like to stay, if that's okay."

Juliet's stomach twisted. "You guys really don't have to do that." The idea of her sisters watching her sent a wave of nervous energy through her. What if no one showed up?

"We want to," Viv said. "It'll be cool to see you all professional and stuff."

"No pressure," Tessa said. "We just thought it would be fun."

"I know what's going on here." Juliet suddenly realized what was going on. "You came to *support* me."

Viv shrugged. "That's what sisters are for, right?"

Just then, Delores and George Teeter rapped on the door and then walked in, holding hands.

"Hello, Juliet, honey," George said with a wink. Delores gave her a big hug, then she hugged Viv, too. "We had twenty more orders for Santa panties," she said, shaking her head. "You and Jack have started something."

Delores must have seen Viv's shocked expression, because she shrugged. "It's only October and we've had a hundred orders."

All because Jack was being goofy, selling them out of a box?

"But I thought you didn't like anything risqué in the store," Juliet said.

"Oh, they're still online only," Delores said. "We can barely keep them in stock, thanks to the social media stuff you posted."

Juliet recalled that Viv had worked miracles with Tessa's and Leo's businesses last year by managing social media and building Tessa's YouTube channel. Which she seemed to like a whole lot better than being an elf.

"Glad it worked out." Viv flashed her usual big smile. Still, Juliet made a note to sit her down for a talk ASAP.

"Thanks for coming," Juliet said to Delores and George, "but what are you two doing here?"

"We came for some counseling." Delores

poked George in the ribs. "He's being difficult."

"I'm always difficult," he said, giving Delores a squeeze. "That's why you love me."

Juliet put her hands on her hips. "You know this is just a community info session. Otherwise, it would be unethical for me to have friends and family here." She had the same suspicion they were here for the same reason as her sisters. "Why are you two really here?"

George helped himself to a pastry and sat down. "It's date night, and we thought we'd come check it out."

"Besides, we're always looking to improve our relationship." Delores settled into a chair. "Hand me one of those little cakes, George, honey."

"Hey, Viv," Juliet said. "I stashed some water bottles in the fridge across the hall. Would you please bring some in?"

Just as Viv walked out, their mother walked in with Leo's dad, Marco Castorini, whom she'd been dating for almost a year.

"Hi, honey." Her mom, dressed in a sweater with a pretty scarf around her neck, greeted her with a hug. She looked happy—and since dating Marco, hadn't got caught wearing her bakery apron in public once. "We thought we'd come learn more about mental health services from our favorite counselor."

"Knock 'em dead, sweetheart," Marco said, looking proud. With his thick gray hair combed back from a widow's peak and his muscular build, he'd come in handy as a bouncer if anyone got out of line tonight.

"Why is everyone showing up?" Juliet was a little freaked out that practically her whole family was here, except for her grandmother.

"Um…because we love you?" Tessa said. "Also, we're a built-in, guaranteed crowd." After seeing Juliet's face, she added, "Not that you're going to need us, but we're good to have in a pinch, right?"

Noah popped his head in. Of course. Because who else wasn't here that she knew? "Hey, Jules," he said, "this is relationship therapy, right?"

"It's just an information session," Juliet said. "I'm going to talk about what therapy is, when people should seek it out, that kind of thing."

"Do you have to be in a relationship to come?" he asked, waving to everyone.

"Of course not," Juliet said.

"Well, guess what," he said, "I *might* be in a relationship."

"Noah!" Juliet embraced him. "How did I not know this?"

"I haven't told a single soul," he said. "I'm sort of holding my breath about it. Like maybe it's too good to be true."

"You deserve the best," Juliet said. "I'm so glad you came."

George moved over and patted the seat between him and Delores. "Sit right on down, son."

Delores smiled. "We want to hear all about it."

This overwhelming support from her loved ones was…overwhelming. "I need a drink," she whispered to Viv.

"All that's in the break room is coffee. I just put some on."

The smell of freshly brewing coffee wafted into the room, making Juliet's heart lurch. "I'm afraid Jack's going to smell that." And come barreling down to stop her.

"Don't worry," Viv said. "I made sure his office was dark and quiet before I brewed. He must have left. Also, you're going to keep this talk generic, right? Because I really don't want to hear any details Mom might share about her relationship with Marco."

"It's definitely not that kind of talk," Juliet said. But they both knew their mom could be an oversharer.

Jack's grandmother showed up, of course, and Juliet went to greet her. "Hi, Adele," she said, receiving a warm hug. "Are you looking for Jack?"

"Heck, no," she said, waving her hand dismissively. "I'm here because I heard something was going on tonight." She dropped her voice. "And I was hoping some single men might be here."

Before Juliet could figure out how to respond, she heard her own grandmother's voice from the hallway. "There may not be any here, but just sign up for bingo at the church on Wednesdays." Her grandmother came into view, wearing a big smile. "In fact, I'm going there right after this. You can come with me."

The two women couldn't be more different. Juliet's grandmother was tall and svelte, with pretty gray hair. Jack's grandmother was half-pint sized, with pure white hair, wearing a jean jacket and a red bandana around her neck.

"Well, thanks, Sophie, I'd love to."

Her grandmother patted Juliet's forearm and kissed her cheek. "We won't make you nervous, will we?"

Just because she was in a professional crisis, and everyone she loved knew it, what was there to be nervous about? "Of course not."

She'd be okay. It was only an info session. What could go wrong?

A young couple walked in and gazed about the room. Juliet recognized Faith Brandenstein, who worked as an assistant at the library; she had been a client of Juliet's in individual therapy during her training at IU. Faith had brought her long-time boyfriend, Axl, who in the past had refused to come to therapy with her.

Which was interesting on a lot of levels. Seeing him here was positive. But part of her wished Faith had dumped him by now. Because Axl was...difficult. Controlling. Demeaning. Everything really bad for a person who was struggling with self-esteem to begin with.

Juliet smiled and hugged Faith. "I'm so glad you're here," she said.

"Hi, Ms. Montgomery. This is Axl. We...we came for the information session."

"Hi, Axl," she said to a muscle-bound guy in a tank and shorts.

He nodded to Juliet. "I only agreed so she stops bugging me about coming to therapy every single day," Axl said.

Oh yeah, Juliet had forgotten that he was condescending, too. "Well, it's great to have you here. Feel free to ask any questions."

Then she walked to her seat in the circle and addressed the group. "Okay, everyone, let's get started."

Viv had set the coffeemaker on the desk, along with a bunch of mugs. And Juliet could tell from the aroma that it was indeed Jack's expensive coffee. Everyone was drinking, eating French pastries, and chatting. A great start. She just prayed Jack was home now, putting his boots up somewhere, singing more offkey songs to his heart's content.

And somehow that made her smile, even though she was still annoyed with him. Which made her realize that she had difficulty tucking him away in the right place—as a business associate she had to temporarily tolerate.

"This is excellent coffee," George said. "I'm going to make sure to order more of this for the hardware store."

Juliet smiled and held up her own mug. "I wanted to welcome everyone here tonight and thank you all for coming. I'm going to talk a little about what relationship therapy is, when to seek counseling in a relationship, and of course, answer any of your questions."

"That's my daughter," her mom said proudly. "She's a licensed therapist." Marco, next to her, beamed.

Before Juliet could be too embarrassed, Daisy woke up, giving a big yawn, and blinked as she noticed the room full of people. Then she beelined over to Juliet, who scooped her up and placed her in her lap.

She petted and cooed to the dog, who was shaking a little. "This is Daisy. I'm dog sitting her tonight. She's a little shy, so, I have to ask you not to pet her until she gets used to everyone." Juliet gave her a soothing stroke. Which actually might have helped to calm her own nerves.

"That dog looks like a wrinkled old man," Axl said, chuckling under his breath.

"I think she's sweet," Faith said.

Great. A man who insults dogs. This was going to be really fun. "Just in case anyone doesn't know me, I'm Juliet Montgomery, and I'm really thrilled to be back here in Blossom Glen where I grew up."

"Way to go, Lulu," George said with a fist pump.

"Thank you, George," she said calmly, fighting the instant blush. "But for the group, please stick to Juliet." There, she was assertive. She had control.

"We're so proud of you." Her mom gave a little wave.

"Thanks, Mom," she said.

"Aren't you the one with all the engagements?" Axl flexed his muscles, showing off all his many tattoos. Which might have been interesting if he wasn't so intimidating.

"Axl, please," Faith said, clearly embarrassed.

And that's when Juliet felt a tingle between her shoulders. She adjusted herself in her chair, pressing her back against it, hoping she was imagining.

But no. The tingle turned into a burn, and then

an itch and a flare.

Her friends the hives were back with a vengeance.

Juliet sat up straight and tried to project confidence. "I have been engaged previously," she said. The room was so quiet, she could hear the traffic on the street. A child's laughter. The distant whine of a siren. "Which makes me human like everyone else."

She tried not to scratch her arms. And pretended like little red flares weren't erupting all over them. As she did some parasympathetic breathing, she thought of a positive. She was so involved in trying to hide her distress, it took her mind off of handling Axl.

Hives or no hives, she wasn't going to let him unnerve her.

She turned to the group. "That's the thing about therapy. People think you have to wait for a huge mental health crisis to seek it out. But therapy can help explore issues, help with communication, and resolve conflicts. Basically, it helps us to understand ourselves and improve our relationships with other people."

"I just love knowing what you do for a living, sweetie," her mom said. "And maybe you can give us all some pointers."

"Well, Mom, I can't practice any therapy on friends or family. That would be unethical. But I can give out a lot of information."

Marco, holding her mother's hand, said, "Um, relationships are important. And…we're always trying to be the best people we can be, right? So, everyone should get some help."

"Why, Marco, that's such an enlightened view," Juliet said.

"And then maybe after therapy, people can head on over to my restaurant for a good meal. In fact, tonight we've got a fabulous lasagna and a veal piccata dish that's to die for. With two-for-one apps." He pointed out the window, where the giant neon spaghetti sign with the blinking meatball was just firing up for the night.

Yes. Always the salesman. But at least he was helping sell the idea of therapy.

She felt a little calmer now, but a big red blotch was now sitting atop her left ankle. She crossed her feet and saw that Noah had raised his hand. "My question is, can you do relationship therapy with a person who's worked really, really hard to overcome issues from his past?"

"Of course. But that person can also use individual therapy, and that's exactly what it's for, to help us become the best versions of ourselves. That can't help but be good for our relationships."

"I'm here because *she* forced me to come," Axl hiked a thumb at Faith, who cringed.

"Well, we agreed we needed some help in dealing with disagreements, right?" she said to Axl. "I wanted you to come and see that just talking wasn't so scary."

Go, Faith!

"I'm not afraid of anything," Axl said, crossing his giant arms. "I'm here to try to make you happy." He snorted. "But that's never easy."

"I think that couples therapy is for ourselves as

well as for our partners," Juliet said carefully.

Axl spoke up. "How can you run this group when you clearly don't know anything about relationships yourself?"

Juliet forced herself not to choke on her coffee. A direct attack—in front of her family and friends. She course-corrected from her shock, setting down her cup and gathering her wits. And rubbing her back against her chair because it took some of the itch away.

"Axl, shhhh," Faith said. To which Axl gave her a glare.

"Now hold on a second," Delores said before Juliet could speak. "No one is perfect and no relationship is perfect. Just because our therapist isn't happily married and her life isn't tied up in a perfect bow doesn't mean she can't help us with our troubles, right?"

"Well, that's real nice, ma'am," Axl said, "but my girlfriend and me need some help. How can we get that from someone who can't help herself?" His harsh gaze rested directly on Juliet. "You told Faith we need to do hard work to figure out what's wrong with us, so how are *you* going to do the same?"

"Well, I can tell you that therapists are often in therapy themselves," Juliet said. *I can do this*, she told herself. *I can be a professional.* "But what I do personally is private. And I've been trained to—"

"Lady, I don't care about your training. All this talk is a bunch of bullsh—"

"Hey," someone said from the door. "I thought

I smelled coffee down here."

Jack opened the door and walked into the room, looking pleasant enough. He zeroed in on her, lifting a single brow as if to ask, *Are you all right*? But that look was nothing compared to the glare he cast at Axl. Jack looked like he wanted to haul Axl out by his large gold hoop earring.

So many feelings churned through her. She was off-balance, thrown by Axl's comment, but getting her foothold. Second, she felt relief at seeing Jack—but not because he had some misdirected cowboy need to save her. She didn't need to be saved. But he'd showed up—so maybe he cared about her as a friend?

He'd told her *business only*. So why was he here?

If he was here to do some bold rodeo lasso trick to save her, she didn't need it.

But on the positive side, at least he didn't look like he was going to boot them all out of this room, which was now the least of her worries.

So that left her with showing him and her family and friends—but mostly *herself*—that she could handle someone throwing her a little bit of shade.

Her dad's voice came to her. *You got this.*

Somehow that gave her a sudden sense of comfort. Daisy had nestled into her lap and fallen asleep, trusting her enough to take care of her. So now she had to trust in herself.

She smoothed her hands over her legs, which she hoped looked like she was preparing to talk, not scratch. "The beauty about therapy," Juliet said, speaking slowly and calmly, "is that you get to pick your own therapist. Someone you trust and have confidence in. That person doesn't have to be me."

Axl sat slumped, his legs extended, his arms crossed. He took a brief survey around the room as if he were debating how far to push. "That's fine, but I don't like a lot of highfalutin', high-and-mighty people who don't have their own lives figured out telling me what to do."

"Therapy isn't easy," she continued in a firm and steady voice. "You have to want to do everything possible to help yourself and your relationship. You have to be willing to take risks and leave all the excuses behind. It's uncomfortable. Change always is."

The weird thing was, Juliet sort of felt like she was also speaking to Jack. Not about suggesting therapy, but about taking risks. Specifically, with her.

And she discovered—at the weirdest, strangest time—that she was angry at *him*, not difficult Axl. Not for barging in, looking ready to jump Axl. But for running away from…well, from their friendship.

From being okay with the opportunity to get to know her.

But she certainly didn't want any more than that. Because he was her polar opposite in just about everything. Plus, she'd tossed enough fodder to the town gossips for three lifetimes. Okay, two and a half.

But even as Juliet looked at him—concerned,

ready to pounce if necessary, and so *handsome*—
she knew she was lying about being friends.

Her feelings for him weren't just friendly feelings.

And that meant that *she* was running away, too.

And why was all this occurring to her *now*?

Axl glanced around nervously. "Well, Ms.
Montgomery, are *you* doing everything to help
understand yourself?"

Whoa. Okay.

"Axl, please," Faith said. "We're here to get
some information, right?"

"Well, that's the only information I want to
know," he said, getting up from his chair. "I'm not
sure what kind of group this is, but I'm outta
here." Then he stomped out.

Leaving his words to echo in her head.

And leaving her free to take her antihistamine.
She may not be able to control her hives, but she'd
stood up to Axl. And that was a win.

CHAPTER THIRTEEN

Jack walked over to Axl's empty chair and sat down. "Well. Seems like I came just in time for all the excitement." He tried to take the temperature of the room. It seemed that everyone was holding their breath.

"Juliet was giving an info session about therapy," Delores said. "And Axl got a little upset."

But Juliet didn't look distressed. In fact, she was assessing Faith carefully, maybe worried more about her than the insult that A-hole Axl had just hurled.

"I'm really sorry, Juliet," Faith said. "Axl is angry. At me, at everyone. Please don't take it personally."

"The thing is, dear," Delores said, "that he was taking his anger out on Juliet. But he wasn't treating *you* very well, either. It's important to have a partner who respects you and doesn't demean you or say mean things to you."

"It's okay, Faith, I'm not offended," Juliet said. "And Axl is right that everyone has to work on their issues. Including me." She added softly, "And including *him*. Red flags in a relationship are someone criticizing and putting himself on higher ground than his partner, being defensive, and withdrawing."

"I'd say Axl was waving all of those flags, honey," Delores said. "He's a red flag danger zone."

Juliet spoke openly to the room. "Life is always throwing us curveballs. Seeking therapy requires a certain openness. An understanding that you can't always help yourself on your own. And a certain humility that you're not perfect, that there's room for change." She looked at Faith again. "Everyone gets to that point in their own time." She paused. "And Axl is right that we should do everything we can to understand ourselves."

Faith stood up. "I'm really sorry," she said. "It was—nice meeting all of you."

"Stay for some sweets," Juliet offered.

She hiked a thumb toward the door. "I'm going after him."

"Okay, Faith," Juliet said. "Thanks for coming."

Juliet was amazing. She was open and honest. She'd handled things professionally and well. Anyone who could talk about feelings like that in front of people and connect with them had all his respect.

Tessa passed a plate of chocolate mini-eclairs, taking one first. The room seemed to be collectively breathing a sigh of relief.

"You're right, Juliet," Tessa said, "life *is* always throwing curveballs. I'm expecting a baby in a month and—and I'm afraid everything's going to change."

"It sure is," her grandmother said bluntly, which made the color drain out of Tessa's face.

"Well, change is part of life and is often a good thing," Juliet said hurriedly, before her grandmother could say more.

Tessa shrugged and smiled, one hand on her

abdomen. "I just love our life right now. Don't get me wrong. I'm so excited for the baby, but I'm afraid that I'm going to be exhausted all the time."

"Life does change when a baby comes," their mother said. "It becomes a different kind of life. A different kind of joy."

"The thing is," Mr. Castorini said, "life never stays the same no matter what age you are. But I don't think we would want it to." He squeezed her mother's hand and winked. "I think because of the losses we've had and what we've gone through, we really appreciate each other."

Jack was slowly realizing that this gathering of family and friends was turning a little intimate. The info session vibe was gone. He was okay with that…as long as he didn't get called upon to say anything.

"I lost my Gabe a long time ago," Jack's grandmother said.

Oh no. Not his granny, too. Talking about… feelings. Jack shifted in his seat. Too bad the water main break was resolved, because he needed an emergency excuse to leave ASAP.

"I have beautiful memories." His granny cleared her throat. "I have a confession, though. I'm not here to learn about therapy. My relationship problem is that I have no relationship. But I want one. Anyone know of any eligible bachelors in this town?"

Juliet's grandmother spoke up. "I think it takes a lot of courage to put yourself out there."

"What about you?" Adele said. "Do you date?"

"Oh, I'm too old for that," Sophie said, her

cheeks coloring. "And too busy."

Vivienne raised her hand. "Gram, I'd like to say that those might be excuses. I mean, you have a really full social life, and you *do* go to bingo, but you tend to hang out with your girlfriends. Maybe it's time to take some chances."

"I'm just going to be honest here," Noah said.

Not Noah, too! Jack was screwed. Everyone was sitting around eating and…sharing.

"I'm terrible at relationships. That's why I avoid them. But I met someone at a benefit recently and—I don't know. I just don't want to mess this one up."

"I'll be honest, too," Vivienne said. "Ever since I've been home, I've been confused. I mean, I appreciate the job at Christmas Every Day"—she glanced over at Delores—"but I'm just not sure what's next for me."

"You're doing a fine job, dear." Delores patted Vivienne's knee. "You're full of Christmas cheer."

"Axl was right about me," Juliet said suddenly.

"No, he wasn't," Tessa was quick to say. "The guy's a jerk."

"Don't listen to him," Delores said. "He's got a terrible attitude and he was lashing out. That sweet Faith—"

"He's right that I have to do more to understand the mistakes I've made. I mean, I've talked about them in therapy. But I need to do more." But what? What could she do? Jack personally thought that a person's past should be left in the past. Lord knows he'd tried to do that with his own.

"Honey, everyone makes mistakes," Juliet's mother said. "You've matured and moved on from them. So maybe you should stop being so hard on yourself."

That was wise, Jack had to agree. The room fell silent, everyone contemplating the wisdom. But eventually, people started staring at him.

"What do you think, Jack?" Tessa asked.

He couldn't even process his thoughts, because everyone was looking expectantly his way. A clock ticked loudly. Except it was his own watch, which he knew was not loud at all. Or maybe that was his pulse skyrocketing. He'd just walked into his worst nightmare. Talking about himself.

He looked at Juliet, surrounded by her family and friends. He truly sucked at saying how he felt in private, much less in a roomful of people, but Juliet had been brave, so he could try to be, too. "I—um—first of all, I think you handled that difficult situation really well. And second… Everybody grows and changes. If you need to explore your past for your own peace of mind, I say go for it. I haven't come across many people who freely admit their mistakes. Most of us hide them. You're able to talk about feelings. And make people feel better. Actually, Juliet, you leave just about everyone you meet feeling better about themselves. You're open and honest and…that's a gift."

Everyone was staring at him. And Juliet was blinking like she had something in her eye. But what he'd said was the truth. He had all the respect for her, even if his personal feelings for her were muddled.

Juliet's eyes grew wide. He hoped he hadn't somehow hurt her by what he said. "Thank you, Jack," she said, sounding a little choked up.

"Jack might have a point," Tessa said. "How would you explore your past? I mean, what could you do?"

"As I said," Juliet said a little defensively. "I've worked on this in therapy. I'm not sure what else I can—"

"How about something old-fashioned." An idea hit him like a big gust of wind. "Just talking with those guys—um, your exes." Juliet sat up, clearly startled. But nonplussed, he continued, "I mean, they were there, too. Why don't you just ask them their take on it?" The more he thought about it, the more he thought his solution was direct, straightforward, and something to actually *do*. Something he was good at.

"I—no," she stammered. "That would be—awkward."

"I mean, we *are* talking big breakups here," Tessa said, jumping in to aid her sister. "Hurt feelings. Relationships that were never the same. That kind of thing."

"Yes, but all that was a long time ago," Jack said. "If you talk to your exes, you might figure out what went wrong and why you didn't fix it earlier. And then...you're done. Fresh perspective, then the past gets put to rest." He dusted his hands together for effect.

"I think Jack is right," her grandmother said. "Because knowing yourself is never a bad thing. It gives you power not to repeat the same mistakes. And to help others."

"Jack, it's thoughtful of you to help Juliet," Mrs. Teeter said, "but what's your own personal takeaway from today?" She smiled gently. "I'm only asking because we've all shared something a little personal, and I thought you might want to, too."

Oh no. Jack's stomach plunged. He'd come so close to getting off the hook. "I'm all for therapy," he said, clearing his throat and tapping his fingertips together. Then he decided he'd have to shut this down right now, because there was no way in hell he was going to mention his own struggles. "But therapy isn't for me. I'm not very good at talking about my feelings."

"I'm going to call you out on that, son," his grandma said. His *grandma*. Why couldn't his family be supportive like Juliet's? "That right there is something you need to work on."

"Well, I'm not knocking therapy in general, that's for sure," he said. "I just don't have the time for it right now."

"The thing is, it's like exercise," Viv said. "No one really has time. But you've got to make time for your health anyway, right?"

"Talking about feelings is hard," George said. "But I believe the benefits are worth the risks. If you can't expose your vulnerabilities to the people you love, how can you have an open and honest relationship?"

"That's exactly right." Delores tipped her head George's way. "We argue, we disagree. Half the time the man's socks don't make it to the hamper, but George has never once failed to call me in thirty-five years to let me know if he's running late. And every Friday he brings me my favorite ice cream, and believe me, that makes up for a lot of little annoyances. And you know what? We trust each other. We know we're best friends and no matter what happens, I know he has my back. And we laugh. And…that special spark that we felt at the beginning is still there. That's what gets us through."

Jack was in awe of the Teeters. They had a long, loving relationship, the likes of which he'd never seen. So it *was* possible—for some people. Maybe the kind who weren't as damaged as he was.

The topic finally shifted to other, easier things, like the holiday lighting contest and this week's gossip. *Thank goodness.*

He looked around at everyone eating and drinking and laughing. Juliet seemed relaxed and happy around her family and friends. She should be, because she'd shown her professionalism and her caring for everyone and had deflected Axl's nonsense just fine.

He'd come in here to save her if she needed it. But he was leaving feeling like he just might need saving himself.

. . .

"So what's up with Jack showing up all tough and angry looking?" Vivienne asked as she gathered the mugs after everyone had left. They were cleaning up and talking about the night, while Daisy snored in her bed in the corner, pooped out from all the excitement. Even Juliet felt more relaxed, her hives all but disappeared.

Tessa stopped collecting dishes and cups and stood up, hands on hips. "First of all, we need to tell Juliet what a great job she did." She turned to her. "You handled yourself very well, and we're proud of you. And by the way, poor Faith. Axl is a handful, and I don't mean a handful of muscle."

"Yes, we're proud," Viv said. "But then, we've always been proud, and there's no doubt in our minds you're amazing. But come on, people, you have to admit it was a little thrilling to see the cowboy show up and look like he was a second away from tossing Axl out on his…well, axle. Staring at Juliet when she didn't know he was staring. Ready to jump to your defense at any second."

"I can see it now—I really think Jack likes you." Tessa used a singsong-y voice, as if they were discussing a high school crush.

Juliet shook her head. "Jack can't help jumping in and coming to the rescue. That's the cowboy in him. And I don't *need* anyone coming to *my* rescue." She wasn't sure if she wanted to club him or…kiss him. For being there if she needed him.

"Jack and I are complete opposites," Juliet continued, as if she were trying to talk herself out of something. "Maybe that's why I'm so attracted to him." She was always attracted to men who were bad for her. Why *was* that?

"At least you're aware of that," Viv said. "So

you don't make a mistake again."

"Jack is a serial dater and a commitment-phobe, just like Jax from last year," Tessa said. "They even have practically the same name. But I still think that it's possible to get down to his heart."

Juliet shook her head. "I think you have a soft spot for him because of Leo. But I'm not looking for a relationship. When I am ready, I want someone who's comfortable with expressing their love. Like Dad. He never failed to tell us he loved us and was proud of us."

Vivienne turned around at the door with her hands full of dirty mugs. "Well, Jack took all of those Christmas panties that some woman tried to return three months late after buying them online. And then helped me to re-sell them on the spot. He basically saved my job."

"Wait a minute." Juliet stopped wiping down surfaces. "Jack *saved your job* by selling those panties?"

"Yep."

Jack had sold the panties to help her *sister?* And Jack had walked in tonight to be there for her. Jack, who wouldn't get caught dead talking about his feelings. Why did she have to keep learning nice things about him?

"The real takeaway from tonight is that Axl was right," she said. "I haven't done everything possible to know myself."

"Juliet," Tessa said, "Axl is a jerk. Can't you just chalk your past up to youth and inexperience, forgive yourself, and move on?"

"Lots of people make mistakes with relationships. But mine seem… I don't know. More serious. I mean, I almost made it to the altar twice." She paused. "Even if I didn't have to worry about my *job*, the truth is that I'm never going to be ready for a *relationship* if I can't figure out why I've made such bad choices."

"You are so hard on yourself," Tessa said. "Harder than anyone else I know. I wish you could just put your bad experiences behind you."

"Tyler came back into the shop again yesterday," Viv said. "He was asking about you."

"He wanted to have coffee," Juliet said. "I don't know, maybe I should do what Jack said. Get Tyler's take on our breakup." Her mind began churning. "And Ryan's, too. Maybe if I talk with them, I can figure out why I waited so long to break things off with both of them."

Tessa shook her head adamantly. "That's opening up a can of worms you might not want to open. I mean, Mom tells me Tyler asks about you every time he comes into the bakery. I know everybody loves him, but I think he's a little… I don't know. Overly optimistic. Be careful he doesn't misread your intentions."

"It seems to me there were good reasons you didn't marry those guys," Viv said.

"Viv's right," Tessa chimed in. "Why do you need them to revisit those reasons?"

Juliet thought about how she'd always attacked every problem down to the studs. "Maybe Jack is right." She hated to think that. Because it would be really difficult. And awkward. And scary. But it also made perfect sense.

Tessa put an arm on her shoulder. "You know yourself best. Whatever you decide, we'll support you, you know that."

"I know it. Thanks to you both." With that, her sisters helped stack the chairs in the storage room and the mugs in the break room's dishwasher. Viv found a vacuum in the closet and ran it over the awful shag carpet. Then suddenly the place was tidy, everyone was gone, and Juliet was left with Daisy, who seemed to be anxiously awaiting her ride home. "You ready to go see your mom, babe?" Juliet asked.

She felt like she'd handled Axl well enough. And she had him to thank for giving her the push to figure out what was holding her back once and for all.

CHAPTER FOURTEEN

After the info session, Jack somehow ended up back in his office, where he tried to brainstorm about the upcoming zoning commission meeting, but his mind kept focusing on a certain redhead who seemed to challenge him in every way.

He turned on the water fountain with the rotating ball and changing LED lights that Juliet had "accidentally" left behind. And watered the succulents. But none of that made him calmer.

He'd gone down to that office to strong-arm Axl if needed, and he ended up questioning himself.

Therapy just wasn't for him.

Neither was Juliet. A therapist. They didn't have much in common. She questioned him at every turn. Made him uncomfortable. Shook him up when things were just fine the way they were, thank you.

Just fine.

He ran his hands through his hair. It wasn't helping that Juliet was gorgeous. But he wasn't going there with her for millions of reasons. He didn't do relationships. She was too vulnerable. And, to be honest, what if he somehow fell for her, only to become another one of her mistakes? That would be a disaster for both of them.

But...he could be her friend, right?

Common sense told him to stay away. That he

couldn't parse his feelings so easily, separate the physical from the platonic.

Yet he couldn't stop thinking about her. Not just physically.

Worrying about her. Was she down on herself again because of that jerk Axl?

She certainly shouldn't be. She'd handled him really well, but he knew how she took her mistakes to heart.

As he turned off the fountain and all the lights and made his way out of city hall, he knew, against his better judgment, that he wasn't headed home.

• • •

After Juliet dropped Daisy off, she started to walk home, thankful for the mild evening. She inhaled the earthy smell of fall leaves, enjoying the crunch of them under her feet as she walked the tree-lined sidewalks of her town. She took big gulps of fresh air, hoping to relieve the confusion she felt inside. Her family and friends loved her. They wanted her to succeed.

But it appeared that there was someone standing in the way of that goal.

Herself.

She hadn't worked so hard for years to get herself educated to be tripped up by her own two feet, right?

Juliet sat down on a bench under a grove of trees. The leaves were still plentiful, but all were showing off their splashiest browns, golds, or reds, getting ready to rest and rejuvenate before a whole new cycle of rebirth. And oh, she longed to feel that way, too.

So she wasn't interested in a relationship, and she needed to figure herself out. Well then, why did she keep seeing the dark, sexy gaze of an Indiana cowboy who always seemed to be interfering in her life?

Speaking of the devil, a big black truck quietly rolled up to her park bench.

"Hey there, Counselor," Jack said, sticking his head out the window. Without his Stetson for once.

"Quit calling me that," she warned. "It's... cheeky. Sarcastic."

He sighed and tapped the door nervously with his fingers. "I'm going to start again. No cheek." He turned his head away and then back, as if seeing her for the first time. "Hey there, Juliet," he said.

And oh, that way was far worse. Because the sound of her name—spoken in his low, rumbly baritone—it did something to her, deep inside. Something heart pumping and a little thrilling. Something she did not understand. And definitely something she did not want to come to terms with.

"Jack," she said with disbelief, feeling like she'd conjured him out of nowhere just from thinking about him. "What are you doing here?"

"Just checking on my constituents." He looked her up and down, mostly with concern. "Making sure there's no trouble."

She viewed the sleepy neighborhood, lights

glowing softly within people's living rooms and kitchens. Birds were singing their final good night song, spreading the news that it would soon be time for flight.

She opened her arms wide. "There's no trouble around here."

He chuckled. "Ah, but you're wrong. I've already found it." He cracked a lopsided grin that was…well, borderline irresistible. Borderline because it was like she was on the edge of a precipice. And if she didn't figure out how to pull herself back, she was going to tumble right over the edge.

She resisted by holding onto the seat of the park bench with all she had. "You're going to find even more if you don't keep on driving."

"You don't mean that." He sounded mock-offended.

She did mean it. Mostly. But the annoying man wouldn't budge. Instead, he turned off the engine, climbed out, and walked over until he was standing before her.

His stride was long and confident, his legs that perfect combination of muscled and lean in faded, soft jeans. And he was so tall, the leaves on the trees ruffled in the breeze right above his head. Without the Stetson, his hair was wavy, a little unruly, and slightly longish, but it suited him—a little wild, a little edgy, and a whole lot sexy. But the thing that devastated her the most was the way he looked at her. A little bemused, a little sympathetic. She saw kindness there, too. And something else.

Desire. If she wasn't mistaken, the mayor was Hot for Counselor.

She bent over, pressing the ball of her hand to her forehead. Her own inappropriate thoughts were complicating her well-hewn plans. Like what nice, full lips he had. And how when he smiled, his blue eyes lit up. And how his Texan jaw could split wood, it was so square and strong.

But these were only thoughts. She had the power to control her behavior. That's what she told her clients all the time.

She was coming to see that Jack was a fixer. He got in there and he fixed things, and apparently, this talent extended to people.

She couldn't let it extend to her.

She couldn't be looked upon as someone who was broken, who needed help. For some reason, that, coming from him, would devastate her.

He sat down beside her on the bench. Around them, the street was quiet. The soft clinking of metal tags reached them as someone walked their dog down the sidewalk.

Her pulse picked up at the presence of him, big and tall, and so close she could feel his body heat. His arm grazed hers as he leaned forward, resting his elbows on his knees, and that little movement sent a wave of tingles cascading all through her.

"You feel sorry for me," she said.

"No," he said, tapping his fingers together. "I really don't."

She frowned. "Then why are you here?"

He turned his head to look at her. "I thought you might need a friend."

She snorted. "Well, I had plenty of those show up for my education session, didn't I?"

"Yes, but that was different. They came to support you. I'm just here to listen."

"I thought you didn't believe in talking, in therapy."

"I never said that. I said therapy wasn't for me."

"That seems a little…arrogant." She couldn't help saying it. Her life was based on the belief that therapy helped people. Anyone who passed that off as nonsense…well, she couldn't really relate to someone like that at all. Even if he did look mighty fine in his blue jeans.

"Actually, it's the opposite. Of arrogant."

That was unexpected. "What do you mean?"

"Well, I'll tell you all about it. But I'd like to take you somewhere first."

Take me somewhere? He sat back and tossed her a slow, steady gaze, like he'd decided on a course of action, and that was that. And even in the dim light from the streetlights, she could see that determination in his eyes.

"Where would you want to go?" she asked.

His full mouth curved up in a smile. "It's a surprise."

She tried to fight her feelings. "Jack, I appreciate that you're trying to make me feel better, but there's really no need—"

"Look," he said, interrupting. "You'll like it. And I promise you'll be back home in your jammies by ten. What do you say?"

Everything about him was charming. But she

had to get something off her chest. "Before I decide, I have one question."

He met her gaze. "Okay, shoot."

"You didn't come down to that office to kick me out, did you?"

"If I say no, I can predict your next question," he said matter-of-factly. "You're going to ask me if I showed up because I was trying to save you."

Bingo. "Well, were you?"

He flung both his arms around the back of the bench, casual and relaxed, and stretched out his long legs. "Juliet, you're among the most competent people I know. But I despise people who are out to take advantage of someone because it helps them to avoid being uncomfortable."

"So you came to my rescue anyway."

"I showed up, but I didn't do any rescuing."

"But you thought I *might* need it."

"I know Axl. Aaron's told me he's trouble. And I don't let trouble happen when I can prevent it. Except I reckon I don't follow that rule myself, because I can't seem to stop worrying about you."

She swallowed hard, suddenly choked up. Why did he have to say all the right things? Acknowledging her competence yet being there anyway. If he kept this up, she was going to fall flat in love with him. "You worry about me?"

She saw him stiffen. "As a work colleague, of course. I mean, if something happens to you, my good reputation goes right out the window, know what I mean?"

Except he wasn't looking at her like a work colleague. He was looking at her like she was a piece of chocolate cake, and it was making her all trembly inside.

She tried to tamp it down. He was dangerous to her heart in ways she couldn't even articulate; he was handsome, and intelligent, and considerate. She hadn't fallen for him blindly, or because of physical attraction, letting her emotions sweep her away into bad situations and relationships, as she'd done in the past. It was just that Jack Monroe had a lot of layers to peel back, and in the peeling back, she was finding someone that surprised her in every way.

Wait...did she just admit she'd fallen for him?

He'd been driving around town looking for her because he knew she might need a friend, and that touched her even more than how devastatingly handsome he was.

A friend, yes, but...what else? And was she ready for the potential *what else*?

Her pulse was pounding, and she felt breathless as she tried to form words that made sense. "Well then, I guess I'll have to just say thank you. For being there. And...I'm sorry for having my info session without asking."

One corner of his mouth quirked up in a smile. "It's all right." He was backlit by the streetlamp as he stood there, tall, broad shouldered, and waiting patiently. The moon was out, the fragrant autumn breeze was blowing, and she reached up and grasped his hand.

CHAPTER FIFTEEN

Jack drove them through town, then out on a state route through some farmland until he made some turns and came upon a dirt road that led to a lake. Surprisingly, the woman next to him was still and silent.

"You're making me nervous," he finally said. "How come you're not questioning me left and right about where we're going?"

She was scrunched down in her seat, half-reclined, looking out the window. As the truck flew down the country roads, the earthy scent of tilled fields was strong. She turned to him. "You said I'd like it. So I trust you." She let that sit before adding, "But I can start questioning you right now if I'm not being annoying enough."

"Too late." He flashed her a grin. "We're here." He pulled up a dirt road and stopped in a clearing surrounded by tall grass and weeds. Then he cut the engine, hopped down, and helped her out.

He surveyed the familiar spot, one of his favorite places in the world. It was fully dark now, and the sky was lit up with bright pinpricks of stars that you could actually see. No city lights here, no siree. Bullfrogs were making low, twangy noises—but if that was a mating call, it left a lot to be desired. He grabbed a small cooler with a handle from the bed of his truck and held out his hand. She took it and let him guide her through the tall grass.

The thing was that he'd taken her hand to help her through the darkness. But it was small and warm and it just felt…right. So he didn't let go, even after they cleared the grass and found themselves walking along the rim of a little lake.

Maybe he was a fool. But he couldn't stop this thing that he'd set into motion.

He took her to a long, weather-worn dock. The moon was shining over the water, big and full and round.

Their footsteps rumbled over the wood. He led her right to the end of the dock and sat down, hanging his feet over the edge.

She followed suit. It was sweater weather, a little cool, but mild. The kind of night that made you inhale the fresh air and enjoy the beauty all around.

"Where are we?" Juliet asked, looking around. "I know all the make-out spots in town, and this isn't one of them." She paused. "I mean, not that you brought me here to do that, but I'm just wondering where we are."

It wasn't dark enough to tell if she was blushing, but she fanned herself, making him think she was. "I *definitely* didn't bring you here to make out."

"Oh." She sounded…disappointed, which made him feel way too good. "I mean, thank goodness for that. Do you bring other women here to…make out with?"

That made him toss his head back and roar. "No. I've never brought anyone here. To make out or for any other reason. And no offense, but most women *want* to make out with me."

She crossed her arms in a defiant gesture. "Well, I'm not most women, am I?"

He gave a little snort. "No, you certainly are not."

Their eyes locked and held. She seemed amused, her eyes lit up with mischief. He found himself wondering what it would be like to kiss her. Except she'd probably whap him upside the head. Or would she? Sometimes the way she looked at him made him believe she was thinking something a whole lot different from what she said.

And for the record, he *didn't* bring her here to make out. But he was sure considering it now.

She nodded at the cooler. "So, are we going to get drunk?"

"No, ma'am." He reached behind them and dragged the cooler closer.

"No kissin' and no drinkin'." She gave a soft chuckle. "Why'd you bring me all the way out here anyway?"

Opening the cooler, he said, "I—well, here, you've just got to reach in there and see what it is."

"Will it bite me?" She started to extend her hand but hesitated.

He burst out laughing again and turned his phone light on.

She reached in and pulled out a roundish carton.

"Ice cream?" She glanced up, looking surprised. *Thrilled*. Which was just what he'd wanted.

"You brought us *ice cream*?"

"Oh, not just any ice cream."

She squinted at the label in the darkness. "Chocolate caramel crunch." Her pretty eyes widened. "How'd you know… You remembered that?"

A little embarrassed, he had no words. Rummaging around inside the cooler for spoons, he handed her one. "Eat up, now, before it melts."

"You were driving around town with my favorite ice cream in a cooler?"

He tried to act nonchalant. And like that wasn't a really strange thing to do. "Well, not for very long."

"No, I mean…you were looking for me," she insisted.

He glanced up at her, but he wished he hadn't. She was assessing him carefully. Wanting answers. "I mean, I essentially knew where to find you. It wasn't hard."

"No, but you were *looking* for me." She spoke slow and deliberately. "You went out of your way to buy me ice cream, and then you went and found me."

Impossible woman. He gave an enormous sigh. "*Yes*." She never failed to push him to his limit. He assessed her out of the corner of his eye. "There, are you happy?"

She shrugged. "I like to hear the words, Jack."

She stared at him like she saw straight through him at all the things he never told anyone. At all the things he felt but kept inside, locked away where they stayed and simmered. He expected more questions. But she didn't ask even one.

As she reached for the carton, their fingers grazed. He was unusually nervous. Not like he'd never been around a pretty woman before—he was around pretty women all the time.

Except this one he wanted to strangle as much as he wanted to kiss.

But the truth was, he did want to kiss her. Bad.

He reminded himself that he was on an errand of human decency. He was being a friend, that's all.

Except the way his pulse was hammering against his temples and every nerve was jumping just from being near her, it sure didn't feel like friends.

She grabbed both pints of ice cream, her mouth agape. "I just can't believe that you, my mortal enemy, bought me my very own pint of ice cream."

"Look, the only thing to do with an open mouth like that is to eat up."

There was another thing to do, too, but he couldn't mention that.

Then her brows suddenly creased and her eyes got watery, like she was going to start crying.

"Hey, please don't be upset," he said. "I swear I only brought you here to eat ice cream. And maybe let you know you were amazing in that session. You handled Axl just right."

"I didn't handle him, Jack. He left frustrated. See, he demonstrated what we call the Four Horsemen of the Apocalypse."

"Say what?"

"In marriage therapy, there are certain bad things that predict divorce." She counted each one out on her fingers. "The four horsemen are criticism, contempt, defensiveness, and stonewalling, and Axl demonstrated all four. Personally, I hope Faith gets the strength and confidence to leave him."

"I don't know anything about horsemen, but I think you nailed it. You're an amazing therapist."

"Look, Axl is difficult. But he spurred me to think really hard about myself, and I'm going to make some changes. And in the meantime…this is just what I needed. Ice cream and a beautiful place to eat it. Thank you." She opened the lid, dug her spoon in, and took a bite. "Oh, so good." He could tell from the way she closed her eyes and an *"mmmmm"* escaped her throat that she was thoroughly enjoying it. "Where are we, by the way?"

"This is the north border of my grandma's land," he said, taking a bite from his carton. Yep, cool, creamy, and delicious. "It's called Lake Begone."

"I've never heard of it."

"My grandfather named it. He taught me how to fish here, right at the end of this dock. And he said it was so beautiful, you'd want to cast your troubles into the water."

She grinned. "So they'd be gone."

He smiled broadly. Because she'd gotten it, just like that. "Exactly." He decided to say what he really came here to say. "Since we're friends now, I wanted to tell you about my dad."

"*Are* we friends now?" she asked, looking a little dubious.

He nodded. "Once you share ice cream with someone, you're definitely friends. And...I want you to understand a little bit about me."

She was getting a little teary again, and he wasn't quite sure if that was good or bad, but he kept talking anyway. Because he wanted to make the effort to explain, even though it was hard. And he didn't want to think too much on why it felt so important for him to do this.

"So my dad was good-looking—like my mom—and he could talk a big talk, but he never walked the walk." He paused and stared out over the lake. The breeze was making ripples in the water, and the moon was shining on them, making them look like silver threads. It was enough to take your breath away.

Somehow, his favorite place gave him the courage to keep going. "He had a giant drinking problem and my momma finally kicked him out, but not after a lot of trouble. She used to complain that nothing ever got done around the house. She'd look at me and say, 'Jackson, I can't wait until you're old enough to help your momma out.' So from a young age, if a repairman came over, I'd attach myself to his side so I could learn how to fix a leaky toilet or jumpstart a car or change a light switch."

"You got good at fixing things, then."

The compassion in her eyes nearly did him in.

"I couldn't fix the dysfunctionality in my house. My mother got rid of my father, then her drinking became a problem and that's when she left. So you could say she got rid of me, too."

Juliet stopped eating. "Oh, Jack."

"No, it's okay. There wasn't anything for her here. She needed a fresh start." He didn't add the part about her being young and wanting to find another man and how dragging a kid along wasn't an asset. But he left it at that. "So my grandma took me."

"Jack."

She squeezed his hand tight, like she wasn't ever going to let go. He felt her body stiffen, like she was feeling his pain, too.

"I'm not telling you this to have you feel sorry for me. Just like you didn't want me to feel sorry for you. I'm just saying that some people can express themselves very well. I'm not one of them. I've always believed that actions speak louder than words. And that's why anyplace where I have to talk about my emotions is always...difficult."

He wagered a glance at her out of the corner of his eye. She was staring at him, taking in everything that he'd just said. Maybe feeling sorry for him. Which he hated, but he was going to get this out somehow in the hopes that it would make her feel less alone. And help her to understand him.

Yeah. He couldn't believe it, but he realized that he wanted her to understand. It felt important all the way down to his gut.

"Thank you for sharing that," she said. "And for my favorite ice cream. It means a lot."

He stared down at their joined hands. Her hand was pretty. A delicate thing, although she wasn't delicate. She was tough as nails, even if she had this compulsive need to figure herself out.

"I wanted to share that with you," he said. "As a friend." There. He couldn't be any clearer. Friends, friends, friends. If he said it enough, he'd believe it. He hoped.

She nodded. "I'm really glad you did." He raised his gaze to look at her. "I had a great time growing up," she said, and he realized she was sharing her own story. "Three of us girls, two hard-working parents who loved each other. Until my dad died suddenly when I was fourteen. We were all devastated, but somehow, I took it extra hard. I-I was really close to my dad. You know how you have this person who just gets you? Well, that was him. So anyway, my grief took a rough turn into depression—not the ordinary kind. A big, whopping, crisis kind. It turned my family inside out at the worst time."

He'd heard rumblings about it at school. And he knew she'd missed a semester. But everyone just attributed it to her dad dying. "What pulled you out of it?"

"Medicine. Therapy. Lots of both. Thank God I had the family I had, or who knows what would have happened to me. Lots of people don't understand that something like that can happen."

He nodded. "So you did okay after that?" Of course she had. Look who she'd become.

"Well, there was a lot of buzz that I had a"— she made air quotes—"'mental breakdown.' After that, I tried a lot harder to get people to like me. I spent a lot of time and energy trying to prove I was…normal." Then she smiled. "You don't seem to care what people think."

"What makes you think that?"

"You wear that"—she pointed to his Stetson—"in Indiana."

"Well, I'm so blunt I needed you to give me PR help. But I do believe that not everyone is going to like you or what you do. That's unavoidable."

"You've got to stand tall and believe in yourself, right? I've heard it a million times."

"Sounds like you just needed to believe it."

"Which brings me back to today. Axl said something kind of remarkable. He asked me if I was doing everything I can to work on myself. I've been thinking about that a lot."

He reached over and tucked back a strand of her hair. He just did it…without thinking. Then he smiled. "Well…my opinion is, you don't need to change. You're perfect as you are."

CHAPTER SIXTEEN

Jack's words melted Juliet for two reasons. One, he'd said them slow and carefully in that low, deep, Texas voice of his that reverberated down to her toes. But the second thing was, he'd said something that no one else had ever said to her.

Don't change. You're perfect as you are.

And the funny thing was that with him, she'd been only herself all the way, the good and the bad. Somehow, she'd never possessed a burning need to impress him. Maybe because she'd never considered the possibility of them as a…couple.

But now he was leaning over. Or maybe she was leaning toward him. She couldn't tell, because she felt a little light-headed. And it was dark, a slight breeze blowing off the water and wrapping around them like a velvety blanket, the frogs and crickets serenading them with their songs.

She couldn't stop staring into those bluer than blue eyes of his. Which right now held a look. That chocolate-cake look that made her feel…fine just as she was.

And then their lips met. His mouth grazed hers so lightly, soft as a butterfly, but the contact sent waves of shock all through her. He curled his hand softly around her neck, his fingers sliding through her hair, firm but gentle, as he turned his head to kiss her fully.

Jack kissed her passionately, unabashedly, as he

did just about everything else. He knew when to barely brush her lips, when to stroke with his tongue, when to kiss deeply and thoroughly until stars exploded behind her lids and she became hot and boneless and breathless. Grabbing his shoulders for purchase, she explored his lips, his mouth, getting lost in the taste of him, ice cream and something heady and earthy and all *him*, and every single thought flew right out of her head. All she could do was kiss him back, press against him, reach for more.

Until she found herself tipping over him as Jack leaned back, their kisses continuing, passionate and unrelenting.

He wrapped her up in his embrace, gliding his hands along her back, pulling her into him. She'd braced herself against him, her hands roaming along the smooth, muscled planes of his chest. The bumpy dock still held warmth from the sunny day, but it was nothing compared to the heat coming off of Jack's hard body. She ran her hand along his lean waist, along the smooth ridges of muscle, the rough scrape of his stubble as she pressed against him, their kisses hot, consuming, and making her lose all sense.

A whimper escaped her as he ran kisses down her neck, and his hands down her body. Fevered and restless, she adjusted herself over him, like a moth diving for the flame, and her hand swept something off the dock. At first, she was dazed, unsure of what had just happened, until the object landed in the water with a *plop*.

Jack tore his lips from hers and bolted upright,

his strong hands gripping her upper arms as he let out a curse. "My keys!"

Before she could fully sit up, he'd dived off the dock straight into the water. Not thinking, she jumped in right after him, lowering herself down, down, opening her eyes to try to see the keys—or anything—but everything was dense, inky blackness.

The water was freezing.

Not to mention it smelled like fish.

They surfaced at the same time, Jack looking like a wet and furious bear. "Why did you jump in?" he asked, scrubbing water from his face.

"To help," she said, gasping. "Why else?"

His thick brows knit down in a frown. "You can't seem to stop getting wet and freezing whenever we're together, can you?"

"Wait," she said, swiping her hair back and out of her eyes. "You're angry at me for jumping in, not because I drowned your keys?"

"Yes!"

"You're worried about me." His answer was to look uncomfortable. To be fair, he likely was, since they were both shivering. "That's really sweet, Jack."

He darted her a glance that could have meant *please stop talking*. "How about I help you back up before you get hypothermia?" He moved to guide her toward the dock.

She tugged her hand out of his reach. "Um, excuse me, but I was a lifeguard and I can dive just as well as you can. And please don't order me around!"

"Um, excuse *me*, but if you die, they're going to blame me. And I really don't want to spend the rest of my young life behind bars."

"You're not that young," came out of her mouth. Which was poking the bear for sure.

She held her breath and went to dive under the water again, but he held her back. When she pulled her head up, they were close enough that she could see the beaded water on his brows from the moonlight. Close enough to feel his breath on her face. And to see the stubborn determination in his eyes.

"Juliet. Please." He seemed to be doing all he could to stay calm. "You are so stubborn. Please get out before you freeze to death. I'm just going to try one more time. And…and yes. I am very concerned and worried about you."

That got to her, a lot more than the bone-chilling cold. And she could tell it took him a lot to say it. So she pulled herself up to the dock, every muscle quivering. It was only October, yet the water felt like the Arctic in January.

Finally, Jack pulled himself up, too, dropping onto the dock next to her, dripping and breathing a little heavy.

"Did you find the keys?" she asked.

"Not yet," he said, catching his breath.

"I'm really sorry."

"Not your fault. I should've known better than to leave them there."

She should've been worried about how they were going to get out of this. But all she could think of was how calm Jack was. Even-keeled.

Kind. And he'd brought her here to support her. No one had ever done anything like this for her before. All of which set off flashing lights of warning in her brain.

Things like this didn't happen to her. They were too…wonderful.

But something else was flashing, too, in the distance. The red and white lights of a Blossom Glen police cruiser as it pulled up next to Jack's truck.

A door slammed and a figure made its way through the tall grass. "If I haven't told you kids a hundred times this is not a swimming—" Aaron stood at the end of the dock, squinting into the dark. "Jack? Juliet? Well, for the love of—"

Juliet's teeth were chattering. She wanted to curl her body against Jack's for survival purposes, but common sense stopped her.

Her head was whirling. She could hear all the lectures she'd given herself about slowing down. About being careful. Using common sense. About not being impulsive. About choosing a man carefully.

They'd all flown out the window with those kisses.

Kissing Jack had been *amazing*.

Was this the old Juliet making mistakes again? Or was this something different and better than a mistake?

The thud of heavy footsteps sounded on the dock as Aaron approached. Suddenly, Jack gripped her arm. He was dripping wet, soaked to the bone. "Hey," he said softly, giving her an earnest look.

Her heart froze. She'd expected...well, she didn't know what to expect. A brush off, probably. But then he chuckled softly. "It was worth it."

"What was..."

"It was totally worth it." He was smiling. "I don't give a damn about those keys."

And right then, she melted for the second time that night. The man might not get his words right a lot of the time, but when he did, *be still her heart*.

He dropped his hand as Aaron strode toward them, shining a giant high-beam flashlight in their faces. And she found herself smiling, too, because she just couldn't help it. Until Aaron said, "What the sam hell are you two doing here?" He took in their dripping, shivering forms. "You're not kids. You're grown-ass adults!"

"My keys fell in when were were...eating ice cream," Jack said.

"Yes," she agreed, suppressing a giant shudder as she wrapped her arms around her torso. "Ice cream."

That's when Aaron began to shake his head. "You came all the way out here to eat ice cream, huh? What are you two, senior citizens?"

"Um, ice cream lovers?" Jack said.

"I've heard a lot of expressions, but *eating ice cream*'s a new one." He expelled a heavy sigh. "Well, you do have all your clothes on. When I bust up the teenagers, they're usually scrambling to zip up their flies."

"Aaron, we're freezing," Jack reminded him.

"I've got some blankets in the back of my cruiser," he said. "Did you find the keys?" One look at Jack's face and he added, "Never mind. Well, follow me. I'll give you two a lift home."

They followed Aaron back through the high grass, Jack's hand at her back.

She sneezed as Aaron handed her a blanket. "It's clean enough," he said. "I think I might have used it to wrap around a homeless pup the other night." She wrapped it around herself, because her teeth were clattering, and prayed that puppy didn't have fleas. "Thanks."

Jack got in the back and Juliet scrambled in next to Aaron. Because the situation was bad enough without giving Aaron the impression that they were a couple.

They *weren't* a couple. There was still time for sense to prevail. Except...she wasn't entirely sure she wanted it to.

Aaron made small talk, saying how he'd responded to another barking dog complaint and checked on a few seniors who lived alone. He joked about finding some business for the next mayor's forum because he mediated a dispute between two neighbors arguing about a cat they were both feeding. "Each one thinks the cat is theirs and wants to bring it inside for the winter." He glanced over at Juliet. "How would you solve that one, Counselor?"

"Which one treats the cat better?" Jack piped in from the back seat. Juliet turned to see a somewhat smug expression on his face. Like he'd come up with the most sensitive solution.

"Absolutely not," Juliet said. "I say, the one who pays the vet bills gets the cat."

Jack guffawed out loud and shook his head.

"I gotcha on that one, didn't I?" she asked, flashing him a satisfied smile.

"I see why you hired her," Aaron said.

Just then, Aaron turned onto her street. "Would you mind dropping me off right here?" she asked. "Mrs. O'Hannigan will be upset if she sees the cruiser."

More like be full of glee and gossip about this for months.

The car rolled to a stop two doors down. She lifted the corners of the blanket. "Do you want this back?"

"You keep it for now," Aaron said.

"Thanks." She got out and closed the door, then leaned in the window. "And thanks for picking us up, Aaron." She glanced into the back. "Jack, sorry again about your keys." She paused. Her heart gave a sudden lurch as she considered her words carefully. Seconds ticked by. Aaron looked like he was wondering why she wasn't leaving. Jack was in the shadows so she couldn't see his face very well. "Hey," she found herself saying, "maybe you should come with me. Um, since your keys are gone."

Good one, Juliet.

"My apartment's unlocked," he said.

"Oh. Okay." Well, that was that.

She bit her lip. Her life passed before her. Her bad decisions, her mistakes. Her determination not to repeat them.

Then she thought about what Tessa had told her about taking risks. That to grow and change she'd have to take them. "Why don't you come in anyway," she said on impulse, her heart beating in her throat. "I—I have leftover pizza." Which sounded ridiculous. But also, Viv had gone to a concert in Indy tonight and was staying with friends. So for once she had the place all to herself.

What had she done? Just propositioned Jack in front of his best friend. And maybe embarrassed him.

Could someone be propositioned with pizza?

But for the first time in a long time, she'd put herself out there. Followed her heart.

Seconds ticked by that seemed like hours. Her cold hands death-gripped the door of the cruiser. Aaron judiciously checked his phone. Jack leaned forward in the back seat. "I like pizza," he said, and climbed out of the car.

"Catch you tomorrow," Aaron said as he threw the car into drive. Then he looked at both of them. "Figured that ice-cold water would cool you two off," he mumbled as he pulled away.

• • •

"I have one question," Jack said as they stood there dripping in the middle of the sidewalk, the lights from the proud old Victorians on the block glowing softly in the darkness.

"Sure," she said in a too-chipper voice.

"Is there really pizza?" he asked.

She locked her gaze on his. "Not a slice."

"Okay, good." He blew out a breath. "Because

I'm not hungry for pizza."

"Jack, I—"

"I'm hungry for you." He said it without thinking, or he wouldn't have said it at all. But that was the truth. He wanted her bad.

Her eyes grew wide. And something in them softened. "Jack, I really, really like you," she said with feeling. "But that doesn't mean I can do serious now. My job is important to me, and I just can't risk any—"

Ha. That was usually *his* line.

"Juliet," he said slowly and carefully, "ever since I met you, I've been upside down. But in a good way. The best way." He paused. Debated on how to say what was in his heart. "And all I can think of is how you'd feel in my arms. When you're not wet and freezing, that is. So, what I'm saying is, I'll take whatever you give me." And then he took a step closer. "Maybe I should have stayed in that cop car. I don't want to hurt—" Oops, that's how he got into trouble the last time. But it was true— the last thing he ever wanted was to hurt her.

"Don't." She silenced him by putting a finger on his lips. She grabbed the front of his wet shirt and pulled him into her, planting a kiss on him. Not a quick, easy kiss either, but a long, deep, drugging one.

The woman could kiss. And he found he loved kissing her back, loved the playful back and forth between them, the way she tasted, the way she softly murmured his name as if she couldn't help it. And somehow, the way they were together...the way she fit into his arms was...perfect. Just right.

He just...loved being with her, plain and simple.

When they came up for breath, she tugged them out of the streetlight. "I think we better go before my landlady's light turns on," she said a little breathlessly. "She sees everything."

He followed her down a gravel driveway lit only by a light in the window of the old house, but halfway to the garage, a window slid open. "Juliet, is that you?" a voice asked.

Juliet froze in place, making wild hand motions that he didn't fully comprehend. It finally dawned on him that she was directing him into some nearby bushes.

"You can't be serious," he whispered.

Just as she managed an oh-yes-I-am nod, followed by more frantic gestures, the entire back yard was illuminated with brightness in the lumen range of a World War II searchlight. Jack dove into the shrubs, only because Juliet looked so panicked. Although he questioned his good sense. *Mayor found crouching on private property*, the headline would read. After which he'd be fired faster than he could pull the burrs out of his ass.

This was the weirdest date he'd ever had. Diving for keys, hiding from a landlady. What would be next?

"I thought I heard a noise," someone said. Peeking through the leaves, Jack saw an older woman in a robe, with curlers in her hair, standing in the doorway. He recognized her as Jacqueline O' Hannigan. She'd helped organize the Blossom Festival for years, but she'd kept to herself ever since her husband died.

"Why, you're all wet," the lady said, followed quickly by, "There'd better not be a man with you."

"Just me," Juliet said with an innocent shrug. "Coming home after a little…swim."

"Oh." Mrs. O said. "Well, you'd better get inside before you catch your death."

"Thanks, Mrs. O," she said. "Have a good night."

Jack had taken part in enough sneaking around in his younger years that he understood how this worked. He waited until Juliet walked up the stairs. Then he crept after her a few minutes later and she quietly let him in.

"I'm sorry about that," she said. "She lives alone and she doesn't want any trouble from tenants."

"I'm no trouble," Jack said, smiling. "I'm the opposite of trouble."

She grinned and shook her head. "Cowboy, you're nothing but trouble." Then she grabbed onto his shirt and tugged him to her lips. And he took her in his arms and showed her just how much trouble they could make together.

CHAPTER SEVENTEEN

At seven fifteen the next morning, Juliet found Jack wearing down the floor of his office by pacing back and forth in front of his model town. He looked up to see her, his expression softening. A little thrown and nervous, she walked over to the coffeemaker, which was pleasantly chugging away.

"Oh, coffee!" she said cheerily, as if they hadn't been lip-locked together for most of the night before—and now she felt brain-locked as well. "Is it ready yet?"

"Just put it on," he said, taking a seat behind his desk.

She decided to say what was on her mind. "You left early, cowboy." Pouring him a mug, she walked it over to him. "Do we need to talk about that?" She may have had an amazing night with him, but she needed to know how *he* felt about it.

"I made sure not to make any noise to wake up your landlady." He grinned. "It helped that I have no car."

Oh no, the sunken keys. With everything else that had happened, she'd forgotten all about them. She looked around the office. "How did you get in here?" She glanced at her watch. "No one's even in the building yet."

"Aaron let me in."

She stood in front of his desk and spoke her mind. "Did you leave early on purpose? Because you don't spend the night? I know we're just having fun together, but I just wanted to know." There. She wasn't going to wonder.

He got up, walked around his desk, took the mug out of her hands and set it down. Then he held her hands, rubbing his thumb over her palms.

"I left early so your landlady wouldn't see me, but mostly because I'm really worried about that zoning meeting. It's just two weeks away and I still don't have a solution to keep my granny in her house. It had nothing to do with you. And as for last night…" He took a big breath.

Dropping his voice, he looked into her eyes. "We have a saying in Texas. 'It's better to keep your mouth shut and seem like a fool than open it and remove all doubt.' So, at the risk of sounding like a fool, I'm going to say that words aren't enough to describe how amazing I think you are." He stroked her cheek with his thumb. "And everything we did last night, I want us to do again as soon as it's humanly possible to do so."

She felt blood rush hotly into her face. And she was getting weak in the knees. If he kept going, she might dissolve at his feet, melted by his words. He wasn't a sweet-talker, but when he put his mind to it…Lordy.

Yeah, somehow this *really* wasn't feeling like a just-for-fun thing. "Jack, I—" She blew out a breath and gave him a smile. "Amazing?" she asked, cocking her head.

He gave a nod. "Mind-effing-blowing."

"Beyond words?"

"Yes." Then he kissed her, short and sweet but

with enthusiasm, which was just right. He smelled like shaving cream and a scent she was coming to recognize as simply *him*. Comforting and irresistible at the same time.

"Well," she said against his neck when the kisses finally ended. "That's how I feel, too." She lifted her head and smiled. "Now, how can I help?"

She walked over to the cardboard buildings, the little plastic people shopping their way down Main Street, and the crabapple trees with tissue paper blossoms, which were in eternal bloom.

"Your pretty model town," she mused, picking up a fake person that happened to look a little like Sharon, with a shock of red hair and heart-shaped glasses. "This can't be an accident."

He sighed. "She made one of me, too, but she said she burned it one day when I gave her too many reports to file."

Sharon was one of a kind.

"Anyway," he said, "the only way I can think of to stop Omnibuild is a real longshot." Worry creased his face.

She lowered herself onto a stool and laid her hand on top of his, which happened to be tightened into a fist. "So hit me with it."

He jerked his head up, looking puzzled.

"Tell me the plan." Her stool scraped on the floor as she scooched it next to him. Juliet hovered her arms over the model town and circled them like a conductor in front of a symphony orchestra. "Why don't you just start from the beginning and tell me everything you're thinking."

"Honey, if you knew everything I was thinking, you'd be runnin' for the hills."

She laughed and shook her head. "All right, ready? This is sort of a brainstorm-y thing. Just let your mind…roll." She found herself looking at the fake people to see if she recognized anyone else. Fortunately, she didn't.

He heaved a big sigh. "Okay, here goes." He pointed to the east border of town. "Omnibuild needs every single acre of my granny's land for the golf course, so it would mean re-routing the river in several places."

Juliet bit her lower lip in concentration. "That's evil, but I get it."

He stood up and pointed over her shoulder. "On the northern end, overlooking the big lake, Omnibuild wants to build a hotel." His arm accidentally grazed her shoulder and she almost lost her train of thought. "Here's where they want to put a high-end shopping center and restaurants. So our Main Street shops would be taken over by chain restaurants and a giant hotel. That isn't Blossom Glen. It's a disgrace."

Juliet noticed something interesting as Jack spoke. He was passionate. And his words were flowing freely.

"See where the old junkyard is?" He pointed to the south of town, where that had been an eyesore for as long as she could remember. "I applied for a federal grant to clean it up. If it comes through, whoever buys the land wouldn't have to spend their own money to clean it up. If Omnibuild used the junkyard land, the river wouldn't have to be re-routed. A golf course could be built, and it could be surrounded by sustainable buildings, like a hotel. At least, that's what I'd propose. And we'd drive new business to our downtown shops, not build chain restaurants or shopping." He paused, leaning over the model. His voice grew soft. "Someday, I'd like to work on this project. As a green architect, not as mayor."

Interesting. "So," she said, "even if Omnibuild decides to use the south land, what would happen to your grandma's land?"

He raked his hands through his hair, a gesture of frustration. "Short of finding Santa Claus to buy it back, I can only think of one idea. I've asked if the park service would want it. That might keep her in her house if they agree to let us buy back a small parcel. The rest would be parkland."

Hmm. Also interesting. But clearly not a good enough solution for Jack, who began pacing back and forth again.

"Don't give up, Jack," she said softly.

He blew out a big breath. "That's a big ask."

"I believe in you. And in what you're trying to do for your grandmother and for our town. You know, we're opposites in a lot of things, but we both really love our families."

He smiled. "I always envied you having such a great family. But you're right. My family might only be one person, but she means the world to me."

"Family's more than blood, and we have great friends."

"Good point." They were both silent for a minute. Seconds ticked by on a wall clock that was probably as old as the building. Juliet could see the toll this whole dilemma was taking on him.

"I'm dry. That's all I've got," he said. She could hear the desperate edge in his voice.

She gave him the tiniest smile. "Maybe it is. But you have something that's the start of a solution—conviction. Passion. That's how you'll get through to everyone."

"It's going to take more than passion to fix this. Plus, I suck at talking about stuff."

Juliet decided to choose optimism, because what was the alternative? "My job is dealing with emotions, and I'm really good with those. I can help you."

He raised a skeptical brow. "How do you propose to do that?"

She gave a smile and a shrug. "Now it's my turn to ask *you* to take a drive."

• • •

They ended up at a little bend in the river with a waterfall, and the first thing Juliet did was take her shoes off and wade right in.

She'd asked Jack to take her here. To his favorite spot on his granny's land.

"The rocks are slippery," he warned. "And the water gets deep right over there—"

She gave him the taunting smile of a toddler about to barrel right into a swimming pool despite her parents' warnings. "Come on in." She beckoned him in. "This is a real creek. You need to get wet."

She kept rock hopping, dancing from stone to stone, scaring the bejesus out of him.

So he had no choice. He took off his shoes and socks, then rolled up his pants and joined her.

"Took you long enough," she said, quirking a smile when he finally caught up to her. She took his hand. "Close your eyes and tell me why this is your favorite place in the world."

He looked at her standing there, closing her own eyes. And he had to admit his favorite place just got even better. He grazed her lips with a kiss.

"Hey, focus," she warned, opening one eye. "You've got a town to save."

"A town?"

She gave a serious nod. "We both know what will happen if Omnibuild gets a hold of this property."

Yeah, he did. So he hunkered down to do his best to explain it to her—and himself.

"Okay, my grandpa and I used to fish here. And after he died, I used to come back here and hang out a lot. Mostly by myself. I'd bring a library book or a sketch pad. But I never brought my fishing pole back."

"Why not? Your grandpa would want you to."

He shrugged. "It was never the same without him."

"I get it." Juliet fell silent, and he had a feeling she was thinking about her dad.

The river was at the base of a hilly meadow, meandering around several curves in the landscape. It was often calm and always clear. Except in the spring when the rains turned it muddy for a while. But even then, it was still beautiful. "This was sort of my hangout place. I used to lie in the meadow, watch the clouds, swim, think about life."

"After your mom left?" she asked.

He nodded. It seemed right telling her, bringing her here. He'd never brought anyone else. "Being here…climbing and swimming and hiking and exploring…it was a way of clearing my head."

The emotion on her face told him she understood what he was talking about. "Look," he said. "I know it's unrealistic for my granny to keep all this land. I just want her to stay in her home and have peace of mind." As he looked out upon the familiar scene, he totally understood the peace-of-mind part. "I grew up without streetlights. Without traffic. Watching sunrises and sunsets. Sitting on the porch in a rocker, drinking tea. Appreciating nature. My grandpa tied a tire to that tree and we used to swing over the water and jump in. Everyone should have a place of peace and quiet to escape to. Not a golf course with a bunch of retail shops and chain restaurants that will suck the life from downtown. Not re-routing the creek and bulldozing it and disrupting all this beauty."

It was the most beautiful place he'd ever known. And it had been in his family for generations.

He was somehow pouring out his heart, and she was standing there in the creek, nodding and smiling. "Tell the zoning commission *that*," she said, stabbing at the air with her finger. "Exactly that. With feeling and passion. *Convince* them not to zone this land commercial."

"Best-case scenario, I get people to see that the Omnibuild developer isn't the answer. But even if Omnibuild doesn't buy this property, someone else will. And she'll have to move anyway."

Juliet jumped over a few rocks and stood in front of him, then wrapped her arms around him and just…stayed.

They stood there for a moment, in the bright sunshine, the water gurgling around their toes, and he drew his arms around her.

He pulled back to find tears on her cheek. For him. For his granny. "One thing at a time," she said, giving him a squeeze.

He reached up and wiped a tear with his finger. "Hush now, don't cry," he said softly. He'd never had anyone cry for him before.

"Jack, I know you can do this," she said, holding him tight. "You can make the town feel what you feel."

"I'll do my best," he promised. Somehow, she made him aspire to be the best version of himself. Even more, she made him think that he could do it.

Juliet had reached a place deep inside him where he'd never let anyone go. For the first time in his life, he felt like he'd known someone forever. That she *got* him. That she made him better than he was.

He would do his best to convey to his town how he felt. And hope that revealing his emotions would be enough to make people understand what was at stake.

CHAPTER EIGHTEEN

A week later, Juliet walked into Bonjour Breads! right after the first wave of the morning rush had passed. Vivienne was helping her mom and grandma behind the counter, and Tessa was sitting at a table with her feet up, working on her laptop and sipping something that was probably decaf.

"Hey, everybody," Juliet said with a little wave.

"Hi honey," her mom said as she quickly and efficiently placed a fresh batch of chocolate croissants into the front bakery case. "Want one?"

Oh yum. The perks of belonging to a family who baked. "Can I have a coffee, too?"

Her grandmother poured her one and added a splotch of cream and a spoonful of sugar, just the way she liked it. Ah, the comforts of home. Well, the bakery *was* her almost-home, where the people she loved hung out. Mostly voluntarily. Or not, in Viv's case.

"How's the town counselor gig going?" her grandmother asked as she handed over the coffee. "We saw the mud photos. That certainly looks like an interesting job."

Oh no, not the mud photos. The Gazette must have been desperate for sales to print that stuff. She decided to focus on the positives as she made her way to Tessa's table. "It's been pretty fun so far. Doni from the book shop and Brandy from the cat rescue asked my opinion about their flower boxes so they can plan coordinated color choices. And the kids in the music studio were playing "Hot Cross Buns" too loudly and disrupting the spa clients next door, so both businesses are going to split costs on some soundproofing. And have you noticed the music that sometimes gets piped in along Main Street? I didn't know that shopkeepers take turns choosing that."

Her mom paused in restocking the napkins. "We chose Bruce Springsteen's greatest hits."

"I love that," Tessa piped in.

"Not everyone was so fond of Metallica," Juliet said. "Mr. Teeter was a little upset, but I think he got over it." She looked over at Tessa. "Everything okay?"

Her mom, grandma, and Viv all eyed Tessa, who was about to bite into her croissant. "What? Do I look not fine? This dough is perfect today, Ma."

"Why are you here?" Juliet asked her sister.

Tessa placed her hand on her back and exhaled. "Nothing terrible, relax. My Braxton-Hicks are really acting up today and I'm having back pain. I decided to come over and work on my books for a little while with my feet up. And get some special loving care from my mom and gram," she added with a smile and a glance back at them behind the counter.

"You sure you're all right?" their mother asked. "You know, once I went into labor, I had every single one of you girls in under an hour. Even you, Tessa."

Yikes. "I just saw Dr. Shah yesterday." Tessa

calmly rubbed her abdomen. "She said I'm doing great and everything looks good." She smiled and looked down. "Just three more weeks, little one." She looked up at everyone. "Then this little loaf of bread is coming out of the oven."

"Awww." Viv made a little rounded loaf with her hands, "that's so sweet."

Tessa chuckled at her own little joke, then turned to Juliet. "Shouldn't you be at city hall?"

"I'm meeting Ryan Malley for a little chat."

That got her a few raised eyebrows, but no commentary. Yet.

"I haven't seen him in ages," Tessa said. "Remember when he used to practically live with us?"

"He was a good kid," Juliet's mother said. "And he still comes in and says hi with his kids. All adorable redheads."

"He and Pam just had their fourth boy," her grandmother reported. "Royce, Ryder, Roman, and Renegade."

From a psychological viewpoint, Juliet couldn't help but wonder, did Pam feel left out as the only non-R name?

"Nice." Viv cracked a smile from behind the bread cart. "They saved the terrifying name for last."

"Why is Ryan coming by again?" her mother asked as she loaded a few perfectly round brioche loaves into the bakery case. "Because it's been what, eight years?"

Yep, eight years since that fated day in city hall where she'd torn up their marriage license right on the big marble steps and dumped him. Hard to believe that was four kids ago for him. "We're just going to have coffee," Juliet hedged.

Vivienne walked over and sat down. "I know that you're doing what Jack suggested in your group last week. But don't do it, Juliet. Nothing good can come of it."

"I have to say that I think Viv is right," Tessa said. "It was a long time ago."

"Look, we grew up together," Juliet said, waving her hand dismissively. "We've known each other for ages. And I've been thinking long and hard about this." Actually, she wasn't really at all sure if this was a good idea. But she needed the closure in order to move on.

"You broke his heart," her grandmother called from the counter. "Not to mention all that flooding. And who knew how expensive fire hydrants are?" She gave a thoughtful pause. "Just saying, but I'd be tempted to let that one lie."

Juliet chuckled a little. "I'm not sure either one of us has lived that down. But I need to know where and how I screwed up. I need to have control over my own mental baggage so I can get my clients back."

"Make sure he doesn't misunderstand your intentions," her grandmother warned as she cleaned the espresso machine. "That happened to me before I met your grandfather. Gaston borderline-stalked me for years."

"You had a boyfriend named *Gaston*?" Viv exchanged a wide-eyed glance with her sisters.

"Yes," Gram said matter-of-factly. "He actually

was very burly and brawny. Everyone thought I was crazy to reject him. He didn't take it well."

"Did he hate women who read?" Viv asked with an evil smile.

"Did he eat five dozen eggs every morning to get large?" Tessa chimed in.

"Was he roughly the size of a barge?" Juliet couldn't resist adding.

"Okay, ladies," her mom called, handing a tray to her grandmother to take into the back. "Let's get some work done here."

"Seriously, Juliet," Viv said, standing up. "This is going to open up a giant can of worms from the past."

"Honestly," Tessa said, "I'd worry about that more with Tyler. He's the one who took things hard. Ryan, I think, has really moved on."

Juliet nodded in agreement. "Ryan's happily married, and we're both way past all that heartbreak." She thought about something else. "Plus, this is a public place. If things go south, I'll have all of you here to bail me out."

"Here he comes," her mother said, suddenly pretending to be very busy cleaning the already-immaculate counters. Her grandmother made the sign of the cross and looked upward.

"Just want you to know I'm not budging," Tessa said with a smile.

Juliet rolled her eyes and ran to greet Ryan with a hug. He was tall and lanky and red-haired, and looked practically as youthful as when they'd started dating, senior year of high school. He'd also brought something with him—a stroller with a sleeping baby tucked inside, a bright shock of red hair sticking straight up from his head.

"He went and fell asleep again," he said as he bent to check on the baby. Juliet smiled at the careful way he tended to him, straightening his booties and tucking the blanket carefully around his sleeping form.

The baby stirred in his sleep. "Renegade. He's so sweet," Juliet crooned.

"Has he lived up to his name?" Juliet's grandmother asked as she and her mom came to *ooh* and *ahh* over the baby, too, while Viv and Tessa admired from afar.

Ryan quirked a smile. "Well, he's definitely different from his brothers. He's learned to hurl his bottle at them with amazing accuracy."

"A free thinker," Tessa said.

"A survival skill," her mom said pointedly.

"A future major league pitcher," Viv chimed in.

It occurred to Juliet that if she and Ryan had had kids, they'd probably have had red hair, too. That felt a little weird, thinking how close she'd nearly come to marrying him.

If Jack and she had babies, would they have his pure blue eyes? Her green ones? Or a combo? And how about his thick, wavy hair? And the cute little dent in his chin that only appeared when he laughed.

She shook her head. What was she doing? She realized she was smiling at her wayward thoughts.

Ryan tucked the blanket around the still-sleeping Renegade and looked around the bakery. "Hey, Montgomerys," he said with a smile, hugging everyone. Juliet couldn't help but remember all the times he'd come in here saying that as a teenager.

This was strange, too. In a time-warp kind of way.

Why had she invited him here? Oh, right. To figure herself out. To get her job back. And for peace of mind, that elusive thing.

"Can I get you something to drink?" she asked Ryan. "I thought we could sit down for just a few minutes."

"Sure, I'll take a coffee." Viv, her mom, and her grandmother were now surrounding the stroller to further exclaim over the baby. As was Tessa from her seat. So Juliet walked behind the counter to pour the coffee.

"Hey, gorgeous," someone said just as she'd filled a cup.

She looked up to find not Jack, but another blast from her past, in a suit and tie, no less. Standing behind the counter, propping his elbows on the bakery case. And speaking in a very flirty tone. "Remember me?"

"Devin Chambers," Juliet said in a neutral voice. "What brings you to Blossom Glen?" He was still as good-looking as ever, with his fade haircut, expensive suit with narrow pants, and pretty hazel eyes.

Juliet remembered being thrilled when they'd both swiped right on a dating app. They'd gone out a couple of times, but something just wasn't right... what *was* it? It had been a few years ago, while she was still in school and working and tutoring.

"I'm presenting a project to the zoning commission next week that's going to be amazing for your little town here." He looked around at the faded but quaint bakery, with its checked tile floor and its faded après-Monet water lilies that Juliet's mom had painted long ago. "You work here?"

Juliet barely heard him. Because her heart had leaped straight into her throat, and she was having trouble swallowing. Breathing, too.

Devin was…Omnibuild?

The relentlessly aggressive developer?

And then the memory came back to her. Devin Chambers had insisted on taking her to a really expensive restaurant on their first date but had tortured the college-aged waitress, asking for his order to be sent back to the kitchen twice, even making her reheat his coffee. Then he bragged about undertipping her, which made Juliet surreptitiously drop more money on the table. Then she caught him checking out the waitress's butt on the way out.

Oh, and didn't he call Ellie "mangy" when he'd picked her up? Mangy!

Yep, a one-date wonder for sure.

She struggled to remember his question. "Um—this is my family's bakery. I'm actually a therapist."

"And still single, I see," he added.

Ugh. Yuck. This dude was bad news.

"I heard the whole town's going to the meeting next week," an older gentleman who'd gotten in line behind Devin said. Juliet looked over to see the elusive Mr. Blossom. She gave the older man a smile and an encouraging wave. "Great to see you, Mr. B," she said. She was a whole lot gladder to see him than Devin, that was for sure.

Devin acknowledged the older man and said, "Well, I've got some exciting plans for this old town. My company's doing an amazing job turning small-town America into profitable America. You should come listen to my pitch."

"That land you want is foreclosure land, son," Mr. Blossom said.

"That's the best kind, sir," Devin said, winking at Juliet. His dimples showed when he smiled, which was attractive, but unfortunately, his personality was not. "*Get it cheap and build it out*, that's Omnibuild's motto."

"Well," Juliet's mother said politely enough, but her brows were tented with worry. "We love our charming town. Whatever happens, we would hate to see its character changed."

Her mom put Devin's breakfast sandwich and coffee on the counter along with Mr. Blossom's coffee. As Devin reached for his bag, he handed something to Juliet.

Please God, not a napkin. A quick glance confirmed that yes, it was indeed a napkin, and he'd written his number on it. "See you at the meeting," was the best she could do as she tore it up into a million tiny pieces under the counter and pitched it into the trash.

As Devin left, Mr. Blossom shook his head sadly. "That man could be the ruin of our town."

While she was behind the counter, she tucked an extra chocolate croissant into his bag. "Yep, and I hope you come to the zoning meeting, Mr. Blossom. Jack's going to need all the help he could get—from all of us. The future of our town really is at stake."

"Well, thank you. Maybe I will be there after all."

She wished him a good day and brought two of the warm croissants over to the table for her and Ryan.

"Just as amazing as ever," he said, exclaiming as he bit into one. "So, what's up, Lulu?" he said. "Besides the big meeting everybody's talking about."

She took a deep breath. Understanding herself suddenly felt a lot bigger than just keeping her job. She realized more than ever that Jack was right—she needed to do this in order to move forward with her own life.

Suddenly, she saw an image of Jack laughing, little crinkles around his eyes forming, making him even more irresistible. And another one...of Jack lying in her bed, a sheet slung low on his hips. Of Jack doing the most amazing things...

Jack as her future? Mr. Do-not-commit?

She pushed all that out of her head. She wasn't going there with Jack, no matter how amazing she felt. She wasn't going to get carried away, and she wasn't going to envision a future with anyone until she figured herself out. Then one day, she could go on and maybe fall in love with the right person and have a family of her own.

She plunged in. "Ryan, we go way back. And we used to be best friends. But I need a little bit of help, and I thought of you."

"Yeah, sure, Jules. Anything." He smiled his usual boy-next-door smile and leaned over. "By the way, I'm completely over that marriage certificate incident. Although people around here might never stop talking about it."

She gave a weak chuckle. "I'm sorry about that. But mostly, I'm sorry about waiting so long to call our wedding off." Waiting until three days before the wedding to break it off was…bad. It had shocked Ryan, wasted a lot of money, and been embarrassing. And it had been heartbreaking to her, too. But she needed to understand why she hadn't done it much sooner.

"Apology accepted." He looked like he was debating whether or not he should say more.

She jumped in to say, "I recently started working as a mental health therapist at Headspace but…but I've been exploring my past, to help me become a better counselor."

He shot her a look that told her he still knew her pretty well. "Jules, everyone in town knows about your marriage counseling clients being on hold."

"Right. Okay!" The familiar embarrassment seeped in. But she kept going anyway. "I just wanted to know from your point of view what… happened with us? I mean, do you have insight into why…why we almost got married?" She felt a little cringy. Like, maybe she should have listened to her grandma and let this sleeping bear hibernate permanently. "You were an important person in my life and I…I was wondering your side of the story."

Juliet tapped her fingers on her mug while she struggled to answer the same question herself. He was a great guy, but they never would have been happy together. He'd wanted to live on a farm and thought she wanted to, also. Why did he think that? Why had she allowed him to?

He polished off the croissant, wiping his fingers on his napkin. "We were friends for a lot of years," he said. "Right up until the day you broke my heart."

"But you don't hold that against me anymore, do you?" she asked, glancing at the sleeping child.

"No," he said quietly. He gave a little smile. "My life worked out great." He paused. "But it took a while."

"I never wanted to hurt you," she said. She'd loved him, she knew that.

"Maybe that was the problem, Jules. We hung on too long because we didn't want to hurt *each other*."

She thought about that. "Well, I wanted you to know…you helped me so much. You supported me through my dad's death. You never thought of me as marked because I was struggling with my mental health. And you helped me gain my confidence after all of that."

"I always knew you'd come out of all that stronger than ever. And we had some great times." He grinned. "Besides, your mom still gives me extra food whenever I come in here."

"My family always loved you."

He nodded. "For a while there, I was part of your family."

She was trying to summon up how she'd felt when she was with him. But it was so long ago. And the most she could come up with was a panicked sense that something just wasn't right.

Yes, she remembered feeling that way quite a lot. Why had she ignored it?

"Since you asked," he said, lifting his gaze to meet hers, "I honestly thought you shared the same vision as I did about life. Frankly, I was shocked to learn that you didn't."

She remembered how furious she'd been that day at the courthouse. He'd described their life—which he seemed to have tidily planned— including her taking her place on his farm. Working side-by-side with him to run his family's business.

She'd panicked. She'd finally seen how deeply he'd invested in that dream. *His* dream, not hers. And he'd somehow assumed that she'd wanted to be a part of it, too.

That was when she'd ripped up the license and bolted.

"Pam loves the farm," Ryan said. "She gets up at five a.m. to help me, then homeschools the kids and does all the business paperwork while I'm working. It's a tough business, but it's fun."

"I'm really happy for you," she said. But *she* never would have been happy with that life.

"I guess I could never understand why anyone wouldn't want a life on the farm." His tone was cordial, as if they were old friends who saw each other every day instead of only at a distance for the last eight years. "It's so beautiful there. The kids are growing up with plenty of fresh air and sunshine." He looked at her. "I never meant to ignore your dreams. I just—thought you wanted what I wanted."

Juliet thought again about the discontent that she'd swallowed for a long time. "Maybe I let you think that, Ryan." But she still wasn't sure exactly why. Had she been that desperate for love? Or not want to hurt his feelings at the expense of herself?

He smiled and shrugged. "Live and learn?"

She squeezed his hand. "Live and learn. Thanks for meeting with me. And for being honest."

"It's no trouble," he said. "I'll always love you, Juliet. We helped each other grow up. You were my first."

She reached over and hugged him. Until she heard someone clear their throat. And drew back to find Jack standing at her side.

• • •

"Hey there, Ryan, buddy. Hey, Juliet." Jack smiled pleasantly—he hoped. Because it was a stretch.

"Oh, hey there, Jack," Ryan said with a friendly wave.

Ryan was nice enough. But *You were my first?*

"What are you doing here?" Juliet asked.

"I was just passing by. You go on and finish your…um, meeting. I'm going to grab some coffee." Actually, Sharon had told him Juliet was meeting Ryan and had hinted that it would be good to find out how it had gone.

Emotional support, is what Sharon had called it. He was so confused. How did you know when to talk about your feelings and when to just listen?

He walked up to the counter. "Hey, Mrs. M. How are you today?" He waved to Tessa, who was sitting at a back table with her feet up, doing paperwork, and to Viv and Juliet's grandmother, who were working in the back room.

"I'm great." She greeted him with a smile. "What can I get you?"

He dropped his voice. "Something strong. I'm meeting with a couple of my architect friends on some ideas for the junkyard land. We're getting a presentation prepared for the zoning meeting."

"How about something with a nice jolt of espresso in it? To really get those ideas flowing."

"Surprise me," he said. While she was making his coffee, he hiked a thumb behind his shoulder. "How did the big talk go?"

Mrs. Montgomery leaned over the counter and smiled. "Jack, it was your idea for Juliet to do this. And she's taken it to heart. Some may question the sanity of it, but…I'm actually changing my mind about that. So I'm sure she'll tell you all about it. And if you're interested, I have a suggestion for you."

"What's that?" he asked as she handed him the coffee and he pulled out a bill.

She folded the bill back up in his hand by grabbing it and pushing his hand back. "First of all, coffee's on me. And second, a guy who listens is sensitive. He's being there for someone."

She gave him a knowing look. Maybe she'd been talking to Sharon, because they were both into this listening thing.

"I see." He didn't, really. Okay, he did. But he really didn't want to hear about Juliet's relationship with another man. Not that he was jealous, but…it was about another guy. A guy who wasn't him. But he reckoned he could bend an ear for her.

"We're just finishing up," Juliet called a minute later. "Want to walk back to the office with me, Jack?"

Juliet's mom gave him a little nod.

"I'd love to," he called. And he meant it. Juliet had been there for him, and he wanted to do the same.

A few minutes later, they were walking down the street in the middle of the midday bustle. "Well, I—um, what did you discover from your talk?" That's what a friendly ear would say, wasn't it?

He imagined himself grabbing her arm, right here in the street. *Ryan is bland, sunny, agreeable, and calm. You are fiery, full of life, and passionate.*

Yes, that was exactly how it was. How it had been between them.

He found himself pointing to a park bench across the street in the park, so they crossed over and sat. It had a great view of the little river that meandered through town.

"Ryan and I had a nice talk. It was healing. I knew that when we dated, I kept pushing down the feeling that I couldn't share the life he wanted. But I somehow kept denying it. Not speaking up about it. Until I couldn't deny it anymore."

"Somehow, Juliet," he said softly, "I don't think that is ever going to be a problem for you now."

She lifted up her head. "Why not?"

"Because…" He couldn't say what was inside of him. Which was too…*emotional*. Yet, she was looking at him with the eyes of someone who needed someone to say *something*. And he knew that the truth he held close inside him would help her. "Because you don't hesitate to say what you feel. You did it today. I mean, anyone who could approach a man they almost married and ask him point-blank about what went wrong is just plain brave. And you're also kind. And you're driven. And…you're going to find your answers. Then you're going to be a kick-ass relationship counselor in this town and you're not going to let anything stop you."

Where had all that come from? It had poured out of him, much to his chagrin. But the next thing he knew, his arms were full of Juliet, who was sobbing on his shirt.

Okay, well, if this is what letting out his emotions did, he should try it more often.

She was holding on vise-tight to his neck. His heart seemed to have somehow turned to the consistency of melted ice cream. But he didn't mind it at all.

"Thank you," she finally said, pulling back and swiping away tears. "What you said was just right."

Great. Now Ryan was hopefully tucked nicely

into her past, which made his day. Jack had somehow managed to say all the right things. Except
acknowledge the truth that he could no longer
avoid.

That this didn't feel casual. And he was in way
over his head.

CHAPTER NINETEEN

"Do you see Jack?" Noah asked as he sat down next to Juliet at the bar in the Foggy Bottom on a Friday night a week later. Jack had texted them that he had some good news to share.

"Not yet," Juliet answered. With just a few days before the big meeting, everyone was on edge, and they all welcomed the chance to come down to the familiar neighborhood bar to celebrate.

The Foggy Bottom was a favorite place for locals to grab a beer and a sandwich. Or, in Juliet's case, the best nachos in town, which Hector G, the owner, had just placed in front of her, along with a whiskey sour. Just as she took the first cheesy bite, she noticed a man in a white shirt and dress pants standing near a pool table across the room. Devin Chambers took a sip of his drink, looked directly across the room at Juliet, and winked.

Juliet immediately dropped her chip and pretended to rummage through her purse. Viv, who was next to Noah, leaned over and said, "Please tell me that isn't who I think it is."

"I'll explain later," Juliet whispered.

Noah frowned. "Did that horrible man just wink at you?" He frowned. "Also, what on earth did you say to Tyler Wells? I ran into him at the grocery store and he sounded really excited about meeting with you."

"When does Tyler *not* sound excited?" Viv asked.

"This appeared to be *extra* excited," Noah said with concern.

Juliet took a big sip of her drink. "Well, my talk today went really well with Ryan, so I texted Tyler and asked to have coffee."

Speaking of Tyler, there he was, waving from near the door. She reluctantly waved back. "I wasn't expecting this."

"So many suitors." Viv suppressed a chuckle by taking a sip of her drink.

Juliet groaned. To make it worse, Devin made a shot, then straightened out and full-out waved.

"You'd better tell us what's going on here, hon," Noah said. "Because I sort of feel that someone's getting themselves in some very hot water here."

"I know Devin from a long time ago," Juliet blurted.

"You slept with him?" Noah's glass of beer hit the table with a *clink*.

"I did *not* sleep with him," she insisted. "It was one date."

Noah shook his head in puzzlement. "Did you tell Jack about this?"

"First of all, I didn't get a chance to. But second, I'm not going to. Jack has enough on his mind. I'm just going to make certain I don't run into Devin again."

"That would be fine if our town wasn't the size of a bottle cap." Noah paused. "What if Devin finds out you work for Jack? No, wait—what if he finds out you *slept* with Jack? Could Devin get angry and then take his anger out on Jack?"

Viv choked on her drink. "*You slept with Jack?*" She looked incredulous. "This is what happens when I leave for one night?"

"Yes, but it's not serious." She turned back to Noah. "I mean, nothing ever happened with Devin, and I can't stand the guy. So he's a nonissue."

"Okaaay," Noah said, looking dubious. "Hope you know what you're doing."

"It's not even a secret," she said firmly. "There's just nothing to tell."

"Okay." Viv caught up to the conversation quick. "So forget Devin. *Tell me about you and Jack.*"

"I told you, it's not…anything." But Juliet's heart knew she was lying. "Until I have myself figured out, I'm not getting serious with anyone."

"You *are* determined," Noah said sadly. "But I think that's a little sad. You may be missing out on the love of your life."

She should have brushed that comment off as a typical Noah-ism, blunt and full of drama. Instead, she broke out into a cold sweat. Because how would she ever really know herself? Or trust herself? How would she ever get over the terror of making another mistake?

"Jack is different," Viv said, her tone earnest.

"What do you mean?" Juliet asked, sounding skeptical. Yet she knew he was, down to her soul. And *she* was different with him than she'd been with her other boyfriends. But she didn't want to admit that, and she didn't even want it to be true, because she wasn't ready for different. The timing was bad. Her life wasn't in order.

Viv assessed her with deep blue eyes that reminded her very much of their dad's. "I can just tell," she said with a little sigh. "You're just yourself with him. You're able to tell him exactly how you feel." She made circles with her finger in front of Juliet's face. "And you sort of have this little sparkle in your eyes whenever you look at him."

"Sparkle, Viv?" That was…ridiculous. Sparkle was a term reserved for little children, ones who wore glittery costumes and shoes and nail polish, not adults. And she was trying very hard to be an adult.

"She's right," Noah said. "I've never seen you so much yourself."

Before Juliet could react, the door opened, and Jack himself walked in. As he stood there, searching the room, her heart gave a flutter. He looked handsome and relaxed and confident.

Being hot was fine, but the thing about Jack that really melted her was that he listened to her and believed she'd figure things out. He believed in her. Now she just needed to make sure she believed in herself.

As their gazes locked across the room, she felt a rush of blood in her ears, a thrumming of her pulse. And she couldn't keep herself from smiling.

Suddenly, Juliet became aware that Viv was staring at her. "See," she said with a smug expression. "*Sparkle.*"

She didn't have time to respond to her

annoying sister. Jack walked over and stood next to Juliet, lightly touching her back with his hand, a move that sent a little shiver through her. Hector G walked over to take Jack's order. "Sorry I'm running late," Jack said, "but I just got some great news," Excitement stirred in his voice. "We got the federal grant to clean up the junkyard."

"That's amazing," Noah said.

Juliet frowned. "But Omnibuild..."

"...has agreed to look over the feasibility study with the green plan that we did for that land." Jack looked pleased. "If Devin can wait for the cleanup, he'll find that this land is actually a lot better suited for what he wants than my granny's."

"That's terrific news," she said, squeezing his arm. She wanted to throw her arms around him and kiss him but she didn't know how he felt about showing affection in public. Since they weren't really dating. So what exactly *were* they doing, then?

"Well, it's a start." Jack gave her a hopeful smile. His gaze was filled with other things, too, affection and a mischievous twinkle that made her blush. "I'm cautiously hopeful."

She was, too. But not just about the land.

Jack got whisked away by some of the city council members, excited to discuss the news. Noah left with him, and Viv went to chat with friends, leaving Juliet alone with her nachos. Which was fine with her. Leo slid into the seat beside her, placed his beer on the table, and stole one.

"Hey, that's my dinner," she said with a

chuckle, grabbing a chip herself and then pushing the plate toward him so they could share. "So, where's Tessa?"

"Resting up." He grabbed another chip. "She passed on coming tonight." Leo smiled and bumped her elbow with his. "We don't often get to talk, just the two of us."

"That sounds like the beginning of a big brother talk." *Actually,* she thought, *Leo really* was *the big brother she'd never had.* They fought over chips and had heart-to-hearts. Lucky her.

"Not necessarily. But I can listen. Especially when it's about Jack."

She rolled her eyes. But secretly, she was amazed at how he'd read her mind. "How do you know I want to talk about Jack?"

"Just a hunch. I mean, you two are going around looking all googly eyed at each other."

"The truth is," she said, looking him in the eye, "I think I'm falling for him." Wait, where had that come from? It had literally fallen out of her mouth, and once the word avalanche started, she couldn't stop it. "I really, really like him. But how will I know if I can trust my own judgment?" She paused and thought about that. "You've seen me at my worst—remember after my breakup last year? You of all people wouldn't want me to get involved with someone who was clearly wrong for me, would you?"

Leo let out a heavy sigh. "Juliet, that's the last thing I'd want." He rubbed his neck, like he was thinking hard about what to say. "Seeing Jack and you together, I guess I've been reevaluating. Jack has so much to give. I love him like a brother. Maybe you can be the one to help him get over his past. I just don't want to see you hurt."

"Leo, it's okay. I was honest with him about not wanting anything serious, and so was he."

"He was lying." Leo stuck his fingers in his mouth and whistled and waved. "Jackie! Over here." Leo rubbed her shoulder. "If you really care for him, don't give up on him, that's my opinion."

Across the room, Jack waved. Leo sent him a thumbs-up. And wow. Leo was giving her his blessing? "I don't want to screw up again and have my heart broken." It was all about fear, wasn't it? "I'm…afraid."

Leo looked at her with a wise smile and shrugged. "You'll never find love unless you learn to trust yourself. And somebody else. Take it from someone who had to learn how to do that." Then he ended the discussion by stealing one last chip. And kissing her on the head.

"Well, thanks for the talk…I think."

"And thank you for sharing your nachos," he said as he washed them down with his beer.

As Jack made his way toward them through the crowd, Leo said, "Uh-oh. Here comes trouble."

But Juliet followed his gaze to find he wasn't looking in Jack's direction. He nodded toward the other end of the bar, near the pool tables.

Devin was gone. But Tyler was waving again. Except this time he appeared to be on the way over.

She couldn't help groaning. "I think I've given him the wrong impression. He's way too enthusiastic."

"Tyler is enthusiastic about everything."

"This feels different."

Leo chuckled. "This is so much fun."

"Watching me suffer?"

He rubbed his hands together in an evil fashion. "How about we make a little wager."

"Leo! Stop. This isn't funny. No wagers."

"Five bucks says Jack's going to do…something."

She narrowed down her gaze. "Do something? To Tyler? Like, threatening?" Jack didn't strike her as the threatening type.

"No, not threatening. *Caring.* Like he doesn't want a guy staking a claim on you."

"That's ridic—"

Before she could finish her sentence, Jack sat down next to her.

"Hey there, Leo," Jack said. "Juliet," he added, flashing her a smile that instantly made her feel like the bubbles in her drink. Light and floaty and fizzy inside.

Jack looked at her glass. She slid it toward him.

Jack had barely taken a sip when folks began to make their way over, probably to congratulate him. And Tyler was halfway to their table. So she said, "Everyone seems excited. How are you doing?"

"Devin's slicker than a boiled onion," Jack said. "I don't trust him one bit. But maybe I bought us a little bit of time. I still need to find a buyer for my granny's land."

"I agree with you," Leo said, popping up at Jack's side. "That guy is not going to give up your grandma's land for a project that costs even more. Especially when he's proven he's about as into green as the North Pole."

As Leo wandered off, Juliet said to Jack, "Before someone else claims you, I just wanted to tell you that no matter what happens, you're doing everything you can. Not just for your grandma. For the town, too. Your ideas are bold. I admire your courage."

He shook his head. "I'm just doing my job. It's time for us to think about doing things differently. Blossom Glen would be ahead of its time with this green project."

As Jack talked, Leo's words echoed in her ears. About trusting herself. About pushing past her fear. "Maybe *we* need to think about doing things differently, too." She moved her hand back and forth between them. *You and me.*

He looked surprised. Just as he opened his mouth to reply, a voice behind Juliet made her heart sink.

"There you are," Tyler said. "You look incredible, Jules." Tyler kissed her on the cheek. "Hi Jack. Mind if I join you all?"

Oh no. This was the worst. What had she done?

"I got your phone message about meeting up," Tyler said to Juliet, "and I thought I might find you over here. Good guess, huh?" He looked around at the throng of people. "You used to love pool," he said enthusiastically. "How about we get away from the crowd and play a little one-on-one?" He waggled his brows in a way that made Juliet want to flee.

Or barf. Or both.

Just as she opened her mouth to tell him there would be no one-on-one *ever*, Jack said, "Hey, Ty, want to rack 'em up with me? How about we play some 9-ball?"

Tyler's eyes lit up. "Hell, yeah!" he said before suddenly becoming subdued. "I mean, that is, if it's okay with you, Juliet."

"Please. You guys go for it." As Tyler turned to walk to the tables, Jack gave her a little wink. A wink that said *I've got this*.

Leo suddenly popped up at her side, nodding knowingly and rubbing his fingers together like she owed him money.

She hated all men.

"Just to warn you, Jack," Tyler said as they each grabbed a cue, "I'm pretty good at this."

"I consider myself warned," Jack calmly chalked his pool stick.

"Let's bet on the winner," Tyler said. "Say… fifty bucks?"

"Fifty bucks?" Juliet whispered to Leo. But he just motioned her to keep watching.

"I probably shouldn't bet," Jack said. "It wouldn't be right for me to take money from my constituents."

"Ha ha, Jack," Tyler said. "Funny. We can play for a round of drinks if you like."

"Okay, Ty. Rack 'em up."

Tyler gathered the balls with the triangle.

"Since you're mayor, I'll let you break."

"Well, I haven't played in a while, so bear with me." Jack took his place at the end of the table, leaning his long form over to break.

The cue ball hit the others with a big smack and they all went scattering.

One ball went in. The nine ball.

"No way," Leo said, sitting up.

Tyler's mouth dropped open and he turned as red as the felt on the table.

Everyone standing around exclaimed and cheered and whooped.

"What just happened?" Juliet asked, taking in the chaos. "I think I'm missing something."

Leo was laughing so hard he was holding his stomach. "Game's over."

"But they only just started." She thought she understood pool. One pocketed ball was not a game.

"If a player sinks the 9-ball on the break, he wins. It's called a Golden Break."

That's when Jack glanced over, a big, confident, satisfying grin on his face.

Jack slapped Tyler on the back. "No hard feelings, okay, buddy?"

"No hard feelings," Tyler said, as they set down their sticks and walked over. "Are you two dating?"

Juliet held her breath. She didn't expect Jack to say yes. Because they had an agreement. Plus if he said yes, the answer was sure to fly around town faster than Mach 3 speed.

Jack stared at Juliet for a long second. Asking her a question with his eyes.

Her heart flew up to her throat, making it hard to breathe.

Then Jack spoke. "Now might be a good time, Juliet, to do things a little differently. Is it okay if I tell Tyler the truth—about us?"

Juliet's heart literally blocked her throat. His words echoed what she'd said to him earlier. And they sounded exactly like what she'd been trying to convey to him earlier.

That she cared.

But did she trust herself to care?

Her pulse pounding at her temples, she gave him the slightest nod.

Jack put his arm around Tyler's shoulders. "Juliet and I are dating."

"Is that what you wanted to talk to me about?" Tyler asked her.

"Um—yes," she said. "Yes, it was. I wanted to let you know." Which was a teeny lie but—she'd seen enough to understand that Tyler might be a great kindergarten teacher, and kind, but he was not for her. And she didn't really need to go any deeper than that.

"Well, congratulations, Juliet," Tyler said graciously. "I—wish you the best."

"Thank, Ty," she said. "I wish you the best, too."

Tyler went to the bar to order a drink. Jack sat down and took another sip of her whiskey sour.

"Where'd you learn to play pool like that?" she asked.

He shrugged. "Didn't I tell you I had a misspent youth?"

He was very near. Everything in the bar—the music, the clinking of glasses and pool balls, the hum of conversation—faded away. "Jack," she said. "So…we're…dating."

He stared straight at her. "You okay with that?"

She stared right back and cracked a smile. "Yeah. I am. But I have a question."

"What's that?"

"How did you do that—that break thing?"

He let out a big laugh. "If you really want to know, I'm happy to explain, but…maybe some other time. I have an idea about a better game to play."

Then Jack Monroe kissed her, right there, in front of all their friends and half the town. A full, steady, enthusiastic kiss that made her go hot and cold and made the room whirl around her like a brightly colored carousel.

A little voice inside of her whispered, *This is it. He's the one.*

Which should have shocked her. Or made her deny it. Except it just felt too good.

And it felt like she'd waited a lifetime for that kind of good.

CHAPTER TWENTY

A little later, in Juliet's apartment, Jack took her arm and led her to the couch. He'd just admitted, to himself and to Juliet, that he was in a relationship. He felt a little stunned. And he wasn't quite sure how it had happened. Just that she'd broken down all his defenses. And for the first time in his life, he felt…humbled. Lucky. Awestruck. And completely baffled, lost in territory he'd never entered before.

But he needed to say something. So he looked honestly into her eyes. "You know, I'd be considered a bad horse to bet on as far as relationships go. You all right with that?"

"You know, *I'd* be considered a bad bet for a relationship, too," she answered right back. "And the whole town knows it." She shrugged, like she knew the truth, but she was now okay to move on from it.

"You're not a bad bet," he said, playing with a strand of her hair. "You're just misunderstood."

She lifted a right-back-atcha brow at that. "Maybe that makes two of us."

She made him feel that he wasn't as impossible a case as he'd thought. Also, he'd never met a woman who could dish it right back at him. In all the best ways.

Jack was crossing a line he'd never crossed before. He wanted to stamp *Mine* all over her, which was…illogical.

He felt fiercely protective of her, even though he knew she didn't need a protector.

She accepted him as he was, but he wanted to be a better man for her.

Juliet was a complicated, emotional woman, his opposite in nearly every way…and he was wild for her. Helpless from want. Jack understood that his feelings were way out of control, rushing through him like a swollen river.

He wanted to tell her how amazing it was to have her in his arms—curvy and warm and wonderful—and how perfect her full, soft lips felt like beneath his. And how he loved being with her and how she was just as fun and amazing and sassy in bed as she was out of it.

He couldn't help but think of Shelby. How he'd thought being with her was the perfect solution for his lifestyle. No feelings, no attachments, just freedom.

What a fool he'd been.

Juliet had been the one to tell him she needed space and time. That she wanted to keep things light. He should have been thrilled with that.

But everything seemed different now.

"Hey, Juliet," he said. "I've been thinking."

She'd snuggled up next to him, her head resting on his shoulder. "Is it really time for thinking?"

"I—I just wanted to ask, are you done digging up your past? I mean, I see why you did it."

She smiled up at him. "It *was* your idea."

Right. Not one of his best. "How about no more old boyfriend interviews?"

"You're not jealous, are you?" *Are there wild hogs in Texas?*

"No, just...wanting to put all that in the rear-view and look ahead. To the future."

"I may not have discovered why it took me so long to figure out that those guys weren't right for me, but I do know that they weren't. And I'm ready to move forward."

That's all he needed to pull her to him and kiss her, slow and deep. Her lips were soft, and she tasted like...heaven. He wanted to take his time and savor every part of her, worship her every-where, because he just couldn't get enough.

"Jack," she said.

"What is it?" He looked up from kissing her neck. Her eyes were misty.

"What you just said—it was beautiful."

Every muscle froze. "Did I just—say that out loud?"

She gave a slow, wicked nod. "I especially liked the *worship me all over* part."

He wasn't quite sure how he'd simply just spo-ken what he thought. "I want to learn how to speak your love language," he said. It was true.

"Yeah, well, I think you must've studied hard, because you get an A-plus." She grinned. "Better be careful, though. If you keep saying things like that, I can't help but fall for you." She pressed her hands to her chest, her eyes suddenly glistening. "That...that's the best thing anyone's ever said to me," she said softly as she drew her arms around his neck. "But...what *is* my love language? I'm not really sure what it is."

"Well, I'm in the learning phase about this, but I'm thinking that it involves expressing plenty of feelings. Which I'm not so great at. But also…" He bent and whispered something in her ear that made her blush. "Okay?"

She grasped more tightly onto him and shot him a dazed look.

Satisfied by her reaction, he mustered a steady, slow grin. "And that's where I've got this all handled. Because honey, I'm terrible at talkin', but I'm *really* good at doin'."

• • •

Early the next morning, Jack heard something crinkle beneath him in the bed. He moved his arm to find a foil chocolate wrapper from sometime in the middle of the night, when they'd gotten hungry for other things besides each other. That brought a smile to his face. But now the day was dawning and next to him, Juliet was fast asleep, her hair tumbling softly around her on the pillow.

Beautiful. In a way that made his heart hurt.

He moved to get out of bed but found a visitor with a bright-pink collar sitting nearby on the dresser, flicking her tail at him in a sassy way.

"Meow," Ellie said. Which he translated to, *What the heck are you doing here?*

Jack got out of bed, pulled on his pants, and continued the conversation in the main room, closing the bedroom door on the way.

"Hey there, Ellie," he said to the cat from her new perch on her carpet-lined penthouse. "I'm not sure we've been formally introduced. I'm Jack."

She bent and snapped her tail again, in true Elle Woods style. He wasn't sure if that meant approval, so he rummaged around the tiny kitchen until he found a can of cat food, which he dumped in a bowl and placed on a black mat covered with painted paw prints and said *I have cattitude*.

Besides the cat food, Juliet's cupboards were pretty bare, so he decided to run to the store so he could surprise her with a real breakfast. He got as far as his truck when a gray-haired woman in a bright floral apron came running out of the big house.

Oh no.

"Mayor Monroe?" she exclaimed, wide-eyed.

"Good morning, Mrs. O," Jack said cheerily. He lifted his hands in surrender. "I'm afraid you've caught me red-handed." The only reason he'd ever say that was to save Juliet from eviction. But to do so, he'd have to think fast on his feet. "You don't know how glad I am that our paths have crossed. I'm in grave need of a citizen of your high caliber to lead our neighborhood watch group on Wednesdays. You interested?"

She'd be perfect. The only trouble was, he wasn't sure how she'd feel about leaving her house since she did seem to be there a lot, according to Juliet.

She blushed, which he took to mean she might be considering, so he kept going. Because he definitely did not want to leave room to field questions about what he and Juliet were up to last night. "It involves educating seniors and other people who are home during the day on what to be alert for in our community. Watching out for people who might be doing things for nefarious purposes. That's how we caught those folks who came across state lines last year with that stolen van. And we busted shoplifters last month because when they were checking out their candle stash in the park right when someone walked by, smelled the candles, and called the police. So it's an important job. I need someone...observant."

He didn't say busybody. Or buttinsky. Or even gossipy. In fact, he sort of saw Mrs. O like Juliet did. Someone who was lonely. Who maybe was searching for something to do to help others.

"Why, Mayor, I—I don't know what to say," she said, clearly disarmed.

"Well, I hope you say yes. You're just who we need."

She put her hand on her chest. "I'd be honored to serve."

"Great." He put a hand on the door handle of his truck. "I'll have my administrative assistant call you with the details, if that's okay."

"I—um—yes, thank you." She looked distracted, like she was thinking hard about his job offer. *Thank goodness.* "Mayor, is it all right if I gather up a few of my friends who would be good citizens for the group?"

Jack grinned. "That's exactly what we need, Mrs. O."

"I want you to know I'm going to take this very seriously."

He grinned. "I just knew you were the perfect person for the job." Then he asked her if she needed anything from the store.

As he turned to get into his truck, he thought about what he'd just done. It started out as a Jack-tactic, a slightly clever way to shimmy out of getting caught—not that he should worry about something like that at his age, but Juliet did have to live in this lady's backyard. But it ended with a total Juliet move—making someone feel useful, better, and appreciated.

She wasn't just rubbing off on him—she was becoming a *part* of him. She'd infiltrated him down deep, body and soul. Which scared him to death, even as it made him smile.

"Oh, yoo-hoo, Mayor Monroe," Mrs. O. said, flagging him down as she ran up to his truck. "One more thing."

She was a little out of breath. The way she'd chased him down, he figured it must be important. "Sure, Mrs. O. What is it?"

"Next time I see your car here overnight, I'll have it towed."

• • •

The next day, Juliet was standing in the middle of a tiny bedroom in Tessa and Leo's house, the walls of which were painted a deep, dark blue and embellished with stars and planets. Her sisters were there, too, as were Leo, Noah, and Jack, and they were all staring at a handful of paint cans sitting in the middle of the floor.

Except Jack kept sneaking looks at her. Ones that were making her remember…well, everything. And once, when she was certain no one was looking, she blew him a subtle air-kiss, briefly puckering her lips and sending it away with a smile.

Despite the lack of sleep, her whole body was buzzing. Oh, not just from a night of really great sex. But also, from another feeling she was afraid to name.

"So I get the primer coats," Jack said as he stooped to examine them. "But which color are the walls going to be?"

Uh-oh. Juliet exchanged looks with Viv. They both knew this was a loaded question. As evidenced from many, many discussions with Tessa over the past several months.

Noah read the names off the cans. "Whisper soft gray, delicate yellow, or white dove." He stood up. "I think someone's wanting a gentle baby vibe here."

"I think we're really wanting a *done* vibe," Jack said. "Because how many weeks away is that due date?"

Tessa patted her belly, which could only be described as…big. Like, really big. "Two."

"That's the problem." Leo was still wearing his chef's apron from working in the kitchen, part of the deal of bartering food for help. He stood stoically crossing his arms, but his expression toward his wife was anything but. "My wife can't seem to decide on the color."

She shrugged. "It's an important decision."

"We could vote," Viv suggested.

"Draw straws and let the winner pick," Jack said.

"Or just grab a can and start painting," Leo said with a good-natured glance at his wife. Which, Juliet noted, was really sweet.

"Fine. Go ahead," Tessa said. "Make jokes at the expectant mother's expense."

"I have an idea," Noah said. Juliet just knew he'd save the day with his design expertise. "We'll do the primer. Then we'll paint a sample of each color and reconvene. Okay?"

"Sounds like a plan," Leo said, clearly anxious to start.

As Noah began prying open the primer cans, Viv said, "I hate to bring this up, but have you two decided on a name yet?"

Someone groaned. Juliet thought it might have been Leo.

"No nice nursery, no bed, and *no name*," Tessa said, counting on her fingers.

Jack shook his head in fake admonition. "That's what happens when you two are so busy getting your businesses off the ground."

"We are terrible parents," Leo said sadly. "And the baby isn't even born yet."

"Okay, we can help," Viv pulled out her phone as the guys got to work. "Here are some suggestions of unique, special, and wonderful names. Are you ready? First, you can keep it simple and name your baby after a single letter of the alphabet."

"No," Leo said with a deadpan expression.

Viv was undeterred. "How about an animal

name like Panda? Or a fantastical name like Twinkle, Sparkle, or Rainbow? Or, focusing on both your passions, naming the baby after your favorite food?"

"We're not naming our baby after bread *or* pasta," Tessa said firmly.

"Why not?" Juliet asked. "Everyone loves both of those."

"How about an adjective like *Precious?*" Viv said, but her enthusiasm was definitely cooling.

"How about a cool name like Chandler, Phoebe, Monica, Ross, or Joey?" Noah offered.

Jack chimed in. "Or good, strong Texas names like Austin, Dallas, Antonio…Stetson…"

That made Leo straighten, armed with a paintbrush, and give his friend a look. "Stetson, Jack? Really?"

"Those *are* all boy names," Juliet noted.

"All right then," Jack said. "How about Texanne, Bluebonnet…or, Blue Bell."

"Blue Bell…like the ice cream?" Juliet grinned. "Finally, one I like!"

"Well, to be fair, a bluebell is also a flower," Tessa said.

"I always thought a Star Wars theme would be cool," Noah said, shifting topics. "Kylo, Leia, Boba Fett…" He surveyed the room, tapping his finger against his lips. "Come to think of it, if you went that route, we could just leave this room as is."

Tessa tossed him a glare. "If you keep talking like that, Noah, I'm going to lock the door so that no one can leave until this job is done."

"How about a family name?" Viv asked.

Leo considered that. "The only ancestor we know of was Guido and he's the one that started the big feud with the Montgomerys."

Juliet knew no one wanted to go there. But that got her thinking, so she started to look things up on her phone, too. "How about something from our French heritage… Jacques, Jean Paul, Rene, Brigitte, Timothée." She looked up and grinned. "Timothée Chalomet Castorini."

Tessa gave an enthusiastic nod. "I *love* it."

"Me too," Viv chimed in.

"Um, I vote no," Leo said. "As in, *absolutely not*."

"How about *Adorable*?" Viv quipped. "Like you two?"

"How about an amalgam?" Noah said. "A combo of both your names. And I have the perfect one. Tesla."

Everyone groaned.

But he didn't have the good sense to stop. "Lotus," Noah said. "Help, I need an intervention."

Jack pretended to strangle him.

"Do you see why we're having problems?" Tessa said. "We've been doing this for *months*."

"Maybe you're going to take one look at your beautiful baby and know exactly what the name should be," Juliet said.

"We can hope," Tessa patted her belly.

Leo walked over and put an arm around his wife. "It's okay, Baby NoName," he said in a high-pitched voice, putting his hand over hers. "We'll figure out your name. I know it." That made Tessa look at him with a silly expression, like she thought that was just too cute. Jack, across the room, seemed a little horrified at his friend speaking in baby talk. "Anyway, thanks everybody, for coming to help today," Leo said. In regular language.

"When's dinner?" Jack asked, just to get a rise out of Leo. But his gaze wandered over to Juliet's and held. Like he was hungry for a whole different kind of dinner.

And that made her blush.

"If you've got the smoker covered, we can handle the rest," Tessa said.

"Covered," Leo said as he spread primer on the wall.

"Smoker?" Jack frowned. "What Italian dish requires a smoker?"

"A surprise," Leo said. He turned to Tessa. "We'll finish the primer then come down and assemble the crib."

"Sounds great," Tessa said. "Come on, ladies."

Juliet walked down the stairs into the living room with her sisters. Tessa sidestepped scattered crib parts, which were lying in the middle of the carpet, and collapsed into a sturdy chair, putting her feet up on an ottoman. "Two more weeks cannot come fast enough," she said. "I'm so relieved that after today, our baby will finally have a put-together crib. And a nursery that doesn't look like a planetarium."

"I kind of like the cosmic vibe," Viv said. But when Tessa shot her a death glare, she changed her tune. "Okay, okay, a nice, *soft* color will look much better for our special beloved niece or nephew."

Juliet surveyed the mess. Headboard, footboard, rails, Allen wrench, nuts and bolts, and... scattered directions. "Did a bomb go off?" she asked with a chuckle.

"Leo and Jack finally started to put it together this morning, but they got a little frustrated," Tessa said.

"How many men does it take to put a crib together?" Viv asked, her lips turning up.

"The real question is, how many *women* does it take?" Juliet asked. She and Viv exchanged glances and pounded fists.

"Leave the guys to the painting, ladies," Viv said. "We got this."

"Hey," Tessa said, struggling to get up. "I can help, too."

"Yes, you can." Juliet handed her the instructions. "You tell us what to do, and we'll do it."

"Okay, I appreciate being the director." Tessa sat back down. "But only on one condition."

Viv disappeared into the kitchen, while Juliet moved the big cardboard crib box against the wall. "What's that?"

"You spill about you and Jack while we work."

She shrugged. "Nothing to tell." But she couldn't seem to wipe the smile off her face.

Viv came back with glasses of iced tea and passed them out. "Your fridge is packed. I'm so excited for dinner. Jack is going to have a cow. Literally."

She was referring to the beef brisket smoking

in the driveway. Not to mention the other smoker full of ribs. And the complete surprise a full-on Texas barbecue was going to be.

"Jack's going to love it," Juliet said. "Thank you for hosting."

"Hey," Tessa said, "you two were here most of yesterday helping with all that food."

Juliet placed two identical metal brackets side by side. "I know, but Leo really outdid himself with the menu."

"We were happy to do it. And Jack will appreciate the moral support." Tessa waved a hand around the room. "Besides, as you can see, we're a little desperate for help here."

"So anyway," Viv said, examining an Allen wrench, "tell us what happened between you and the cowboy. Because he can't stop smiling that toddler-at-a-birthday-party smile, either."

"Okay, fine." Juliet knew she'd have no peace from her sisters unless she dished. "He told me how he felt."

"And...?" Tessa gave her an expectant look.

"And...I don't know." Juliet suddenly struggled for words. "I...I'm afraid to talk about it." She looked at her older sister for understanding. "Like, if I say something, it will all go away." All of a sudden, she got teary-eyed.

"Oh, honey, no," Tessa said, making Juliet so grateful to have sisters. "You know, that's exactly how I felt for the longest time. Life can just beat you down. But I can tell you from experience, you need to embrace it, revel in it, and be happy. Because you deserve it."

Viv nodded her approval. "Jack's a great guy."

"I mean, we…we haven't said the L word," Juliet rushed to say. "And in the beginning, I told him this was just for fun. Because I wasn't ready for anything serious. But he just…he just got to me, you know?" Then the tears really started falling. "I just… I can't resist him."

Tessa teared up, and Viv, too, and Juliet instantly felt bad because she knew Viv was going through some tough times herself. "Viv, I'm so sorry. I didn't mean to—"

Viv stepped over some crib rails and gave her a giant hug. "That's not why I'm crying. It's because I'm so happy for you."

Tessa tried to get up but ultimately just stayed put, reaching out her hand and wiggling her fingers until Juliet grabbed it. "Don't be afraid to reach for your happiness," she said. Looking Viv's way, she added, "You'll figure things out, too, honey. It just takes time."

"Hey," Viv said with a shrug, "At this rate, the Santa panties will fund my next European trip. So it's all good."

CHAPTER TWENTY-ONE

When Jack entered the living room with the guys a few hours later, he came upon a sight. All three women were sitting on the couch looking at something on Tessa's phone and laughing. And the crib was sitting in the middle of the living room, completely put together. With a bow on it, a special touch someone added probably just to be funny. It was also hard to miss the wonderful smells coming from the kitchen. Which smelled a whole lot better than paint primer.

"Nice job, ladies," Leo said.

"Yeah. It was like those directions were printed in another language," Jack said, joining Leo, more than eager to rub it in.

"We couldn't make heads or tails of them," Noah added.

"We would've gotten it eventually," Leo said, his male pride seeming a little tender. But Tessa was squinting her eyes down at him. "Okay, maybe not," he said. "It looks amazing. Nice work." He flashed a special smile at his wife and touched his chest. "I say that humbly."

"I love it when you're humble," Tessa said, joining Leo and giving him a kiss.

"It was easy." Juliet grinned, clearly trying to make trouble.

"Isn't it beautiful?" her older sister said, focusing on the positive. "Our offspring has a bed!"

Noah examined the crib. "Just think. A little person is going to be sleeping in there in just a few weeks."

"Wow," Leo rubbed his neck and looked incredulous, as if it was suddenly dawning on him that life was going to be a lot different.

"Scary, isn't it?" Viv said.

It occurred to Jack that life would change not just for Leo and Tessa, but for all of them. But that might not be a bad thing.

"I better stick to what I know best and go check the smoker." Leo headed for the door, seeming a little too eager to escape.

"I need help setting the table," Tessa said, gathering Noah and Viv. "Jack, can you please help Juliet bring out the sides?"

While Tessa herded everyone outside, Jack promptly grabbed Juliet's hand, tugged her into the back hall, and kissed her.

"What was that for?" she asked, a little out of breath. But smiling. Still. As he was.

"I missed you," he said. He'd been waiting to do that all day.

"It's only been a couple of hours."

"That's two hours too long."

"Well, look at you two," Noah suddenly said from the sliding door.

"They can't keep their hands off each other." Viv was standing there, too, shaking her head and smiling.

"Hey, break it up over there," Leo called. "It's dinner time."

"Jack," Tessa said looking around them. "We

have a little surprise for you." Her eyes were twinkling.

"We're grateful for all the help," Leo said, putting an arm around his wife, "and we wanted to make everyone a nice meal. But the meal is really for Jack." Jack had a suspicion that, as his granny would say, mischief was afoot. "We know what a stress this zoning meeting has been, so good luck and...go get 'em."

Jack stared at his best friends, completely thrown. He was stunned speechless, his limbs suddenly threatening to bend like rubber beneath him.

"It was Juliet's idea," Tessa whispered as she led him outside.

Of course it was.

A pop-up banquet table was set up on the patio, covered with a red-and-white checked tablecloth. And tons of food covered the surface—not just any food, but all the fixings of a proper Texas barbecue. And standing next to all of it was his granny. And Juliet's mom and grandma. And Leo's dad.

"Surprise!" they all held up glasses of iced tea.

He swallowed past a sudden lump in his throat. Stole a glance at Juliet, who was beaming. She'd done this? They'd *all* done this...for him?

Calling himself shocked would be a mild term. His granny was smiling from ear to ear, which he hadn't seen since the day he'd finally graduated from college. So was everyone else, in fact. And Juliet...well, her eyes were sparkling with the fun of the surprise. And something else—something deeper that completely bowled him over.

He felt supported. More than that. He felt *loved*. Tomorrow he'd fight the last fight. But he'd do it knowing that everyone was with him.

It wasn't like his mother was taking the fast train away. Leaving him behind, a discard.

Oh, he knew life was more complicated than that. But as a young kid, you don't understand complicated. You understood being alone. And not being good enough for your own mother to keep.

There was a huge platter of beef brisket in the middle of the table—aka, barbecue. As he approached, he caught sight of a giant platter of ribs and a baking dish loaded with macaroni and cheese. There were pickled jalapenos, sweet potato casserole, a giant salad, and corn on the cob.

"Have a sweet tea," Viv said, handing him a drink. She pulled out a tall can of beer from behind her back. "Or maybe you need this."

He took the beer. Everyone was smiling at him. His granny gave him a big wave and blew him a kiss.

He was…thrown. And something else that he rarely was, uncomfortable. He turned to Juliet, who was now at his side. "You…you did all this?"

"We all did," she said, waving her arm to include everyone.

"Barbecue," he said. "You all did a real Texas barbecue."

"With all the fixings," granny yelled.

He turned to Leo. "You've been holding out on me, buddy," he said, slapping his friend on the back. "I thought you were a one-horse rider."

Leo laughed out loud. "Do you actually have such little faith in me that you think I can only cook Italian food? Better taste it and see for yourself. But truthfully, you gave me an excuse to try out my new smoker."

"And just wait until you try my blackberry cobbler," Noah said.

Jack must have given Juliet an SOS look because she whispered, "Just say thank you," Then she shrugged. "Simple—oh, except this time…you might want to keep the prayer separate."

"Thank you, friends." Jack's voice cracked. Juliet smiled and gave him an encouraging nod. And hey, he didn't even turn the thank you into a prayer service…yet. He looked around the little backyard and realized that everyone he loved in the world was right here.

For so many years, he'd felt like that kid left at the train station. Broken, damaged, beyond repair. But that wasn't true.

He had friends who had become his family.

"I'm sincerely touched. I—I have no words." Then he realized that that was probably his usual condition. So he tried to one-up it. "But what I can say is that…I feel truly loved right now. I love y'all."

"We love you, too," someone called. He thought it was Juliet's grandmother.

"Now go kick that developer's ass," Leo said, holding up a beer.

"Jackson, will you please lead us in the meal prayer?" his granny asked. Then she looked around. "Oh, that is, if everybody's okay with that." Everyone immediately folded their hands.

"Before that," Tessa said, "we're very thankful for everything. Including the nice bed for our baby. And a room that doesn't look like it needs a telescope in it."

"And we're thankful for all of you," Leo added.

"All right then," Jack said, bowing his head. He squeezed Juliet's hand under the table. She glanced at him, gave him a quick wink, and squeezed back. "Thank you," he whispered, keeping it simple. He'd never meant those two syllables more.

She flashed him a radiant smile. "You're welcome."

And he held on tight.

• • •

On the morning of the big meeting, Juliet stopped at the boulangerie on her way to city hall.

"Is Jack nervous?" her mother asked as she poured a giant dark roast for Jack.

"Yes," Juliet said, "he's been working day and night on his presentation."

"Well, make sure he knows we're rooting for him," her grandmother said, handing her the strong coffee for Jack and one with a lot of cream for herself. Juliet left with the good luck cheers of her mom and grandmother spilling out onto the street behind her. Their support of Jack meant the world to her and bolstered her spirits, too. She hoped it would make Jack feel that he wasn't fighting this battle alone, no matter what happened. She only crossed her fingers that the rest of the town would rally around him, too.

As she made her way up Main Street, someone fell into step beside her.

"Good morning, Juliet," Devin said, dressed in a navy suit and expensive Italian loafers, that cloyingly expensive scent he must have poured all over himself making her suppress a sneeze. "You're up and at 'em early." He flashed a bright white grin.

"It's really hard to sleep in when everyone in your family routinely rises at four thirty a.m. to go to work." It was true. She had early rising built into her genes. And also, all the jobs she'd held to get herself through school had made sleeping in a luxury she could never afford. Except she had slept in like the dead the other morning when Jack stayed over. And woke up to the smell of a delicious breakfast burrito he'd made just for her.

"You always had a lot of ambition, Juliet," he said, giving her a side glance. "Just like me."

Oops, back to reality. Good thing she was just a block from city hall. Juliet made a little go-get-'em fist pump. "Well, Devin, I hope that your vision and ambition are all geared up for this meeting today." She pressed a hand to her chest, suddenly feeling a desperate pang that made her send up a silent prayer from the depths of her heart. In truth, she didn't want Devin being part of their town at all. And she knew he would never be motivated by altruism. But she hoped with her whole being that he would see opportunity in the south side land. Or, frankly, just build his golf course somewhere far, far away.

"Yes. Um, about that." He slowed his pace, which unfortunately made her slow hers, too. She really did not want to stop and have a discussion with him in the middle of Main Street. Or anywhere, for that matter. "I had a few questions about the meeting. I wondered if you might want to have coffee?" He looked at her two coffees. "That is, unless you're headed somewhere."

"I'm the town counselor, not the town architect," she said, not unkindly. "I think Jack's the one you should direct your questions to." There. That got her off the hook. Job done. Because... what the hell?

"Oh, and I definitely will," he said. "But I wanted to get *your* take on it." He pointed to the same park bench where she'd sat with Jack the other day.

"Why do you care about my opinion?" she asked honestly.

"Well, I know that you know everyone in town. They all seem to love you, and I also know that you have your finger on its pulse. Maybe you can give me your take. After all, if I get involved in a project here, I'd like to get involved with the community. Community input is essential for success in these kinds of decisions."

Juliet wasn't sure what he was up to. Or if he really cared at all about anyone's opinion, much less hers. He'd struck her from the beginning as a determined businessman more concerned with profits than the will of a tiny dot of a town on the

Indiana map.

And that dot meant *everything* to her.

But, if he was reaching out sincerely, she owed it to Jack and to her town to sell the idea that would preserve their town as well as Adele's home. "My take is fully and positively for the green project," Juliet said firmly as they both sat down. "I'm completely in love with the idea." If he was using this as some kind of means to flirt with her, she wasn't going to bite. "Also, everyone's really excited about the clean-up grant. That junkyard has been a real eyesore for a long time, and the possibilities for the community are really exciting."

He raked a hand through his expensively cut hair. "Juliet, that's *just* what I need to hear. How the townspeople are reacting. What everyone is thinking. What the citizens want. I—I know how difficult it must be for Ms. Anderson to lose land that's been in her family for generations."

"You do?" Her empathic powers were not giving her a handle on him. He had blue eyes, too, not as pretty as Jack's, but she just couldn't get a read into his soul.

"Well, I feel it vicariously, anyway," he said.

She started to reach for her coffees so she could stand up and leave when he lightly touched her arm.

"Now let's talk about something more fun."

"More *fun*?" A prickly feeling skittered up her spine.

"When this project gets underway, I'm planning on moving to Blossom Glen. At least temporarily. So I can supervise everything. And I can really use some help finding my way around town, some advice about the best place to live. Would you be interested?"

She somehow managed a polite smile. "I can set you up with a great realtor. She sold my sister and brother-in-law their house. She's fantastic, and she'll explore all the neighborhoods with you."

He looked at Juliet intensely. Then he took up her hand. "Thanks for the referral. But I was hoping you might want to tour me around. Informally, of course."

She withdrew her hand. Faster than if she'd touched a hot stove burner. She eyed him calmly and coolly. "Devin, I'm not looking for a personal relationship."

"Well, I can understand that right now. But as soon as this deal is done, maybe we can make it personal. If you're interested."

"Hey, Juliet, Devin," Jack said.

Jack, with his silent way of suddenly being there. Standing on the sidewalk, smiling a tight smile.

CHAPTER TWENTY-TWO

"Hello, Jack." Devin rose from the bench to shake Jack's hand. But Jack's hand seemed to be balled into a tight fist, and he was trying his best not to use it as a weapon.

Devin smiled. "Juliet and I were just about to catch up on old times."

"Old times?" One glance at Juliet showed her flushing. Which made his heart sink. Because that meant it was true.

There'd been old times with *Devin*, of all people. But were they *good* old times? And like, exactly how good were they? "You two know each other?"

"Oh, we go way back," Devin said with a flick of his wrist. "How many dates did we go on, Juliet? Two, maybe three?"

Juliet smiled sweetly. "One and only one."

Devin chuckled. "Well, I always wanted it to be more."

"Thanks," she said, turning to him, "but I'm seeing someone." She looked pointedly at Jack.

Jack should have been relieved. But his relief was completely overtaken by anger.

He loosened his collar, because he was having trouble getting enough air. How could she not tell him that she knew the guy who was about to buy his grandmother's land? And that he was apparently still interested in her?

"I'm actually in a relationship," Juliet pressed.

It dawned on him that Devin might be playing them. Pitting them against one another. For fun or for another reason, he wasn't sure. Probably to cause division. So that during the zoning meeting and the auction, it would cause friction between them, and also prevent Jack from mobilizing his town.

That's when he realized what Devin was really up to, and it made Jack's heart plummet into his stomach. Devin had made a show of wanting to listen to the other option, but it was just that, a show. Jack was 99 percent sure he wasn't even considering it. At all.

Devin wanted his grandmother's land. And it also appeared that he wanted Juliet.

"Jack," Juliet said, spearing him with her gaze. "You're really not going to say anything?"

Jack shrugged. "Nothing to say." He knew he was being an asshat. He was just so *angry*.

"Oh, and just to let you know, Jack," Devin said, "we ran the numbers. Turns out, it's easier to move the stream and get going on the original land than to wait years for a clean-up that hasn't even started yet. We would make enough profits in the years we waste waiting to start the project to pay for everything. Sorry, Jack. I feel for your grandmother, but this is about the bottom line."

As Devin said his goodbyes and left, Jack's head was whirling. He'd expected this. Not in this manner, but it made him furious that Devin would use Juliet to get to him.

He would have to readjust his strategy…but

what was left to adjust to? The green project was dead. The only thing left was…his people. His town. And he'd have to rely on making an emotional appeal.

In front of everyone. His worst nightmare. Even Juliet, who had believed in him and got him to open himself up, was wearing a wary look.

"Why didn't you tell him we were dating?" Juliet asked in a hurt tone.

He rubbed his hands over his face in frustration. "How could you not tell me that you dated *him* of all people?"

She heaved a heavy sigh. And swiped away a tear. "Because he was a jerk then and he's a jerk now, okay? I saw no point in it. I never thought it would become an issue."

Jack snorted. "You didn't think telling me that he was still interested in you would make a difference?"

"Would it have really mattered if I did?" She did face him then, throwing up her hands. "It was one date a million years ago."

"It would have mattered…to me. I'm about to fight for my grandmother's land in front of our town and I suddenly learn that you knew Devin all this time?"

"I didn't even find out he was Omnibuild until a few weeks ago."

He poked the air. "That's a few weeks too long." She was the last person he should be fighting with, especially at a time like this. But he couldn't seem to help himself.

Juliet crossed her arms, a wounded expression

on her face. "So you can't admit in front of a guy I don't like that we're together? Because you're angry with me?"

"That's a pretty big secret to keep." What he really wanted to say was that he was just…hurt. Why hadn't she told him? And now she was fixated on him not saying what she needed to hear.

"Maybe you didn't tell him about us because you're not sure about us," Juliet said. "Maybe you didn't *want* to tell him about us. Or you didn't think it was *important* to."

"You're perfectly capable of standing up for yourself," he said. Panic clogged his throat. He knew that was the wrong thing to say. The burning pain in his chest told him so. The right thing would have been to tell her how important she was to him.

But she was already doubting him.

"Yes, I am perfectly capable of standing up for myself," she said, straightening her spine. "But I needed *you* to stand up for *us*."

It was hard enough in the best of circumstances to say what she needed to hear. But he felt chastised. And wronged. And orneriness made him not want to try.

She speared him with her gaze. "You're really not going to say anything, are you?" She looked disappointed. Like he'd let her down. Maybe even like she'd expected him to let her down all along.

This was why he didn't open himself up. Why he stayed away from relationships. They all went bad.

Jack shrugged. "Not right now I'm not." Why

should he open himself up when she'd already decided he was a mistake? That he was incapable of proclaiming his love.

Love was about pain. About betrayals and dishonesties. He'd seen it for years, all through his sad youth. He should have known better than to try with her. Or with anyone. It was best to keep things simple. Not to give all you had to someone and then be crushed.

He stood steely-still, unbudging. She searched his face, needing him to say something. Anything. But what was the point? It was better to be alone. Better to keep his damage to himself and let her move on.

She bit down on her lip, and he could see she was trying not to cry. "Okay, Jack. Have it your way. I—I'm leaving."

She gave him one long, hard look. And then she turned and left.

Devin had used her to get to him. It hadn't changed anything about the land or the meeting, but it was one tool in his toolbox to throw Jack off guard, to wreak havoc on an important day.

And it had worked.

•••

Noah was the first one to come up to Jack before the meeting, standing before him at the podium with a concerned look. "Are you all right?"

Jack straightened his tie. He took a brief glance downward. Shirt. Tie. Pants. "Don't I look all right?"

"Your hat's on backward."

Jack swiped it off his head and straightened his hair. Wearing a hat backward was bad luck for sure. "Thanks."

He just needed to focus. He had to convince his town that his grandmother's land should not be zoned for commercial use. It was the only way to stop Devin.

Then he could only pray that the state park would bid on her land at auction.

That was all he had.

So, in a sense, he'd failed his grandmother. She'd have to leave the land regardless of how it was zoned, because he had no other options to pull out of a hat.

No wide outdoors. No trees she loved. And no daily visits to his beloved grandfather's grave just over the hill.

He'd failed Juliet, too. He knew he had as soon as she'd turned away. He'd let his hurt and anger prevent him from speaking out. She was the first woman to get through to him in years. And the only one who got through deep.

He sucked.

Noah was standing there expectantly. It dawned on Jack that he'd just said something. "What?" he asked.

"I said, you seem a little frazzled."

"I'm fine," Jack answered. "But thanks, Noah. Thanks for coming. It…means a lot." He paused. "You're a good friend. I'm not sure if I ever told you that."

From now on, he was going to tell everyone everything he was thinking.

Because clamming up hadn't gotten him anywhere.

"Oh." Noah stared at him like he was seriously worried. Jack *was* shaky and sweating. And completely miserable. "You're a good friend, too, Jack."

Then Noah backed away, the concerned look not abating. Jack tried to read his notes. Then he flipped through his slides, but all the words were merging into nonsense.

He'd never choked in front of a meeting in his life.

He'd never been so nervous before a presentation.

But now he was sweating so bad he was afraid he'd have to go home and change his shirt. The zoning commissioner came up to him with a couple of questions, and he hoped that whatever answers he gave him made some kind of sense.

At six forty, he glanced up to see Noah again, this time with Leo at his side. "We, um, wondered if we could speak to you a minute," Noah said. He gestured with his head toward the hall. "In your office."

"Can it wait until after the meeting?" Jack asked.

"It absolutely cannot." Noah gave him a look more stern than his granny's when he broke curfew as a teenager.

"Yeah," Leo said. "It's um…important."

Jack followed his friends out into the hall. Except that the hall wasn't good enough and they weren't satisfied until he'd walked with them all the way down to his office and locked the door behind them. Leo made him sit down in one of the chairs in front of his desk.

As he sat, Juliet's fountain caught his eye.

And made him upset all over again.

Something else caught his eye, too. A piece of paper speared by Bevo's horn. The air conditioning clicked on, making it flicker a little in the breeze.

He stood up and plucked it off.

Then let out a curse. It was a resignation letter. Short and sweet and signed by Juliet. He sat back down and put his head in his hands, stifling a groan.

He ached all over. His head hurt. His *heart* hurt.

"Jack!" Noah was shaking his shoulders. "Have you been drinking? What's wrong?"

Leo and Noah exchanged worried glances. "Just tell us what's going on, buddy, so we can help you."

"Do I look that bad?"

"You're sweating buckets and you're pale," Noah said. "And then there was the matter of the backward hat."

"So the answer is *yes*," Leo said.

Jack glanced up at his friends. They were worried because they cared. And he knew he had to tell them what was wrong. "I did something stupid." Something that was going to cause him to lose his town if he couldn't get himself together.

"What else is new?" Leo said but Noah speared him with a look. "Sorry. Just trying to crack a joke."

Jack pinched the bridge of his nose. "I did something *really* stupid. I saw Juliet talking to Devin. He said something about them going out before, probably just to get me hot under the collar. At first I didn't even believe it. Then I got angry that she kept it from me. So I didn't tell him that I was dating Juliet. I didn't stand up for her— I mean, she didn't *need* me to stand up for her. What I mean is, I didn't stand up for *us*." He paused and thought about that. "I ruined things with Juliet not because I had trouble saying what I felt about her but because I was too stubborn to do it."

"Maybe it's not that bad," Leo said. "What did you actually say?" Leo asked.

"Nothing." Jack blew out a breath. "I said… nothing."

"That's pretty bad," Noah said.

"Yeah," Leo said solemnly. "You blew it."

Jack started pacing. "I was just so…angry that she kept that from me."

"So what happened with Devin?"

"He never intended to buy into my plans. He's planning to buy my grandma's land at auction. So if the zoning committee tells him he can, that's it. Not only is it the end of my granny living there, it's the end of our town as we know it."

"If you're too upset, we can give your talk for you," Noah offered.

"Thanks, Noah," Jack said. "But I've let enough people down today. I need to be the one to tell everyone exactly how I feel." Somehow, he had to do it. It was his last shot at helping his grand-mother. But how was he going to put his heartache over Juliet aside so he could function?

"Jack," Leo said, laying a hand on his shoulder. "You're right. That's exactly what you need to do. You have to focus. Don't hold anything back. People will at least appreciate hearing it directly from you, no matter what happens."

Jack nodded. "I've wrecked things with Juliet," he said, raking his hands through his hair. "I've lost her for good."

"We're sorry, Jack," Noah said.

"Wait a minute," Leo said. "You've only lost her for good if you don't do what people do when they screw up."

"Say I'm sorry?"

Leo counted on his fingers. "Grovel, apologize, and beg for forgiveness."

"In that order," Noah added, nodding.

"Right. Except she told me she needs someone who's not afraid to tell her how they feel."

"This is it, Jack," Leo said. "You know what you need to do."

Noah opened his thumb and index finger and held them up in demonstration.

Jack stared at the hand sign and had no idea what it was. "Are you trying to tell me that I'm a loser?"

"The L-word," Noah said. "Get it?"

Yes, he got it. He did love Juliet. With his whole heart. And he somehow had to find the words to let her know that.

"I just hope it's not too late." Jack sighed. He

stood up and hugged his best friends. "Thank you for always being here for me," he said. "I'm lucky to have you." He knew they would always be there for him, no matter what. He glanced at his watch and forced himself to focus on what he had to do. "I need to do something right now before the meeting. I need to talk to my grandma."

CHAPTER TWENTY-THREE

Jack found his grandmother in the courtyard gardens, sitting on a stone bench next to Juliet and surrounded by several of her lady friends from church. Juliet's mother, grandmother, and sisters were there, too.

"Granny, can I talk with you?" he asked. He sent a glance in Juliet's direction, but she only seemed concerned with his grandmother.

"Of course you can, Jackson." She sounded so positive. So trusting. And that almost killed him. "There's certainly a big turnout for the meeting tonight, isn't there? Better than for the old theater during dollar night."

Her friends laughed at that. His grandmother patted Juliet's hand and smiled. Juliet managed a smile for her but didn't even toss him a nod.

Which stabbed him.

He offered his elbow to his grandmother and walked with her down the garden path until they came to a little wall overlooking the river where a lot of city hall employees ate lunch on warm days. A riot of sunflowers had just finished blooming on the other side of the wall, which everyone enjoyed while hanging out during lunch hour.

They took a seat on the wall itself, which had a ledge made just for sitting. He took up both her hands and looked his grandmother in the eye. "Granny, I—" His voice broke.

He would rather be anywhere but here, having to wreck his grandmother's simple dreams of living out her life in the place she loved.

He would rather do anything than fail her. And he *had* failed her. In the worst way. Her property was going up for auction. Devin was going to buy it. And he couldn't stop it.

Just like he'd failed Juliet. But he couldn't think of that now or he'd never get through this.

But this time, he was going to man up. At least his granny would hear the terrible news from his own lips. He opened his mouth to try again.

Suddenly her eyes welled up with tears. "No, Jackson," she said, stopping him before he'd even begun. "Shush now. No need to say a thing."

"Granny, I—"

She squeezed his hand. "You see, I already know what you're about to say." Her voice was quiet and calm—soothing. Unbelievably, she was taking it upon herself to soothe *him*. "It's all right, son. You did your best. I don't mind leaving, and I don't mind not having the land. I just don't want to leave Gabe there."

Jack's stomach twisted. "I'm so sorry." His voice came out as a strained, hoarse whisper.

"If only we could give our land to a good cause instead of to that…that man. That's the only thing I regret, not letting it pass on in a good way. That's the second way I let Gabe down. I lost his land, and I lost it to someone who's going to ruin our town." Her eyes welled up with tears.

"No, Granny. You didn't let anyone down. I did." He wanted to offer her hope, to tell her there was some inkling of a miracle, but he knew in his heart there wasn't. And he wouldn't raise her hopes for nothing.

"Well, there's nothing more to discuss," she said. "We'll deal with it as we do with everything else." She sat up and jutted out her chin in that determined way of hers. "Now, what's happened between you and Juliet? Did you two fight over this mess?"

He was about to deny it, to not upset her further, but he knew she'd already seen right through him. "No, Granny. It's a long story, but leave it to say I was a fool. I didn't tell her what she needed to hear. I didn't tell her my true feelings."

His grandmother cast her wise blue gaze on him. "Jackson, I've always stayed out of your private life. But if anything good comes from all this trouble, it's that we've got to use our pain to grow. And with that in mind, I think I have to tell you something that you need to hear." She took up both his hands. "It's not your daddy that caused the trouble in your life. It's good to be a doer. You learned that lesson well because he wasn't one. You learned to be *better* than your father. All your real trouble comes from your mama."

He sucked in a breath, surprised and a little confused. Of course, his mother had left him. But he'd survived that just fine. So what was she talking about?

She gripped his hands hard. "I love you like a son. God knows, I've raised you like my own, and you *are* my own." Her voice cracked, but she continued. "And I love you with all my heart and soul.

But it was your mother's behavior that made you close off your heart. If anything good comes from this, it's that you've got to open yourself up to people in order to be able to love them and be loved back. That's what you've got to think of, son. I'll be fine. But if you don't figure this out, your life is going to be…empty."

Her words walloped him in the head. He knew that he could be an emotional Neanderthal at times, but he'd always attributed that inability to express himself to his dad.

But his *mother* as the reason he avoided relationships?

Also, his granny was more worried about him and Juliet than her land? That was typical. She never put herself first. But that made him want to help her all the more.

"Granny, don't worry about me and Juliet. We need to focus on the land right now. I want you to know I'm not giving up. I'll make more phone calls. I'll—"

She touched his cheek. "I know you've done everything you can. Don't ever think that I felt you didn't. I've known this day was going to come for a long time, and I've accustomed myself to it. But you've got your whole life ahead of you. I want you to live it fully. I want you to be able to reach out and love someone." She paused to let that sink in, and man, it had hit him like a whopper. And made him more confused than ever. "I love you, son."

Jack hugged his grandmother hard. "I love you, too, Granny."

• • •

Jack slammed down his gavel, determined to get through this meeting, which was packed to the gills. The men and women of the zoning commission were in the front row. As were the town trustees. And so many of the townspeople had showed up, too, shop owners and city employees and teachers and farmers, many of whom he knew by name.

He tried not to look in the third row, where his grandmother sat next to Juliet and her family, and just focus on his task at hand. He was focusing so hard that the creak of the heavy wooden double doors to the meeting room as they swung open made him startle. It was just old Mr. Blossom walking in late with a *tap-tap-tap* of his cane on the wood floor to his seat.

"Ladies and gentlemen," Jack said. His voice cracked, and he had to force himself to speak loud and clear. "As you've probably already heard, Omnibuild would like to make a bid on my grandmother's land." The fact that Juliet was holding his grandmother's hand tightly made a lump form in his throat. He didn't deserve the privilege of Juliet being there for him, but he was grateful that his grandmother wasn't alone. But then, it was just like Juliet to be there despite everything.

He wasn't sure he was going to get through his speech. But he knew he had to. Not only did he have to get through it, but he also had to make the people in the room feel what he was feeling. This was bigger than just his grandmother, and he somehow had to find the words to make them see that.

He closed his eyes and pictured Juliet as she'd stood near the waterfall, making him see everything through her eyes. Making him feel everything that she felt. And then he took a big breath and began. "I used to think that the best decisions were made without getting emotions involved." He looked at Juliet, which might have been a mistake, but he couldn't help himself. "I was wrong." For a moment, he lost his train of thought. But he plowed on. "A memory is a memory, a person is a person, and our town is our town." He cleared his throat, finding it clogged with emotion. He hoped Juliet heard her own words to him as he spoke. He hoped she saw that he'd learned something—so many things—from her.

"Omnibuild's not interested in the idea I recently proposed about converting the old junkyard into a golf course. They want to buy my grandmother's land at auction. So we're here to make a zoning vote. But before we do, I want to present to you *my* vision of the future of our town."

He had to find a way to tell his town how he felt. And show them the alternative he believed in. Even if he couldn't save his grandmother's land from being sold, he could save it from being sold to the wrong person. And Omnibuild—Devin— was the wrong person. Not just with regard to his grandmother, but for the entire town.

"I can't prevent my grandmother's land from going on the auction block. But I can tell you how I feel about how it should and shouldn't be used."

First, he showed drone photos of the southside land. The junkyard.

He looked around the room at all the polite faces. Someone stifled a yawn. Old Jed Barton was asleep, his head bobbing. Even Daisy was snoring gently at Louise's feet in the front row.

What he was doing wasn't working. So…*screw this*.

He clicked his presentation forward ten slides, past the feasibility study numbers, past the statistics, *click-click-click*.

He halted at the colorful renderings that he'd done. *His* vision for the future. He spoke like he was talking to Noah and Leo over a couple of beers about his dreams for a golf course that would follow the slow rolling hills and overlook a small lake and stream. And the possibility for a modern, low-lying, completely sustainable hotel that would blend in with the trees. "And finally," he said, "here's an example of a brand-new road leading directly from the new golf course to downtown to drive visitors to the best of Blossom Glen—us. Our businesses. *We* are the heart of our town."

The room suddenly hushed, like someone had put it on mute. People were sitting up and staring. *Listening.* He stuck the PowerPoint remote into a cup holder on the podium and walked in front of it to speak directly to the people. *His* people. "The folks at the park service are interested in my grandmother's land, but to be honest, if the zoning changes to commercial, Omnibuild will surely outbid them. Omnibuild will reroute the river. They'll dam portions of it and the wildlife will be displaced. Pollution will build up. Ecosystems will be disturbed. The high-end hotel they plan to build is a high-rise. A *high-rise* in our town." He shook his head in disgust. "Ask yourself if that is what you want. They'll bring in chain restaurants and shops that will overtake our Main Street businesses."

Devin stood up, looking a little flustered. "I object!"

"Sit down, Chambers," Bob Hutchins, the head of the zoning commission smacked his gavel. "You'll have your turn. Let the mayor speak."

Surprisingly, Devin obeyed, even though he sat forward on the edge of his seat like he was going to spring up again at any moment like a jack-in-the-box. For the first time in his life, Jack had everyone's attention. He reached down deep inside to his own desperation. Cracking his knuckles, he continued. "When you think of success for our town, is that what you mean? We would have revenue, yes. But what happens to *us*? What happens to all the wonderful things that make Blossom Glen our town? Like our candle factory. Teeter's Hardware. And Christmas Every Day. And The Foggy Bottom. And Castorini's. And Bonjour Breads!." He looked at the Teeters. At Hector G. At Leo and his dad, and at the Montgomerys.

Jack spoke with the passion he pulled out from

deep inside. That's what Juliet had taught him to do.

Was that enough? Was he done? He'd said his piece. He glanced over at Juliet, who was staring straight at him.

She gave him the slightest nod, the slightest lift of her brows. *Keep going*, he read in her expression. *Pull out all the stops*.

Okay. All right. Here goes. He sucked in a breath. "We can only stop Omnibuild one way," he continued. "Just one way." He paced back and forth in front of the rows of people. Sweat trickled down his back, but he felt strangely cold. He stood and looked straight at everyone, making eye contact with everyone he knew. "We can stop this by refusing—*refusing*—to rezone my grandmother's land. Which I believe with my whole heart is integral to keep Blossom Glen...Blossom Glen. I beg you to consider the whole picture here, not just for us, but for our kids and grandkids."

As soon as he stopped speaking, the room was abuzz with murmuring. The zoning commission talked heatedly among themselves. Jack felt no pride in his words. He only felt that he'd been honest. But that wasn't going to bring them a miracle.

He quelled the urge to run outside and suck some cool, fresh air into his burning lungs. But there was one more thing he had to do first. He walked back to the microphone. "I want to thank everyone for standing up for our town. And for each other. That's what I love the best about us." Hiring Juliet had helped neighbors to be more neighborly and helped people to put their kindness before their animosity. And it had helped him to see people as…people. Not as constituents with complaints he was too impatient to handle.

All around the room, friends, colleagues, former teachers, business owners—everyone he'd come to know—were waving at him, giving him a thumbs-up. His heart swelled with pride and sadness. Because in that moment he realized why he'd become mayor. Yes, to help save his grandmother's land. That was the main reason in the beginning, but now, he realized, he loved his town.

"I have to say that this issue has been on my mind since the day I ran for office. But I've come to realize how much of an honor and a privilege it's been to be your mayor."

He was prevented from getting too big for his britches by the sight of Devin striding to the front of the room. Outwardly, Devin's emotions seemed contained, but Jack could see his gaze darting back and forth across the room, his angry frown, his fists balled at his sides. Like maybe he was worried. Seriously worried. At least Jack hoped so. Bob Hutchins finally called for order, rapping the gavel multiple times to get everyone to settle down.

"Omnibuild is all about progress," Devin said, not even bothering to use the podium. "Financial stability. Looking to the future." Jack had to admire him for managing to speak smoothly, with confidence. "Who wouldn't want all the revenue our plan could generate? Yes, it would change the town, but change is good. Not only that, change is *essential*."

Jack stepped away so that Devin could begin his presentation, a series of dry, sleep-inducing slides. He didn't get too far before George Teeter stood up and spoke. "With all due respect, Mr. Chambers, I for one love our town just as it is." Delores stood up, too. And then Marco Castorini and Mrs. Montgomery. And all the other Main Street shop owners. Followed by, one by one, everyone in the room. Every single person, as if they were at the end of a magical, tear-inducing Broadway play. Even old Mr. Blossom got up, leaning heavily on his cane.

"Would anyone else like to put their opinion on record before we take a vote?" The zoning commissioner asked, not even calling for order so that Devin could finish his slides.

The room was so silent you could hear Daisy's dog tags clink as she twitched in her sleep. No one was protesting? That could be good or—terrible. Jack held his breath, his entire body frozen still in his seat.

"Those in favor of rezoning Ms. Anderson's land as commercial, say 'aye.'"

Jack fought the urge to squeeze his eyes shut. Instead, he set his jaw and waited.

The silence continued.

"Those opposed say 'no.'"

A resounding chorus of nays sung through the air.

"All right then, the noes have it." Bob nodded at the zoning commission members in the front row and gave a satisfying smack with his gavel.

"Mayor and citizens, we've reached our decision, after reviewing the plans, talking to experts, and listening to our town. The zoning commission votes a unanimous *no* to turning this land into commercial property."

Praise Jesus.

Over the clapping, whistling, and cheers, Devin headed for the door, looking like he was fixing to tump over, bless his heart.

Once again, Jack's gaze gravitated to Juliet, who hugged his grandmother hard. In fact, *everyone* was hugging her and patting her on the back. Suddenly Juliet glanced straight at him, tears in her eyes. She might have given him the slightest smile. Which might've just meant that she was proud of him for what he'd said. It made his heart swell with hope.

Amid all the chaos, his granny got up and walked to the podium. "Jackson, I want to say something," she said quietly. So he got out of her way.

"I know there's still going to be an auction," she said, "and I'm still going to have to move, but I feel so much better that the land will stay as it is. Thank you all for your love and support." Short, sweet, and to the point, no words minced. That was his amazing granny.

At first, the room was as dead silent as a movie theater at a spellbinding moment. But then one person clapped. Joined by another, and another. When the applause became thunderous, everyone stood again. And kept clapping.

Everyone was rallying around his grandmother. Jack examined their faces. They wanted the best for her. They were sorry that she'd lost her land. He felt proud to be mayor, and prouder to be her grandson.

When the applause finally died down, old Mr. Blossom slowly came to his feet and rose to his full but slightly stooped height. "I'd like to say something," he said.

"As you all know, I've had some losses in the past few years and haven't been as involved in the community as I used to be. So on that note, I want to thank you, Juliet, for welcoming me back into the community. That's meant a lot to me."

Juliet looked a little puzzled as Mr. Blossom glanced around the crowded room. "It warms me to see that our town still has a heart. But that heart needs to be protected, and not by building fancy golf courses and shopping centers. And so I have a suggestion, but I was waiting for the zoning commission to make their decision. I believe our town needs a beautiful place for people to enjoy. Trails to walk on, bike trails, a place to bring a picnic and gather with family and enjoy the beauty of nature. And so I'd like to ask you, Adele, if you'd mind sharing some of your land with us. I'd like to work with the state park and donate money for its purchase. That way your beautiful property would be protected for generations to come. And as repayment, you'd stay in your home. You'd be involved in all the decision-making and keep any of the adjacent land you'd like for your descendants." He turned to Adele. "So, what do you say?"

"You're telling me the land would be a park

for everyone to enjoy?" She had tears in her eyes. "Gabe would have loved that. I love it, too. That's perfect, Alfred. Just perfect." She clutched her chest. "Thank you from the bottom of my heart."

"After all, what's better for the mental health of the community than parkland?" Mr. Blossom said.

That made Juliet smile. "Thank you, Alfred," Jack said.

"You've been a good mayor, Jack," the old man said. "But if I were you, I'd take some of that land and build yourself a house. Get some real roots here." He didn't hesitate to glance Juliet's way.

As everyone broke out into applause again, Jack realized that his time as mayor was coming to an end. But he was okay with that. What he wasn't okay with was his life without Juliet. He looked around for her…but she was gone.

As he ran out of the room, he sent up a silent prayer. If he could say his feelings in front of the whole town, maybe he also could say them in front of Juliet.

CHAPTER TWENTY-FOUR

Juliet left the meeting barely holding it together. She was relieved at the outcome. And happy for Adele and also for Jack, who had worked so hard to protect his grandmother.

But she could not forget what had happened between her and Jack. And she couldn't compromise herself for a man again. She just…wouldn't.

When she walked out of the meeting room, she found Char leaning against the wall in the hallway, finishing a call. Jordan, her somewhat-perfect colleague who was temporarily taking her clients, stood next to her, scrolling her phone. "Juliet," Char said, stepping forward. "We're so relieved about Ms. Anderson's land. I hope things work out well for her."

"Me too," Jordan echoed. Then she added, "We heard…about you and Jack. We're sorry about that, too."

Here we go again, is what part of her thought. Another failed romance she'd be forever remembered for. *Another mistake.* But then something happened. Out of the ashes of her misery, the wiser, more sensible part of her popped up and decided that she wasn't going to make this about her love life.

Eff her love life. She was not her love life. It only interfered with her job because she'd *allowed* it to.

What she'd been essentially doing all this time was not standing up for herself. Letting her past control her. In other words, not letting it be the past.

And it was time to start changing. Right now.

Juliet managed to look them both in the eye. "Thanks, but everything worked out in the best way." She didn't believe that about her and Jack, but that was all right. She'd survive. She flicked her gaze up to Char. "I've enjoyed my time as town counselor, but I'd like to take my clients back. I'm ready, Char." There. She was more than ready to do what she was born to do, and it was time she stood up for what she wanted.

And this time, her body was cooperating for once. There wasn't a hive in sight.

Jordan smiled. "Thank goodness! If one more couple comes in asking for the town sweetheart, I'm not sure what I'm going to do."

"The town sweetheart?" Was that better than being called Lulu? Hmmm. It might be a toss-up. On the other hand…maybe it wasn't so bad after all.

"Everyone loves you, Juliet," Jordan said, and that was the most honest thing Juliet had ever heard her say. "Apparently, everyone's been following all the disputes you've helped settle as town counselor. They all want you to counsel them."

Did she just hear that right?

"And I have some exciting news," Char said, glancing over at Jordan. "We've decided to bring Jordan into the practice, too."

"I'm really excited to be a part of Headspace," Jordan said. "Maybe you can give me some tips about getting clients."

Well, all right. Maybe Jordan wasn't so bad after all. Also, Juliet had clients lined up?

Juliet stuck out her hand and smiled, because why not? "Welcome to the practice."

A minute later, as Char walked with her down the hall, she leaned over and whispered, "It really wasn't about your past relationships at all, you know. It was about your attitude about them."

Juliet nodded. She did believe in herself now, in her abilities, even if she didn't always make perfect choices. And Jack had helped her to get there. But even without him, she knew that she was going to be okay.

She marched down the hallway to her office, where she could finally have a moment to herself. But she opened the door to find her entire family there. Tessa sat looking uncomfortable, half reclining in a hard-backed chair, her mom and grandma sat together on the orange couch, and Viv was watering her rubber tree.

"We were, um"—her mom assessed her with a shrewd look—"just checking to see if you're okay."

"I'm okay," she said, but it came out like a croak. Maybe the emotion was finally catching up with her, and with family, she could finally let down her walls. "I *am* okay. Really." She had to be. "I have to lead an info session in the church basement in an hour."

Juliet sat on the one remaining chair, the

orange plastic one behind her ugly desk. "Are *you* okay?" she asked Tessa. "You look…uncomfortable. Want to sit here?" She patted the pumpkin orange armrests, excited to soon have her real, twenty-first century office back.

"If you couldn't touch your feet and your ankles looked like grapefruits, you'd be uncomfortable, too," Tessa said with the tiniest little touch of a smile. "In other words, I'm fine."

That was Tessa, always seeing the positive. Always bucking up in the face of discomfort. Always teaching her lessons. She found herself blinking back tears.

"But your toenail polish is really cute," Viv said, perching on the arm of the couch.

"Leo did it for me, God love that man," Tessa said.

Her grandmother leaned over to see it more clearly. "I might have to borrow that one."

"Anyway." Their mother got down to business. "You should be very proud of yourself, Juliet. You helped Mr. Blossom feel connected to the community again. And he paid it forward. It's a miracle, really."

Juliet pressed her lips together and nodded. "I can't take credit, Mom. I was just being nice to him. Jack…he worked hard to get this all to happen, too."

"We're so proud of you," her mom said. "You're always kind to people. I can't help feeling that everyone rallied because they feel like a community…a family, really."

"You've always loved helping other people,"

her grandmother said.

Yes, that was what she did.

Help other people. That was her superpower. She glanced at her watch. "I'd better get going."

"Are you going to be okay to lead your session? We know about you and Jack," Viv said. "People are talking about it."

Of course they were.

"And we're sorry about that, too," her mom said.

"I—I don't think I can talk about it now," Juliet said. In front of her family, her tears decided at that moment to just let go.

Viv jumped up and ran out the door, coming back with a roll of toilet paper and tossing it to Juliet.

"Th-th-thanks," she managed.

Her grandmother reached into her paisley tote bag and pulled out a black binder.

"Are you here to interrogate me?" Juliet asked with a partial smile as she wiped her tears. She had no idea what was in that giant binder, but it appeared stuffed with newspaper clippings. "Don't bother. I'll tell you what happened. Jack doesn't do relationships. And this time, I know what I need. Someone who can stand up for our relationship."

"Oh, that's disappointing," her mother said.

"Jack is a classic commitment-phobe," Juliet said. "His dad was never around, his parents had a dysfunctional relationship, and his mom left. I knew it from the start, but I got involved with him anyway. But the truth is, I don't feel like I did with my other mistakes. I really cared for Jack. With him, I didn't try to become what someone else wanted me to be."

She hadn't compromised who she was for Jack. She hadn't tried to force herself to want a certain life like she had with Ryan, or talked herself into loving someone who seemed perfect on paper like Tyler. And she hadn't fallen for him just because he was hot, like she had with Jax.

She knew herself enough to not try to desperately mold herself to fit someone else's dreams. And she didn't need anyone's approval anymore.

Jack had never asked her to bury her desires and wants.

He'd helped her to achieve her dreams. Encouraged her. He'd believed in her.

She loved him. Yes. She did.

She *really* loved him.

But she loved herself enough not to compromise herself. And if he couldn't say that he loved her and believed in her, well, then...she wasn't going to stick around and hope that one day he could.

"You were just yourself—" Tessa let out a sudden loud *aah!* And rubbed her belly. "Oh my. Sorry, this little one is really kicking up a storm today. Must be those stuffed peppers I ate for breakfast."

"Stuffed peppers for breakfast?" Viv made a face as she sat winding and unwinding the old blind cord around her fingers. "That's disgusting."

Her mom gave her a little smile. "Juliet, your relationship with Jack struck me as a mature relationship."

"I thought he was the one, Mom." With him she was not just unabashedly herself. She was the *best version* of herself.

Her grandmother stood up and stood in front of the ugly metal desk. "Juliet, this is between you and Jack. And it's up to you two to resolve or not resolve your troubles." She slid the black binder in front of her. "But I finally dug this out of the attic and thought you should have it. It might help."

What did an old binder from the attic have to do with all the chaos swirling around her head right now? And her miserable, broken heart?

The room was suddenly silent. Viv even stopped fidgeting with the blind cord.

Juliet frowned and took the big black book. It had pink construction paper hearts tucked into the clear plastic cover. "I remember making these in like, second grade." She took a careful look at the lace-lined hearts. "There are valentines I sent you. This is a scrapbook?"

Her grandmother smiled and ran a hand over the faded pink paper. "Yes, well, I actually made one for each of you girls."

"So when were you planning to give us ours, Gram?" Tessa asked. "When we die?"

"That's enough, Tessa dear," her grandmother chided. But she was smiling. "We are busy women, and it's taking me a while. But I felt it was important to give Juliet hers today."

Juliet opened the book. In the front was a giant pile of...stuff. Her vaccination records, an award certificate for running the fifty-yard dash in sixth grade, a bunch of girl scout patches that never got sewed onto her vest.

Hmmm. Interesting, but…not exactly things she wanted to keep for posterity. Well, maybe her vaccination record.

"Like I said," her grandmother said, "it's not tidy and complete. But turn the page."

Juliet flipped a page containing the cardboard postcard that said *It's a girl!* that must have been attached to her bassinet in the hospital. There were photographs of her dad holding her as an infant.

Dad. Her aching heart swelled even more, but mostly in a good way. What would her dad say if he saw her now, heartbroken and imperfect?

"Oh, Gram," she said, "I've never seen these before."

"You can look at them all later." She made a forward motion with her hands. "Keep turning the pages."

A chart of milestones. A handwritten index card filled with adorable things written in her mom's handwriting that she'd said when she was two. A birthday photo of her, Viv, and Tessa with their dad and their yellow cat.

"Oh, remember Monet?" she asked.

Tessa leaned over to see, and Viv came up behind her.

"We had a cat named Monet?" Viv asked.

"We had Van Gogh, too," their mom added.

"But Van Gogh is Dutch," Tessa said, "not French."

"Don't be a stickler," her mom said. "Your dad picked the names."

"I do remember him. We called him Go-ey," Viv said. "You know, sort of like Joey with a G."

"You actually called him GoGo," Juliet said. "Because you were like, three. He was a sweet cat."

Her grandmother let out a patient sigh. "Did you get to the newspaper articles yet?"

One more page flip, and there was a bold headline from the *Blossom Glen Gazette*. "Toddler Scales Water Tower," read the title. "Returned unharmed to anxious family."

"Oh no," Juliet said, her cheeks heating. "Not this." She'd finally come to terms with part of her adult past—but now she was going to be forced to examine the toddler part, too?

Her grandmother nodded wisely. "Oh yes. Read it."

Her mom caught her eye and smiled. "It's time you read the full story."

"Out loud," Viv added. "We all want to hear it."

So Juliet read, her voice cracking a little, her eyes blurring. "Local toddler Juliet Montgomery, age three, went missing while her family was at the Blossom Festival. Her father thought she'd fallen asleep in her stroller but the toddler apparently decided that setting out on an adventure was far more exciting than nap time."

Juliet couldn't help chuckling. "Dad thought I was in the stroller, but I left?"

Her mom nodded. "Oh, you know how your dad was. Always talking to everyone. He thought you were fast asleep, but you woke up and decided you didn't care for the Blossom Festival. When

I met up with your dad, you were gone. It might be amusing now, but we literally thought that someone kidnapped you."

Juliet shook her head. "That must've been terrifying."

"Everyone searched for an hour," her grandmother said. "They made announcements over the speakers. Then it started getting dark. We were all in a panic. So was the whole town. And then the lights on the water tower came on."

"What happened then?"

Vivienne tugged the book from Juliet's hands and skimmed the rest of the article. "Someone looked up and saw you against the white of the water tower. Six men from the volunteer fire department scaled the tower with flashlights, and a ladder truck pulled up with a giant beam."

"How embarrassing," Juliet said, her head in her hands.

"Six firefighters rescued you?" Tessa exclaimed.

"Oh, they didn't rescue her," Gram said. "Your dad was the first one to scale the ladder on the tower. The rest of us gathered at the bottom, wringing our hands and praying you wouldn't slip and fall. You were so small, we feared you'd slip right through the fencing."

Viv continued the story. "The other men—Mr. Parker, Mr. Santangilo, Mr. Teeter—didn't want your dad to go first. They were afraid he'd be too emotional. Or you'd get so excited to see him, you'd forget where you were and lose your footing."

Her mom rubbed her temples. "I'm shuddering just thinking about this."

"Tell her what Francis told you before he went up there, Margo," her grandmother said.

Her mom got teary-eyed. "Your father held me by the arms and looked into my eyes and said, 'That little girl was strong enough to climb all the way up there. That was the hard part. So we'll pretend it's a game and get her down. I promise.' And he kissed me and up he went."

"I'm getting goose bumps." Juliet rubbed her arms. "So what happened when Dad found me?"

"You'd fallen asleep on the narrow landing that runs all the way around the curve of the tower. Dad woke you up, and you wrapped your arms around him and said, 'I want ice cream.' And your dad said, 'Honey, we'll get you all the ice cream you want.'"

Everyone let out a sigh—and a laugh.

"That certainly hasn't changed," Tessa said. "Also, ice cream sounds so delicious right now."

Juliet rolled her eyes. "Finish the article, Viv!"

Viv read from the article. "'While Miss Juliet was enjoying a chocolate caramel crunch ice cream cone from the Blossom Shop, this reporter asked her why she scaled the highest structure in three counties. 'Because I wanted to touch the stars,' she said, completely unfazed."

"Ballsy, motivated, independent, adventurous, reaching for the sky," her mom said.

"Extraordinary," her grandma said.

"Anyone who can do that as a toddler gets all *my* respect," Viv said.

"Viv, I was lucky to come out of that alive." Juliet snorted. "Life was so much simpler when you don't know enough to worry about everything. And second-guess yourself."

"Juliet," her mom said, squeezing her hand. "You're still the same bright and curious person. Don't ever stop reaching for the stars. And don't settle."

That made the tears fall fast. Her family loved her unconditionally. Her gram was sweet to bring the article. And to remind her to be her best self.

Everyone came in for a hug. Even Tessa, who needed help getting up. "I love you, fam," Juliet whispered. "Thanks for being here for me. Thanks for reminding me who I can be."

"Who you *are*," her grandmother said.

"I know what I am," Viv said. "Starving. I vote we go get ice cream."

"Does anyone else have something we need to have a family discussion about?" their grandmother asked.

"Don't look at me," Tessa said. "I feel like I'm eleven months pregnant and I have no other stress but to get this baby out of me. And then figure out how I'm going to stay awake for three months straight."

"You really didn't start sleeping through the night until you were nine months old," their mother offered with a wicked little laugh.

"Wait," Viv said. "What did you ever decide about the nursery walls?"

If Juliet wasn't mistaken, Tessa blushed.

"Tessa, what did you do?" Viv asked. "Choose

something bizarre, like remember Oliver Webster from preschool? Didn't he have black walls with flames in his bedroom?"

"He *did* grow up to be a firefighter," their grandmother pointed out.

"I — did something," Tessa said. "You know how they say you nest right before you give birth? Well, I got a burst of energy and I...wallpapered it."

Everyone gasped in suspense.

At least she'd made a decision. "So? What kind of paper?" Juliet asked.

Tessa gave a little shrug. "Roses. Tiny pink roses." She shrugged. "The paper was on super-clearance, so I bought like, twenty rolls. And...it just felt right." She looked around at Viv and Juliet, who were wise enough to keep any opinions they might have to themselves. Besides, who said boys couldn't enjoy rose wallpaper, right? "I just wanted to say that I hope my baby gets to experience the joy of having sisters."

Everyone *awwwed* at that. Then Juliet decided that if she was going to start embracing the kick-ass little girl she once was, she was going to have to take some risks. "Vivienne," she said, "Mrs. O' Hannigan tells me you've been crying a lot."

"Good move, Juliet," Viv rolled her eyes. "Thanks for shifting the attention off of you and onto me."

"Look, all my dirty laundry's out there flapping in the wind." Juliet waved her hand in the air. "Time to get yours on the line, too."

Vivienne sighed. "Okay, fine. I'm looking for

some kind of art-related job overseas. And I'm saving up money to get there."

"But you just came home," her mother said sadly. Her grandmother gave her mom a look. "Okay, I mean, go spread your wings and do what you need to do, but I'd be lying if I said I didn't want you to stay on this side of the ocean."

"The thing is, I've never felt like I belonged here," Viv said. "Starting with my gluten problems."

"But you've made Christmas Every Day a windfall," Tessa said. "And you helped Leo get the restaurant off the ground. And my shop. You've got great PR skills."

"My time in Paris taught me I'm a mediocre artist." She sighed. "It humbled me. And made me realize that I never had a Plan B. I've only got a minor in PR. So here I am, home for almost a year and I…have no clue what to do next. Maybe take some more PR classes. But I know I've got to make some changes." She turned to Juliet. "The first one is, I'm going to move out of the apartment."

Oh, *yay*. The words Juliet had been longing to hear. But she actually had a different plan in mind. "Viv, I've been thinking about that. Why don't you keep the apartment, because *I've* decided to move out. I love Mrs. O, but I've had enough of someone watching everything I do."

"I'm not planning to be here much longer," Viv said. "So I may take you up on that."

Her mom looked like she might want to say something. Maybe like, *Can't you figure out your life without leaving town?* But she bit her lip and instead she said, "I love you girls. My three chickens." She gathered them all together, and Gram joined, too. "With all my heart." Then she turned to Juliet and stroked her cheek. "Now go out there, my darling, and kick some Lulu ass."

"Whoa," Viv said. "*Mom.*"

Juliet laughed. "I'm honored to be the one that made you say *ass.*"

Her mom shrugged. "Well, it's true. It's time you embraced the wonderful person you are."

Tessa let out a short, sudden gasp. "She may have to wait a little while to do that, Mom." Her expression was unreadable, surprised and concerned at the same time, her brows creasing. Resting a hand on her abdomen, she suddenly made a little cry of pain, then breathed in short, quick breaths until it passed. "My water just broke," she said with a shaky voice and wide eyes. "I think the baby's coming."

CHAPTER TWENTY-FIVE

"Oh, hey, Jack," Delores said as he knocked on the door of Christmas Every Day. A glance at his watch told him it was five thirty. She was carrying a broom as she let him in. "We close soon," she said. "You need something?"

"I need a card," he said. "I can pick one out quick."

"Sure thing. You don't mind me if I keep tidying up while you look, do you?"

"Go right ahead," he said. "I'll just be a minute." Jack confronted the wide array of cards with all their pre-written sentiments. His head was still spinning from the meeting, jumping from Juliet to his grandmother to the zoning commission decision to…to his mother.

His grandmother had hit him with that out of the blue.

Your mother's behavior made you close off your heart.

What did his mother have to do with losing Juliet?

She'd been gone for years. Years! The yearning and sadness that had stabbed at him so brutally was mostly just a bad memory now, and he'd long ago learned to live his life without her. Admittedly, he thought of her sometimes, but only with short, quick pangs of regret. But then those would leave and his mind would settle onto other, happier things. He wasn't a man who dwelled in the past.

But what he'd done had hurt Juliet, and he wasn't sure if she'd forgive him. Maybe he didn't deserve to be forgiven.

And maybe he hadn't forgiven his mother.

But he was going to try on both accounts. In the most courageous way he knew how.

Even in May, the shelves were full of Christmas stationery and cards. But there was a section of all-occasion cards, too, which made Christmas Every Day a quick stop for a last-minute birthday or anniversary.

Jack stood and looked for the *for her* section. Surely there had to be something here to help him express what he felt.

What *did* he feel? He closed his eyes, and all he saw was a big, giant void.

A void without Juliet. Long days and nights without her.

He picked up the largest, fanciest card he could find. It had a painted bouquet of roses that popped out when you opened the card. *You and I are meant to be,* it read. Too…formal.

Another with a puppy. *You're pawesome!* It read. *I don't need a special day to think of all the ways you make me happy.* Cute, but…this was serious.

There was a little gray cat like Ellie. More cats with sunglasses. Cats batting at Christmas ornaments. Cats being naughty, cats saying *You're purrfect.* Cute but…how he felt wasn't cute. It was…desperate. Anguished.

Cards said *I love you, I don't want to spend a single minute without you, I'm thankful for you.* Others had entire poems that went on for ten stanzas.

Some were cheesy. Some over the top. And some were sexy. But none of them were *him*.

The vacuum cleaner turned off. "Hey, Jack," Delores said. "It's about that time, and George is waiting on me to get home and watch *The Great British Baking Show* with him."

"Oh, sorry, Delores. Here I come." As a last-ditch effort, he grabbed a blank card, left a bill on the counter, gave a wave and a thank you to Delores, and left.

• • •

An hour later, Juliet stood in front of a small crowd in the newly remodeled church basement, with its polished wood floor and newly painted pale-blue walls.

Tessa was in labor, but the doctor had assured her they had an hour. So she'd decided to do her info session after all and then run straight to the hospital.

As usual, her mom, sisters, and Noah had shown up again, too. "Coffee's better here than the hospital waiting room," Viv had said. But Juliet knew they had come yet again for support.

"My name is Juliet Montgomery," she said to introduce herself to the new handful of people who had shown up, a few people she knew from town, and a few new people, too, who must have seen the info session advertised. Which was a little exciting. Not that she didn't love her family. "I'm a licensed relationship counselor, and I'm here today to talk about toxic relationships."

Faith waved from the third row, and Juliet gave a wave back. Axl, however, was absent, but she really couldn't feel too badly about that. Char had promised to come today, but she wasn't here yet.

Juliet started by talking about all the different kinds of toxic relationships. And the reasons people might stay in them. She talked about self-esteem. And empowerment. And counseling. "Love should never cost you your joy, your peace, your happiness. If you're always feeling unhappy, if your self-esteem is suffering, if you feel that you're suffering physical or emotional abuse, disrespect, or being undermined—these are all red flags and reasons to seek help. Are there any questions?"

Faith raised her hand. "I'd like to say something."

"Sure, Faith," Juliet said, proud of how she was the first to want to speak out. "Thanks for coming. Go right ahead."

"I dumped Axl," she said. "He was *my* toxic relationship. And I signed up for more individual therapy to figure out why I stayed with him so long."

"That was very brave of you," Juliet said.

Faith smiled and shrugged. "Maybe one day I'll have it together like you."

Oh gosh. No.

Juliet could just let that go. After all, she was

the professional here. But it wasn't honest. And she felt like she really wanted to be honest. And not present a front to the world that seemed perfect when the inside of her was far from it.

"Faith, I don't have it together at all. I mean, everyone has struggles, right?" Juliet thought about the past few weeks. How an almost-lost job had led to changes she couldn't have imagined.

She'd lost Jack, but what had she gained from it all? A lot. She might be devastated by Jack's loss, but somehow, she knew she was going to be all right. She looked around the room. Her family was smiling and nodding, supporting her as usual. Before she could think too hard about it, she started to talk.

"After my dad died, I had a bout with depression that made me feel different from…well, from just about everybody. When I went back to school, everyone treated me differently. Like I was fragile. Or just…weak for what happened.

"So I started to try to get people to like me. I spent years being a people pleaser to the nth degree. I mean, I was always pretty nice, but then I became…well, *really* nice. Very helpful. Always volunteering for projects. Always trying to help people. And all of those are good things."

She looked at her mom, Gram, and sisters. "I think that might be why I hung onto men until I just couldn't hang on anymore—until I was practically at the altar. I didn't want to be thought of as failing at something. Or different. Or flawed. And so I tried to blend in.

"And with those guys, I compromised and did

everything I could to make things work until I just couldn't stand it anymore." She thought of Ryan and the farm. Tyler and his endless enthusiasm. All the things that didn't seem to fit but she had tried to tolerate. "But now, I don't want to be like anyone else." She gave a little shrug. "I just want to be me."

Being helpful or self-sacrificing was wonderful unless you took it to an extreme—where you could lose yourself trying to please other people.

She'd somehow never felt the need to be who Jack wanted her to be. Maybe because he'd liked her just the way she was. That thought made her a little teary, but she fought through it.

But even with Jack, she'd hid her shame about making bad choices—or she would've just told him about Devin. But she didn't want him to know that she'd gone out with a loser like that.

"Juliet, you've matured a lot," her grandmother called out. "You're going to be a great therapist."

"Thanks, Gram."

"Ms. Montgomery, you've helped me so much," Faith said. "You've helped me learn to stand up for myself. And learn to talk about my feelings."

"Juliet helped me learn to talk about my feelings, too," someone said from the back of the room.

That voice. Juliet jerked her head up. Jack was standing there, and with his characteristic long-legged strides, began heading her way.

This was probably the most unprofessional info session ever, even more so than the one she'd held at city hall. Good thing Char wasn't here.

Jack walked up and stood in front of her. "I didn't think I could talk about my feelings, but I learned that sometimes you have to, because that's how we communicate with people we love. Words are important."

The room got very quiet. Jack looked at her with an intense expression that had her pulse pounding loudly in her ears. A million thoughts flew through her mind. He'd come to her info session. Not to save her from difficult people but to talk about *his* feelings. She couldn't have imagined that if she'd tried.

He spoke right to her. "Juliet, I knew from the moment I met you that you were going to be the person who challenged me the most, because you saw right through me at what was holding me back. You challenged me to express my feelings, and I'm going to take you up on that in more ways than one."

He sat down in the empty chair beside her. He shifted his weight and surveyed the room, nodding in that polite cowboy way of his to everyone. She could tell he was nervous because he was nervously tapping his foot, and he kept squeezing his hand into a fist. Then he drew a big breath. "First of all, I'm sorry for thinking I had an excuse for not needing therapy. That was just me being a big old chicken." He cracked a little smile. "No offense to chickens, of course."

"But second of all, I'm sorry for getting upset over Devin." He paused and sighed. "I-I was angry." Rubbing his neck and looking up at Juliet, he said, "Yeah, I was just plain angry you didn't tell me about him, and my bullheaded stubbornness was why I didn't stick up for us."

Okay, he had her at *talking about my feelings*, but she let him keep going.

"I never told you this," he continued, "but when I was in Austin for grad school, I went to see my mother there. She kept me on a string for months, pretending that she wanted to see me. And she finally agreed to meet me, but in the end, she didn't show. Kept me waiting in this restaurant for hours. So I guess...I need to forgive her. Because...because I think she did the best she could by leaving me with someone who loved me and gave me a great home. Or else I'd just subscribe to the belief that love is hurtful and it's just easier to close yourself off than to try with people. And...and I don't want to be that way."

He took her hands in his and, looking straight into her eyes, said, "You helped me to understand that when you love someone, you've got to let them know it."

Juliet's heart was pounding wildly. She felt jittery. And hot and cold. Deep inside herself, her soul was jumping for joy. Because Jack was...The One. And he was telling her everything she needed to hear.

She didn't need perfect, and she didn't need iambic pentameter poetry. She just needed sincerity and truth. And Jack had got that exactly right.

"And third, I owe you a thank you. You brought the whole town together. You helped people get along and be neighborly, and you helped everyone rally for my grandma. And you helped me to start listening to people and not avoiding coming to know them. Because you're so full of love. And one more thing." He handed her a card.

A card? Everything he did was more and more surprising. On it was a cat that looked just like Ellie, staring at a glass ball on a Christmas tree.

She took the card with a shaky hand and opened it.

Then she gazed up at him, a little confused. "Jack, this card is blank."

He took the card back and closed it. "I know. Because there's not a card in the world that can express how I feel about you. And there's no one who can say it for me." He took hold of her hands and looked into her eyes. And she looked right back into his gentle blue eyes. He shook his head, gave the slightest smile, and gripping her hands tightly said, "I love you, Juliet."

His hands felt so warm, so strong, so…right. Between her heart pounding and her knees feeling like they were going to give way, she was glad he was holding on to her.

He gave her the slightest nod and faced the crowd. "I love her," he said a little louder. Then he said, "I'll tell the whole world every chance I get if you'll take me back."

She let out a sob. "I'm sorry I didn't tell you about Devin," she said through tears. "The truth is, I didn't want you to think that I was a terrible judge of men. Going out with him just seemed to prove it even more. But Jack, I learned something about myself, too. I stayed too long with those guys because I wanted to be loved—even if it meant losing a part of myself. I never felt that way with you, though. I feel more myself than I ever have before. And...I love you, too."

They both stood at the same time. She wasted no time wrapping her arms around his neck and giving him a full lip-lock kiss in front of everyone. And he wrapped his strong arms around her and held her tight. His lips were warm, his kisses were perfect, and he tasted like peppermint and Jack and...her future.

When they broke apart, everyone was laughing and congratulating them. Someone tapped her on the shoulder. It was Char, who apparently had been watching from the back of the room. "I'll expect you to report to work Monday morning," Char said. "We've got a full lineup of clients."

Oh *yay*.

"I have news," Noah suddenly said, holding up his phone.

Juliet froze and exchanged puzzled glances with Jack.

Juliet's grandmother pressed a hand to her chest. "My heart can't take much more of this."

"The baby's coming," Noah said. "We have to leave now."

"Well, I think we're about done here anyway," Juliet said. "Thanks for coming, everyone."

"Good luck to all," Char said as they headed out. "Don't forget, Juliet, nine sharp."

"I'll be there," Juliet said, unable to disguise her joy. And this time, she was going to be sure to crack open her rainbow sticky notes.

• • •

Turns out the baby wasn't in that much of a hurry to be born.

And good thing Leo had a sense of humor, because Juliet, Viv, their mother, and grandmother were all present for her birth.

Actually, Juliet thought Leo was quite relieved to have a little bit of distraction from all his worry. He seemed to feel every pain, and stress over every contraction, and didn't rest until he was at last holding his beautiful daughter safely in his arms.

And her sister…well, Tessa was amazing, birthing that baby like a champ. And she only cursed Leo out once.

Little Rosalia Genevieve Castorini, all eleven syllables of her, waved her baby hands in the air in rhythm with her zesty cries, causing a big ruckus, as everyone looked on. Good thing her parents decided to call her Rosie for short. And good thing her name matched her brand new wallpaper.

She had a giant welcome from everyone. Uncle Noah kept taking photos from every angle.

"I think she's got Great Aunt Alberta's chin," Gram said.

"Gram, how on earth can you tell?" Tessa asked.

Their grandmother shrugged. "And she's got Francis's eyes."

Aw. Juliet hoped her brand new niece did have her dad's eyes. She couldn't tell at all, but she also knew that this debate could go on for hours. Her gram was the queen of deciding which body parts came from which ancestor.

"She's as pretty as a cactus rose," Jack's granny said. "She's going to give those two a run for their money."

"I think she might have the Castorini nose," Marco said.

"Would you really wish that on her, Marco?" Juliet's grandmother asked, making Juliet wince. That kind of comment could start a family feud.

"She's perfect," Juliet's mother said judiciously, and no one had any trouble agreeing.

Everyone *oohed* and *ahhed* as they watched every little movement, and when Rosie precociously shoved her entire fist into her mouth, you'd have thought a receiver just ran a ninety-yard touchdown.

Even Jack's eyes grew melty at the wonder of it all. "Hey, baby," he said in a high-pitched voice. "You love your Uncle Jack, don't you? I'm going to be your favorite uncle, yes I am."

Juliet had to admit, the sight of Jack talking baby talk was...pretty surprising. And it punched her straight in the heart. He was like an onion, all these wonderful layers to discover.

"Not so fast, Uncle Jack," Noah said, elbowing up beside him. "Here comes Uncle Noah, Rosie. Your *fun* uncle."

"This is the perfect end to the day," Juliet said with a sigh a little later.

"Well, yes," Jack said. His expression told her that it had been quite a day. Lowering his voice, he said, "But...I'm thinking of another way to end this day that might be just as good."

"Oh." She looked around the room. "That sounds fun." Then right there, he kissed her, leaving her breathless and dizzy, and so happy she flung her arms around him and kissed him right back.

"Hey, you two, get a room," Noah called out.

"Buzz off, Noah," Jack said, his lips quirking upward. "We're busy."

Then, in the midst of everyone they loved, he kissed her again.

EPILOGUE

It was a warm, breezy day up on the hillside, where the frame of a new house sat, no roof or walls, just long planks of fresh smelling, cleanly-cut wood.

And near the front door, which was really just an opening now, Jack stood waiting for his bride, shifting his weight a bit nervously from one foot to another.

Leo squeezed his shoulder. "You okay, man?"

"Yes. Definitely," Jack said. But the truth was, he was hyperventilating. A little. And he could feel sweat dripping down his back despite the cool day. He adjusted his black felt Stetson that matched his tux coat.

"You're not worried she's not coming, are you?" Leo asked as bluntly as only he could.

Jack glanced at his watch. Five minutes had become ten. Juliet was never late. Except she *did* have a tendency not to show up at her weddings. He cast his friend a wary glance.

"She loves you," Leo said, flashing a grin. "Believe."

He nodded. He loved Juliet with all his heart. And he was pretty sure Juliet felt the same way. And he couldn't wait for the rest of their life to begin.

She'd left all her doubts about those past relationships behind her, hadn't she? And despite his past, she didn't have any doubts about him, did she? Because he'd left his at the door a long time ago. She wasn't going to bolt, was she?

Just then, the strains of a violin were lifted sweetly on the cool autumn breeze. From the audience, he caught his granny's eye. She was a vision in blue, with a sassy hat to match. She waved and blew him a kiss, and he blew one right back.

Around the tent the caterers had erected near the bottom of the hill near the creek, Tessa appeared. She walked carefully up the incline until she reached the grassy aisle between the seats, smiling. As she walked up the aisle, she waved at her daughter in Mrs. Teeter's arms. Little Rosie waved back with her chubby baby hands.

Viv turned the corner next, also smiling widely.

The tension between his shoulders eased a little. Okay, he'd learned that if the sisters smile, then all is well with the world.

Noah was next, loving every minute of his walk up the aisle, showing off his black tux with a teal tie to echo the bridesmaids, which was perfect for his dual job of walking the line between bridesmaid and groomsman.

Then the music changed, and suddenly there were Juliet's mom and grandma, standing on either side of Juliet and linking arms.

And Juliet...well. He'd gotten better at using words but had none at all for his bride. She was a glorious cloud of white, her long dress blowing out a little in the gentle breeze, a simple crown of flowers in her hair. As his gaze locked onto hers, her beautiful lips curved up in a joyous, bright smile directed straight at him.

And that's when he knew that she was not having second thoughts, that she loved him despite whatever baggage he might carry, and that those fears he had about being left…well, he supposed those did stem from his momma. But he'd gotten past that. He'd forgiven her. And hoped she'd come to peace with her new life. Juliet wasn't going to ditch him like his mom had. And as far as she was concerned…third time's a charm, right?

Then she kissed and hugged her mom and grandma and left them to walk up the aisle to meet him.

. . .

The sun was out, the sky was pure blue, and the bright fall day smelled like wildflowers and pine. The creek was gently gurgling, and the colors on the trees were brilliant hues of gold and red. Juliet hugged her mom and grandma, adjusted her crown of flowers, and pointed herself up the aisle, toward the home that one day she and Jack would share. The one they'd planned together, that Jack had designed to sit perfectly on this beautiful hill overlooking the creek. Where Jack had already taught her how to fish in honor of his grandfather.

Come to think of it, it really didn't matter where their home was. Because Jack was her home, no matter where they lived.

Everyone she loved was there. Besides family, there were the Teeters. Sharon. Jerry Caldwell and Sam Iverson, who had given them the gift of a small magnolia tree, just three feet tall and already planted it in their yard-to-be. Louise was there, too, and Doug, but today Louise had left Daisy behind. Aaron and Hunter were there, too, Char and her colleagues at Headspace. And Jordan, who turned out wasn't so bad after all.

Juliet caught Jack's eye. He looked relieved, and maybe a little nervous. But then he smiled, his eyes full of love and the easygoing charm she'd come to know so well. Then he raised his hand to remove his dark felt hat, a cowboy sign of respect.

That day so long ago, when she'd run into city hall, she'd asked her dad for a sign, and he'd sent her Jack.

Now, in the far distance, the water tower sat, nestled in among the fall colors coating the hills. Today the tower was hung with a giant banner, *Congrats Jack and Juliet*, a gift from the Teeters, who had the hardware to make it work.

"Thank you, Daddy," Juliet whispered to the heavens. "I didn't know it at the time, but you sent me just what I needed."

This was what she wanted. A man who she could be herself with, who loved her just as she was. And you know what? She was all right with who she was. A work in progress, but a good work. And good progress.

Jack stood there, his eyes glued on her, like he couldn't look away. And she was grinning from ear to ear, so wide that her cheeks hurt, but she couldn't stop.

As she got closer, she looked into his eyes, the same color as the autumn sky. In those eyes she saw everything she'd ever need. He gave the tiniest nod.

Then, without wasting another moment, she gathered up her dress and stepped joyfully through the framed entrance and right into the rest of her life.

ACKNOWLEDGMENTS

Thank you, dear readers, for journeying along with my swaggerin' Indiana cowboy Jack and my therapist-with-a-big-heart Juliet, two people who have to learn to let go of their baggage in order to find love.

Those of you who read my books know that I love to write about families and friends, the choices people make, and how, like life, it all runs together in one big, wild, and wonderful mess. Sometimes, like Juliet, we find love while we're on the path to our best selves and don't feel ready for it. But surprise! I reckon you've got to grab it when it hits.

I hope, after reading this story, you give yourself a hug and accept that we all screw up in life, but that's okay because we learn and grow.

My sincerest thanks to Publisher Liz Pelletier for taking me on the Amara team, and to my editor Lydia Sharp who is indeed as sharp as they come. Thanks also to everyone on the Entangled team: Relationship Manager Heather Riccio, Editorial Director Jessica Turner, Publicity Manager Riki Cleveland, publicist Debbie Suzuki, copyeditor Greta Gunselman, Production Editor Curtis Svehlak, formatter Toni Kerr, proofreaders Arianne Cruz and Kristin Curry, cover artist Elizabeth Turner Stokes (who made kitties rule!) and Art Director Bree Archer. As always, thanks to my awesome agent, Jill Marsal.

And thank you, dear readers, from the bottom of my heart, for reading my books. I hope you leave with a smile on your face and a warm spot in your heart, because that's what I get from you. Never hesitate to drop me a line. I love to hear from you!

Miranda Liasson
mirandaliasson.com

The Sweetheart Fix is a charming, heartwarming, and humorous romance ending in a satisfying happily ever after. However, the story includes elements that might not be suitable for some readers. Death of family members in character backstory and mention of a major depressive episode in a grieving teenager are included in the novel. Readers who may be sensitive to these elements, please take note.